GW01605821

I'VE MISSED YOU

WARNE C. TOWNER

If you are affected by any storyline in this book please reach out to people and if needed please use one of these numbers, you are not alone.
Samaritans :03300 945 717
National domestic abuse helpline: 0808 2000 247

Edited by Cameron-Rose Neal

"Out of suffering have emerged the strongest souls; the most massive characters are seared with scars."

– Khalil Gibran. Lebanese American writer and poet

Prologue

Julia was a confident, professional sort of woman. Her hair was cropped short, she remained well-kept at all times and always seemed to be wearing a freshly pressed suit jacket. She was stern—always demanding the best from her employees. Her office door was kept open so she could keep an eye on her office and employees any time of the day.

She was contacted, one day, by a friend of hers who had just let a young man go, asking Julia to take him on. "He really is a hard worker… but his attitude started to cause rifts in the office. He just needs someone like you to give him a leg up," she had pleaded. All Julia needed to hear was hard worker. She offered him an interview via email for the next day.

Bright and early, a dishevelled young man sat opposite Julia. He perched on the chair meant for guests on the other side of the desk in her office as though he were waiting to bolt. His tie was wonky and loose. His hair, which covered most of his eyes, was greasy and he smelled like he hadn't showered in a few days. There was a large window—taking up eighty per cent of the wall—behind Julia's desk but, despite the fact her office was flooded with light, the man before her looked to be encased in shadow.

"So, you must be Patrick," Julia said and the young man—Patrick—nodded. "I hear you are a strong worker and you're looking for a job. Am I right?" He nodded again, which lit a fire inside Julia. "If you're going to be walking into an interview dressed like that, the least you can do is move that hair out of your eyes and look at me while you speak," she raised her voice and scowled at him, which seemed to shake the man sitting in front of her.

He bolted upright and pushed his hair to one side his eyes in an instant.

Julia was pleasantly surprised and sighed softly. "Look, Patrick, I didn't have to give you this opportunity, but I was told about your work ethic and that is exactly the kind of person I like to have working here but, I do demand a level of professionalism." Julia paused and squinted over her desk.

Now that Patrick had moved the hair from his face and Julia could properly look at him, she could see his face was sullen. It didn't look as though he regularly ate or slept and, as Julia looked into his eyes as she spoke, he appeared shocked and sad.

Julia hadn't expected to be met with such broken eyes. Without another word, she got up, walked over to her door, and shut it.

Heading back to her desk chair and sitting down, Julia's tone lightened. "Patrick, if I were to offer you somewhere to work, would you accept that what I ask from you isn't just what's good for my business but also to help you?" Patrick cocked his head slightly in confusion; the way Julia talked to him tugged on a faint memory.

"Okay."

It was the first word he had spoken during the entire interview, and Julia was pleased to hear it. It was sincere and to the point. He looked Julia dead in the eyes, and neither broke eye contact for a notable amount of time.

"I will be harsher on you than anyone else in the office—I'll tell you that right now. But it would help if you remembered that I'd be doing this for *your* sake, not mine or anyone else's. Do you hear me?" Patrick nodded. "I said, *did you hear me*?"

Julia's annoyance at his lack of speech was notable, and Patrick scurried to answer. "Yes, I understand."

Julia pulled a piece of paper from her desk and started writing.

"You will be starting on Monday next week. I expect you to turn up with a haircut, showered and wearing clean attire, ready to work. Understand?" She wrote out a list of things for Patrick to do and obtain before his first day as she spoke and handed it to him. "This is a new start for you, Patrick. All I expect from you is what we have spoken about today. Work hard and remain professional. Any problems and you come to me—don't make me come to you; you hear me?"

Patrick turned the list over and read it, expressionless.

"Now," Julia said. "Stand up, shake my hand and I will see you at 8 am Monday."

Wordlessly, Patrick rose and held out his hand. Julia grasped and shook it slightly, looking Patrick dead in the eye.

"Do not let me down.

Chapter 1

PATRICK

It was 7 am in the quiet suburbs of the capital city. The air was fresh, and the only sounds were the squawks of ravens, which had gathered to nest in the green directly opposite the office Patrick had stood outside of a week ago.

He had spent the week since ticking everything off the list Julia had given him and had visited a barber to get his hair cut and styled like the businessman he saw on TV, bought a new suit, shirt and tie—, and even bought a work bag like Julia had requested. He had arrived an hour early on purpose.

The way Julia had spoken to him was unlike how anyone who had spoken to him for a long time. Her tone reminded him of someone he could faintly remember but couldn't make out. It had triggered him to do what she said and not let her down.

He stood outside for the next hour, watching the other people who presumably worked at the office slowly trickle in, each offering him a puzzled glance as they passed. The anxiety was building inside of him; what had changed? He'd had many jobs before this but was never nervous. A big part of him wanted to turn and run but it was as if his beaten-up shoes were glued to the spot.

At 7.55 am, Julia arrived, stepping out of a car and spotting Patrick standing in front of the building instantly. She leaned over and kissed the woman in the driver's seat on the cheek and, as she got out of the car. Julia smiled at her and walked towards Patrick.

Julia approached Patrick, "Ah, good, you're early." Patrick's heart skipped a beat.

"Erm, good morning... Julia," he nervously muttered.

She circled and looked him up and down a few times before nodding once. "See? Now, this looks like one of my employees to me..." she said with a smile. "Do you feel ready to work hard today?"

Patrick nodded, which caused Julia's eyebrows to raise. "I mean... yes, Julia."

Julia sighed and turned towards the office door. "Well, follow me. I'll introduce you to everyone." Patrick followed attentively behind.

This was the part Patrick hated the most; he had never managed to connect with anyone from his previous jobs or even had a proper conversation with them outside of work. It had gotten so bad that he had given up learning their names, as he didn't see the point anymore. He walked behind Julia, looking at his feet as he did.

As Julia opened the door and stepped inside, he quickly scanned the area like a meerkat on the lookout for predators. A receptionist sat behind the front desk and two people were laughing in the open kitchen. It was one of the quietest offices that Patrick had ever been in.

"Freya, Albie—come over here," Julia shouted across the room, beckoning them with her hand. Before Patrick fully understood what was happening, he was standing before three strangers, who were all looking at him.

"This here is our new data entry guy. He's a bit shy, but he's gonna do great things for us. So, welcome him but let him get settled so he can do his job." Julia pointed towards a good-looking guy who was about the size of a wardrobe. "Especially you, Albie. I'm watching you!"

The man lets out a hearty laugh before approaching Patrick. "'Ello mate, how you keepin'?" He stretched out his long arms and held out a giant hand to Patrick.

Patrick looked over to Julia, who raised her eyebrows in turn as though to remind him of what she told him in the interview. Patrick nervously reached out a hand and Albie grasped it firmly, squeezing and shaking it. Patrick grimaced. He hadn't realised how strong Albie was in comparison to him. It was as if he were shaking hands with a gorilla who didn't understand their own strength.

The woman charged over to Albie, slapping him on the arm. "Oi, you big oaf." To Patrick's surprise, she pushed him aside like a feather. "Heya babes, I'm Freya. Let me know if this idiot causes you any problems, yeah?"

For a moment, Patrick was stunned. Freya was tall and strikingly beautiful to an almost scary degree. He watched as she quickly walked off, pushing Albie away on her way back to the kitchen. Patrick immediately feared her presence; her aura practically screamed not to cross her. Julia sighed audibly before directing Patrick's attention to the receptionist.

"And, finally, this is Iris. If you have any problems with the office or need equipment, she's the girl to come to." The girl behind the desk shot up like a flag. Her mouth curled at Julia's words, and she pushed her shoulders back as she strode towards Patrick. "You must be Patrick; Julia told me to have everything prepared for you," Iris said. "Follow me."

Patrick clutched his bag tightly in his fists and Iris walked off, leading the way to his new desk. Patrick had met someone just like Iris in every position he had been in—the busybody, office manager's pet. He couldn't stand them, but he followed closely behind as Julia headed to her office.

It took a little while for the people in the office to realise that Patrick wasn't particularly interested in socialising. After a few failed attempts by Albie to strike up conversation, the rest of the office left him to his own devices and only ever ventured to his desk for topics pertaining to work.

As Patrick settled into his role, he grew more and more comfortable. He knew he could come in on time, do his work and go home to Doc.

Three years passed in the blink of an eye before Patrick realised that he was experiencing something he hadn't felt for most of his life: contentment. He wasn't worried as much as he usually was, and he felt comfortable not having to worry about the other people around him.

'Being part of a team wasn't something he'd ever thought about but now he at least felt helpful.

Chapter 2

ISABELLE

"I need a job… God, any job would do at this point," Isabelle pleaded to herself as she scrolled through the endless job listings on her phone and stomped around her bedsit.

After leaving university with a journalism degree, Isabelle had thought that she was on the road to the big time but, unfortunately, life is never that easy. This was something that Isabelle had quickly learnt while moving from city to city, chasing her dream of being an on-air interviewer and running up a weighty debt in the process. Now years later, the lines of credit had dried up and she needed a stable job.

Isabelle had wanted to be a journalist all her life—from the first time she saw a woman with a microphone in her hand talking to passersby on the TV, she knew that was what she wanted to do with her life. Her parents had helped support her while they lived in the same country but now, they'd taken up travelling in their retirement years, she was left to fend for herself.

After moving out of the capital she moved out to the suburbs so she could afford rent and still live if she found some easy work. She'd started working at a tea house in the city, but it didn't last long; her boss said she was 'too much of a chatterbox.' Isabelle didn't quite understand this. All she had done was try to learn more about her regular customers… she thought that was a big part of the service industry but, perhaps she had just wanted to know everyone's story. She was a firm believer that everyone she met in life had a story to be told.

Still pacing, her eyes trailed a new listing and Isabelle stopped in her tracks. "This is perfect," she murmured, brows rising slightly as she jumped onto her bed and read the job description. Feeling a spark of excitement, she grabbed her laptop and sent an email. "Why didn't I think of getting a temp job at an office? This will be a breeze!"

In only a few days, Isabelle managed to get herself an interview. But to her surprise, the interview was scheduled to take place at a coffee shop on a Saturday morning. She'd hoped to go to a bar with friends as usual on Friday night but, when she received the meeting invitation, decided to miss this one despite her confidence in her interview skills. Isabelle had interviews locked down; she wore the same grey pantsuit, pulled her hair into a sleek ponytail, put on a subtle amount of makeup which made it look like she wasn't wearing any and headed to the coffee shop where she was supposed to meet a woman named Julia.

Isabelle only had a few minutes until she was supposed to be at the coffee shop, and she was franticly jogging down the street in her heels to get there on time. Sweat beaded off her brow and she was certain her concealer would be creased beneath her eyes, ruining her polished makeup before she even got there.

With barely a minute left before her interview was scheduled to start, Isabelle arrived dripping and panting. *Rachael's* was a small mom-and-pop café. The married couple who owned the place were the only ones who stood behind the counter and there was hardwood everywhere. Everything seemed hipster yet old-fashioned at the same time.

The bell tinkled overhead as the door swung closed behind her and Isabelle made her way over to the counter, discreetly trying to blot the sweat from her face as she did so.

"Hey there—I'm so sorry; I have an interview here right now so could I please order a latte, and you bring it over? I'm so sorry—I love this place—but, yes, a latte please and thank you!" Isabelle was trying to be as polite as possible while she scanned the room for someone who looked like they were here for business.

After a moment, she caught the eye of an older woman with a laptop who beckoned her over. Isabelle straightened her suit, let out a breath and headed over. Hand stretched out, she smiled brightly and said, "Hello! I'm a tiny bit late but I am here."

She was using her cheesiest smile but, to her chagrin, the woman—who she supposed was Julia—only stood and coldly took her hand.

"Not the best first impression, is it?"

Isabelle's smile dropped slightly. This was no pushover that she could easily charm.

"My name is Julia and I'm the office manager you have applied to temp for—"

Before Julia could finish her sentence, Isabelle jumped in, ready to say anything and everything that Julia could want to hear. "Thanks so much for the opportunity—"

Isabelle barely got through her opening line before Julia's piercing eyes shot through her like a bullet. She froze. "Thank you, I'll continue," Julia said. Isabelle felt like she was being lectured by her old principal. "We're a small office with just five current employees but space for one more. You would be taking the role of a utility man for us; meaning that anyone in need of an extra pair of hands will approach you for support with their workload. The role is currently being advertised as temporary, however, there is the possibility of it becoming permanent following a review."

To each sentence, Isabelle simply nodded along, waiting for the opportune moment to sell herself.

"This will be our first new hire for a few years now; the team is tight-knit and works well together. Do you think you could work in an environment such as this?"

This was her chance. "Thanks so much, Julia. I've always wanted to work for a strong woman like yourself and would be willing to do whatever it takes to become not only a valued member of your team but someone you couldn't imagine having not hired. I've always wanted to work in Data Management—" Julia sighed and Isabelle stopped abruptly.

"Right, okay, thanks for that," Julia said monotonously. "The final question I have to ask you is, where do you see yourself in five years?"

Isabelle sat for a moment. She knew that if she stuck to her usual, prepared response to this question, she would never hear from this woman again. What would Julia want to hear right now?

"I'll be honest with you, Julia," she began, eyes lighting up. "In five years, I see myself interviewing the most interesting people in this country, shown live on TV in every household." She paused, suddenly feeling embarrassed. She had never told a stranger her goals like this before.

But Julia looked up from her laptop screen and squinted at Isabelle over the table. "Interesting," she said. "Go on."

For the next couple of minutes, Isabelle descended into autopilot and told Julia the crux of her dreams. Her view on people, her desire to host her own show—everything.

All the while, Julia sat and watched the younger woman who had a fire inside her—who spoke so passionately about her goals and dreams—and listened.

"Oh my God," Isabelle blinked as a light blush stained her cheeks. "I'm so sorry. I didn't mean to..." She suddenly remembered that she was interviewing for an office job and that this wasn't the time to go on like she was.

Julia rose, put away her laptop and started to put on her coat.

Isabelle panicked. "Please, I'm so sorry. I really need this job—don't leave just yet." Isabelle was near begging Julia at this point.

"Not to worry, I've heard everything I need. You'll be hearing from me by Monday." Julia stood up and held out her hand.

Face crumpling, Isabelle brought herself to her feet and limply shook Julia's hand. "Chin up, kid," Julia smirked, turned to thank the owners and left.

Isabelle slumped back into her chair and softly blew out a breath. "I've fucked it."

She had never failed a job interview before but had met her match today. Her grim mood was only broken by the man from behind the counter as he approached. "I'm so sorry, miss—there was a slight delay with your coffee." He sounded so kind and sincere that Isabelle instantly snapped out of her mood.

"Not at al—thank you so much, this looks amazing!"

The latte was just the treat she needed, and she took a long sip. Just then, the owner placed a small plate on the table. It was a slice of lemon cake.

"Oh," Isabelle started, "I didn't order this—"

"It's on the house Congratulations on the new job." He gave her a knowing grin before walking away.

Chapter 3

ISABELLE

A week after her interview with Julia, Isabelle stood outside, ready to enter, her new office. It was a horrid, rainy sort of day, and her umbrella had broken when she was just halfway to the office.

"It's fine, it's fine. I've got this," she told herself before pushing open the door and looking around. "I mean, she said small office, but this is ridiculous," she muttered to herself again and swept her wet hair from her neck, wringing it out as subtly as possible. She had gotten into the bad habit of speaking her mind beneath her breath and thinking no one could hear her.

"Good morning, you must be Isabelle—our new temp."

Isabelle whirled around and spotted the receptionist who was sat behind her desk. "Oh God—you got me there," Isabelle laughed, dropping her hair in favour of swiping beneath her eyes to ensure her mascara hadn't run down her cheeks.

"We're meant to arrive by 8 am but, as it's your first day, I'm sure Julia won't mind. I'm Iris. It's nice to meet you."

She seemed cold, and Isabelle was confused about what she could have done to her. "Hi, yes, I'm Isabelle. Is Julia in?"

Iris walked around her desk and pointed to a door to their left. "She's waiting for you."

Isabelle nodded once to Iris and began walking across the corridor to Julia's office. "God, she's got a stick up her—"

Before she could finish her sentence, Julia was there, crossing her arms as she stood in the door's frame. "You're not good at first impressions, are you? Follow me."

Julia led the way to the front of the room as Isabelle screamed in her head, *What the fuck! How does this keep happening?* She clutched her bag tightly, frustration getting the better of her.

"Right, a quick rundown, your desk is over there..." Julia pointed, then paused before tossing over her shoulder, "Iris, where the hell is Patrick? He's late!"

Iris looked up from her computer at the front of the room and shrugged her shoulders.

Julia let out a deep sigh and turned back to Isabelle. "Anyway, where was I? That's right, your desk is over there; your first assignment will be waiting for you. Normally, I would do introductions but since you're late, you'll have to do that yourself over lunch." With that, Julia turned and walked back to her office.

Isabelle slowly shuffled towards the desk. She felt like the new kid at school who had just discovered they had an evil teacher. *God, how do I keep fucking up around that woman?*

Trapped in her thoughts, she wasn't aware of her surroundings and a man charged into her shoulder on his way past and nearly knocked her over. "Hey, watch where you're walking!" she called after his retreating back.

The man froze. Isabelle narrowed her eyes as he slowly turned around, looking at the floor as he did so. "I'm sorry," he murmured. "Please excuse me." No sooner had the words left his mouth than he had turned back around, scurrying to the desk opposite the one she had been assigned. However, before he sat down, Julia bellowed from her in her office and he was off again, on his way to her.

Isabelle trailed him with her eyes, anger morphing into curiosity. His suit was soaked, raindrops glistened from his forehead, and he hadn't even taken the time to adjust the wet hair which had stuck to his forehead.

"Oh, don't mind him, babes—he's harmless." A woman about Isabelle's age was gliding towards her, two coffees in hand. "That's just Patrick—he's a quiet one. Oh, I'm Freya, by the way."

She passed one of the coffees to Isabelle, who gladly accepted it. "Oh my God, you're a lifesaver. I needed this." Freya laughed. Isabelle was just about to take a sip of her coffee when she got her first proper look at Freya and blurted, "Goddamn—you're stunning, you are!" Slightly embarrassed, she quickly looked away and took a sip of the coffee.

Freya shot her a movie star smile and pulled her hair behind her ears. "Oh," she laughed. "Thanks, babes. We'll get along like a house on fire."

Somehow, while they were speaking, a hulk of a man managed to sneak up behind Freya's slender figure. "Flattery will get you everywhere with this one," he chuckled, nudging Freya with his elbow good-naturedly.

Freya shot back with a sharp elbow to the stomach—which barely fazed him.

"How you doin' darlin'?" he asked, grinning at Isabelle.

Isabelle glared at him with one hand on her hip. "I ain't your *darlin'*, mate. Wanna try again?"

Albies Bellowing laugh filled the room, reverberating off the walls.

Freya interlocked her arm with Isabelle's and offered a grin of her own. "Oh, babes, we are definitely going to get along," she laughed before leading Isabelle the rest of the way to her desk.

"That idiot is Albie. He's… well, he's Albie," she rolled her eyes. "He's an idiot but he's alright."

Isabelle put her bag down and sat at her desk, took another sip of coffee and gave a noncommittal *hmm.*

"We'll do lunch today, yeah? On me," Freya said as she walked off.

Isabelle took a moment. *Blimey, that was one way to meet my coworkers, I guess.*

She turned on the computer in front of her and found her task for the day waiting for her, as promised. Reading through the task, she watched as the man who had bumped into her left the bathroom. He must have been using the hand dryer to dry off as he looked different, now with the hair off his face, Isabelle could spy thick eyebrows bordering intense, bright blue eyes.

"I didn't expect that..." she muttered to herself as she glanced at him.

He looked somewhat haunted, yet handsome—with pale skin and a slim figure which seemed almost awkward. In fact, everything about him seemed fragile and innocent. Everything but his eyes…

She violently shook her head and made herself look back to her desk. *Calm down, girl. Let's get to work.*

***

Isabelle was so intently locked in on her work that she was only taken out of it by a tap on the shoulder from Freya. "Come on babes, it's lunchtime. Let's go. Albie and Iris are waiting outside."

Surprised at the time, Isabelle grabbed her coat and followed Freya past Patrick's desk towards the office door and, as they walked, she noticed he was still working. "You joining us?" she playfully asked while on her way.

But Patrick continued typing as though she weren't there. Isabelle stopped in her tracks. Her mouth dropped. How could he so blatantly ignore her?

Before she could say anything, however, Freya linked an arm through hers and pulled her towards the door.

"Is that guy just a dickhead then?" Isabelle asked once they were out the door, enraged.

Freya laughed and shook her head. "Oh, don't worry babes—he's lovely, really. He just doesn't really do the whole social thing, you get me?"

Isabelle frowned slightly before shrugging and offering a laugh. *Why worry about it?* She thought. Isabelle laughed and followed the group to lunch.

After properly meeting her coworkers, Isabelle was on cloud nine. Everyone seemed like her kind of people and, going to lunch with them had really brightened her day. Well, minus Iris, that is... But Isabelle got the feeling that everyone thought that way.

The rest of the day flew by, and it was 5 pm in no time. Data Entry was mind-numbing, sure, but it wasn't anything she couldn't deal with. When she saw Freya and Albie putting on their coats, she knew it was time to go home and the exhaustion hit her. All she wanted was her bed.

After saying goodbye and swapping phone numbers with Freya, she headed home and that night, they spent hours talking on the phone and getting to know each other. The conversation flowed like they had known each other for years and Freya made sure Isabelle was given details on everyone in the office.

After, Isabelle flopped into bed. Looking at the ceiling, she realised that the only person Freya didn't talk about was Patrick.

"What was that guy's problem?" she mumbled to herself. She hadn't let go of him being rude and ignoring her when she asked him to lunch.

And there, late at night in her bed, the memory resounded until she felt newly irritated by his actions—or lack thereof—that she resolved to find out what he had to say to himself when she saw him the next day. That night, she fell asleep with a fire in her belly.

Though, as it went, it took days before she built up the courage to approach him.

Chapter 4

PATRICK

Patrick's morning was chaotic. He woke up late and had to run home to feed Doc, and when he got into the office, he sat down to realise that his morning's work was all wrong.

He knew he would have to redo it. His mind hadn't slowed down since the new girl started. The office felt cold and everything inside was the same yet, suddenly, different. Occasionally, he would look up from his monitor and see her glancing at him from the corner of her eye in a way which suggested she was less than pleased with him. Only… he wasn't sure what he'd done. He hadn't even spoken to her yet. The tension was starting to make him feel like he had at his previous job, and he found, more and more often, that his skin would turn blotchy and red.

Just then, Patrick's stomach growled, and he sighed, jerking his attention away from his monitor and to the time on the clock. He hadn't eaten breakfast because of all the running around this morning and it was finally lunchtime. As he bent down to grab his lunch, a shadow crept over his desk and hovered there until it became an imposing presence.

He slowly raised his head and, there she was, standing before him with her hands on her waist. The look in her eyes told Patrick that she wasn't here for a work issue.

This is how it started last time, he thought. He'd found it much harder to stay under the radar at his last job since his old colleagues used to blame him for their mistakes and he couldn't bring himself to confront them about it.

Just thinking about the behind-the-back whispering and laughing quickly had his temperature rising and the air suddenly feeling heavy.

He hadn't been looking after himself at his old job. He didn't eat, didn't shower and, in the end, it became too much to handle. Ever since Julia had taken him under her wing, however, he had gained enough weight to look healthy rather than the shadow of a man she had interviewed. He was feeling less stressed than ever, and he didn't want to go back to being stressed all the time and potentially risk this position.

The last thing he wanted was to lose this job.

Squeezing his lunch box hard, Patrick stopped mid-motion, just staring at this terrifying woman ahead of him. *Not again* was the only thought running through Patrick's mind as he subtly looked her up and down to try and get the measure of her. But, as his eyes rose, he quickly noticed how petite she was and, as he got to her face, he paused. Even with the intimidating expression on her face, he couldn't help noticing her heart-shaped face, her deep brown eyes or her soft, rosy skin…

Oh. Wow, she's cute. Patrick quickly focused his attention elsewhere when he realised what he was doing and began rummaging through his lunchbox, instead. No one had said a word—it was five seconds at most—but, for Patrick, the moment had felt like five hours.

"So, er—" Isabelle murmured. "Hi?" She waved at him sarcastically "How come you ignored me the other day? You haven't even properly apologised for bumping into me." She seemed annoyed, yet her tone was playful, and she gave him a relaxed smile which seemed genuine. "I think you need to come to lunch to make it up to me."

"Oh, I'm sorry," Patrick said, rising to his feet. He didn't realise how much he would tower over her; there was about a foot between them. He held out his hand. "Nice to meet you. I'm Patrick… I hope we can work well together."

Isabelle's face scrunched and while she didn't seem angry anymore, she didn't hold her hand out. "Right… Yeah—well, we're going for lunch. Are you going to join us today?"

Embarrassed, Patrick pulled his hand back, sat down, and looked down at his lunch box again. "Sorry—I can't. I'm going to eat this and carry on working." His insides felt like they were on fire. His hands were sweating so much that he could feel it on the lunch box.

There was no response except the sound of heels clacking across the floor. She had left with the rest of the office. He was alone.

Patrick put his head in his hands and groaned loudly. He started eating his lunch, but his appetite was gone so he put the lid back on, entering his own little world.

Hours flew by with him tapping away at his keyboard. Sometime during, everyone returned from lunch.

No one said a thing to Patrick for the rest of the day. 5 pm flashed on his screen and he looked up from his desk to see he was the last one in once more.

He took a deep sigh and headed off home.

***

As soon as he put his key into the door, he heard Doc running to the front door. As soon as he entered his flat, A half smile rose to Patrick's face for the first time that day but dropped almost immediately as Doc rubbed his lean black and white body on Patrick's leg.

That night, while cooking, fish for himself and Doc, Patrick turned to Doc, who was sitting on the kitchen counter, and asked, "How do I fix this?" he sighed. "I don't want to lose this job. I don't want to have to—"

Doc jumped down from the counter and drank from his water bowl. As If he'd received an electric shock, Patrick's bolted upright.

"That's it!" he laughed to himself, looking at his cat. "Great idea, Doc. How'd you get so smart?"

Doc simply stared at Patrick and meowed before cleaning his face with his paw, almost in agreement. Patrick smiled. He named him Doc because of how the cat seemed to respond to Patrick's questions, like a TV show he had seen with a psychiatrist in it.

After they'd eaten, the pair headed to bed and drifted soundly to sleep.

***

The next morning, Patrick woke up an hour earlier than usual and started getting ready for the day. Doc plodded a bit grumpily through the kitchen and headed into the living room to go back to sleep.

"Hey," Patrick called after him. "This was your idea, remember? Right, I've put some water and food in your bowl. I'm sorry it's early, but I have a job to do here!" With that, he left for work but, as soon as he stepped outside, the heavens opened.

Rain fell heavily upon him. He didn't have time to go back for an umbrella so he instead decided to sprint to the coffee shop nearest to work called *Rachael's* where he stood for a few minutes, trying to figure out what to buy, he realised he had no idea what Isabelle would like, before the owner's wife suggested he try their latte.

"No one can hate a latte," she said with a kind smile.

He agreed, thinking to himself, *She's the expert. How could she be wrong?*

He bought a coffee and headed to the office, finding he was the first one in.

"Thank God—the plan is going perfectly," he muttered to himself. He didn't want her to be there when he dropped the coffee off.

Moving to his desk, Patrick grabbed a marker and, while regularly checking the door over his shoulder, wrote out the word 'Sorry' on a Post-it note. It took him a while to figure out what he should write, tapping the pen on the table repeatedly, he finally settled on a simple apology.

Once satisfied, he sheepishly crept over to her desk where he paused, looking it over. Her desk was cute—ridiculously cute, in fact. After only being with the company for a week, she had settled in, and it was like she had been here for years.

Everything she has on her desk is cat-related; even her pens have paws on them.

Patrick spun back around to his desk, arched over and grabbed his pen. He carefully drew his version of Doc on the Post-it under the word 'Sorry.'

Hoping it wasn't too much, he put the note on top of the coffee and placed the two on her desk like it was a precious artefact. He then stood, looking at the coffee on her desk for a moment before he heard a car pull up outside and quickly sprinted to his desk. There, he took a deep breath and started to tap away at his keyboard.

People started to slowly trickle in from the rain. Julia came first and, pleasantly surprised to see Patrick at his desk and working, decided not to interfere. The rest of the office got to work in the next few minutes. That is, all except Isabelle.

That's when Patrick realised, he'd made a colossal error; the coffee would grow cold before she arrived. The minutes ticked by and, eventually, Isabelle stumbled through the door soaked through.

Patrick watched, —even though she was soaked, she wore a big smile. Freya handed her a towel which she used on her hair, and they laughed as they headed to the bathroom to dry off. They remained in there for a while before leaving, still making jokes.

How is she laughing? Patrick thought. He hated getting stuck in the rain.

Isabelle thanked Freya and headed to her desk. As she sat, however, she noticed the note.

Oh God, she's just sitting there. She's probably thinking that some weirdo has left her a stone-cold coffee. Patrick sat, stuck to his seat, yet wishing he could run over and throw the coffee out the window.

The next moment, she picks up the coffee and stands. *This is it, I failed. She's going to keep on hating me. Why did I bother to try—*

Patrick closed his eyes as she walked over to the small office kitchen, heels clicking against the tiled floor. Then, he heard the microwave.

His eyes popped open, head flicking up like a light switch. *She's heating the coffee.*

His shocked eyes connected with hers for a moment before flitting away and Patrick focused on resetting himself enough to return to work. His smile was hard to hide, though.

As lunchtime arrived, Patrick diligently typed away while his colleagues headed out for lunch. The rest of the day passed smoothly and all he could think of was celebrating with Doc at home.

As the day came to an end, people started leaving one by one. Patrick was last. He'd had to finish fixing the work from the previous day.

As soon as he finished, he grabbed his things and left. As he turned the corner, however, he was met by Isabelle—who leaned against the car park wall, waiting for him.

Chapter 5

ISABELLE

EARLIER THAT DAY

It was a gloomy-looking morning, but all Isabelle could think of was how excited for the day at work she was. She'd formed a fast friendship with Freya and couldn't wait to chat more at lunch and during their breaks.

She spent a little time styling her hair, then grabbed a banana and headed to work. As the sky appeared cloudy, she threw on a jacket for her half-hour walk there. She managed to get a reasonable distance from her flat while scrolling through the news on her phone before little raindrops hit her phone screen.

"No, no, no," she cursed. "Please don't rain!" She started picking up her pace, trying to get to work before the rain hit but the onslaught grew heavier and heavier until she was forced to take shelter under a bus stop to call Julia.

"Julia, I might be a few minutes late. I'm so sorry! I didn't check the weather and I'm getting drenched in the rain. I'm gonna wait at this bus stop for a few minutes to see if it will calm down. Is that, ok?"

Julia could hear the desperation in Isabelle's voice. "Next time, please check the weather and bring an umbrella," she said. "I may not be as lenient next time." Julia tried not to be too harsh about it, because she appreciated Isabelle calling her.

Isabelle messaged Freya, asking her to bring a towel to the door before starting her run in the rain. As soon as she reached the office, she caught a glimpse of herself in the door's reflection.

"I'm so glad I spent that time doing my hair this morning," she laughed to herself. She walked into the office, thankful that Freya immediately spotted her and came over to help her dry off a bit. As Freya approached, Isabelle struck a pose. "Don't I look amazing?"

They both cracked up laughing as Freya threw her the towel. "Follow me. You're a disaster," she chuckled again. "Let's get that dress at least a little bit dry."

They headed to the bathroom, drying her dress off by using the hand dryers as best they could. "I thought I'd have to buy you a dinner before I could get you like this," Freya giggled.

In a few minutes, the dress was dry, and they left the bathroom. "Now get to work, you, before Julia comes round to moan," Freya instructed before heading to her own desk.

Right, let's start the day, Isabelle said to herself. Sitting on her chair, she realised that her dress was still very damp but as dry as the hand dryers could make it. Switching on her monitor, she noticed a coffee sitting to the side of the screen with a small note which read 'Sorry' atop it.

Sorry? She stared at the cup for a few seconds,

Who left this here? And why are they sorry?

Curious, she picked up the note and saw a little drawing of a cat and her questions disappeared.

"Cute!" she exclaimed aloud without thinking.

You know, a nice hot coffee is just what I need right now. Thanks, kind stranger, she thought to herself, launching herself up and heading towards the kitchen with a smile.

She carefully transferred the coffee into a mug and placed the mug inside the microwave, switches it on and turns around to look around while leaning against the counter. While scanning the room, she caught Patrick's piercing eyes.

He was smiling.

Isabelle hadn't seen him smile before. She smiled back on instinct.

Wait... was it, Patrick?

"That's adorable," she said beneath her breath. Looking back up, she realised Patrick's head had dropped again, however, she could still see him smiling. *Who is this guy?* she thought to herself, cheeks slowly turning red.

She turned to get her coffee from the microwave and headed back to her desk. As she passed Patrick's desk, she hooked her hair around her ear and looked back at him, finding him intently looking at his monitor, unable to hide the slight grin from his thin lips.

God, this is exactly *what I needed,* she thought, taking another sip. She wanted to thank him, but he was in his own world. "I'll thank him later," she resolved.

After a morning of arduous work, Isabelle could still feel the caffeine buzz from her coffee. Freya asked her to lunch, and they went to *Racheal's* for more coffee and a sandwich. While they were eating, Freya suddenly paused. "So, I've got to ask—what was happening this morning?"

"This morning?" Isabelle's brow scrunched. "What do you mean—me being late? Oh, I spent too long doing my hair and then the rain hit, so I—"

"No!" Freya interrupted. "I mean the coffee and the note! When I came in this morning, it was already there and the only person in was Patrick." She put her sandwich down and stared at Isabelle, waiting for an answer.

"I don't know," she said, cheeks reddening. "I mean, I didn't even know it was from him to start with—I only realised when I looked over and saw him smiling when he saw me put it in the microwave. I sort—"

"Shut the front door!" Freya gasped. "You saw him smile? What did he look like? Was he hot?"

At this point, Isabelle was very red and her cheeks flush. Freya noticed and grinned.

"So, one more thing has been killing me—what did the note say? And why did he leave you a coffee?" Freya was leaning forward, her sandwich completely abandoned. Isabelle pulled the note from her purse and handed it to Freya.

"'Sorry?' What for? What did he do? Also, who would have known Patrick, of all people, could draw a cute picture of a cat!"

Isabelle snatched the note back and put it back in her purse to protect it before sighing. "Well, yesterday—when I asked him to come to lunch with everyone—I joked and said he needed to apologise for bumping into me. I think he took that literally."

"Oh, Patrick, babe—you're a cutie. That's just too adorable! *Isabelle*! What did you say to him?" Freya asked, and Isabelle began to relax.

"Well, I kinda haven't said anything..." Isabelle bit her lip guiltily. "He was so into his work that I just wanted to leave him be—but he seemed happy."

Freya gasped again. "You didn't thank him? What the hell, Isabelle! You need to talk to him."

Isabelle snapped back in defence. "I mean, I was always gonna talk to him… I was just going to wait till after work."

Freya held her hands up in surrender.

"Woah there, I'm just checking." They both laughed, finished their lunch and headed back to the office. "Well, message me later tonight and let me know how it goes, babes." Freya blows a kiss into the air. "Good luck."

Isabelle was confused. *Why would I need luck? I just wanna thank him for the coffee...*

The day seemed to fly by, and Isabelle met with Julia at the end of the day to discuss how she was settling in—which made her love where she worked even more. She initially only went for this job to make some money to help pay her debts but feeling so wanted after just a few days was nice.

Ten minutes before the end of the day, Isabelle's mind drifted from work to Patrick. Why was she thinking about him? He was just some guy. *All I'm gonna do is say thanks for the coffee. I'm not expecting a long conversation… even though I would quite like to talk to him.*

She was so caught up in her thoughts that the time to leave popped up on her screen in no time, and she started getting her stuff together. She then said her goodbyes to Freya and looked over to Patrick's desk, finding him still consumed by his work.

I'll just wait outside for him, she thought to herself and did just that, posting herself up against a wall of the car park, thinking that he would be five minutes at most.

Twenty minutes passed and he didn't show.

"Are you joking? What am I *doing* right now?" She was getting irritated and stopped leaning against the wall, about to head home, when he finally appeared.

Chapter 6

PATRICK

What was she doing here? Was she waiting for him? Panic grips Patrick's stomach as his heart races, and he clings to his bag. Isabelle slowly starts walking over to him.

"Hey, Patrick," Isabelle started as she finally reached him.

Just get through this, then you can go home. He takes a noticeably big breath.

"Hi, how can I help you?" he asks. "Or are you waiting for someone else?" Why had that never even occurred to him? His heart raced faster and sweat accumulated in his palm.

Isabelle places her bag on the ground and tucks her hair behind her ear. She looks stunning in the dusk light.

"Sorry for waiting for you outside like this but I didn't want to interrupt you while you were working. I just wanted to catch you before you went home."

Patrick started to feel slightly calmer and focused on controlling his breathing, however, he didn't say anything.

"I—I just wanted to thank you for the coffee and note this morning." She looked directly into Patrick's eyes. Although he usually avoided doing so with anyone, her sincere, deep chocolate-brown eyes held his gaze. "You really didn't have to do that," she continued. "I was only joking when I said you should apologise. I'm sorry if I made you feel guilty."

Patrick suddenly came to life and began to gesticulate wildly with his arms. "No, please don't worry. I didn't do it because of you, I promise. You did nothing wrong, I was talking to my cat, Doc, and—" Patrick cut himself off, his pale cheeks flushed with colour. He almost stumbled back. "Erm—no, I mean…"

No one in the office knew he had a cat, and he'd just told her that he talks to him like they had full conversations with one another. He completely loses his composure, and it feels like time has stopped. Stuck in his mind, imagining the worst outcomes, everything around him is suddenly tinged with pitch black. Endless possible disasters spin around him.

“Oh my God!” Isabelle squeals and the darkness rescinds without warning. “You have a cat?” She lunged toward Patrick, grabbing hold of his arm. “Do you have any pictures? I need to see them!”

Stunned, Patrick instinctively pulls out his phone and shows her his lock screen which a picture of Doc asleep on his lap waits.

As he turns it to show her, she unclenches her vice-like grip on his arm and covers her mouth with her hand. “Aw, look at that cutie! They are just adorable—I can’t even.”

Patrick glanced at her and was taken aback by how adorable she looked, gushing about Doc.

“Now, I just know there’s a story behind such a strange name. How about you tell me tomorrow over lunch?”

Patrick didn’t know how to respond. The last time she asked him to lunch, he ignored her. This time, he knew he had to give her a proper answer, but he hesitated too long, and her face twisted uncomfortably.

“Yeah, okay—I guess I could,” Patrick said, looking towards the ground.

“Really?” Isabelle’s face lit up and it was clear that she hadn’t expected him to agree but the idea of rejecting her twice made Patrick feel guilty. Usually, people ask him once and then leave him alone.

"Sure, we can go for lunch if you'd like to?" Patrick couldn’t help himself from cracking a slight smile at her obvious excitement.

“Yes, of course I want to!” Without warning, she swiftly snatched up her bag and began to walk away. “Right, I'm looking forward to it. I’ll see you tomorrow!”

Patrick simply watched her walk away.

“What just happened?” he groaned to himself before raising a hand to his eyes and rubbing them.

Chapter 7

PATRICK

Patrick stood still for a few minutes before slowly walking home, his mind replaying the conversation over and over. Had he really agreed to go to lunch with Isabelle?

The walk took him over an hour as opposed to the ten minutes it usually took. He opened his front door, and, like every day, Doc came running over and rubbed his head and body on Patrick's legs, twirling delicately between his feet. "Hey buddy," Patrick yawned and bent down to pick Doc up. He cradled him in his arms and headed straight to the sofa to sit down. Patrick flopped down with Doc on his lap.

"Doc, I think I've messed up bad," Patrick sighed, scratching behind Doc's ears absentmindedly as he leant his head back and stared at the ceiling. "Today has been a long day."

Doc looked up at him, purring softly.

Patrick began to regale the feline with a narration of his day, up to when Isabelle was waiting outside for him. "Now, Doc, this is the kicker—as I left work, the woman I brought that coffee for was waiting outside. I thought I had fixed the problem of her wanting to speak to me and, when I saw her, and thought that she was going to have a go at me or something! But—God, bud, was I wrong." Patrick picked Doc up and dangles him and looked into his eyes. "She asked me to go for lunch with her. *Again.*"

Doc meowed.

Patrick had always bounced ideas off Doc to help him process whatever was bogging him down but, to him, it most likely sounded like bizarre human ramblings.

"No, Doc, you don't get it. When she asked me to lunch, I said *yes.*" Patrick paused, then suddenly put Doc down and sat up sharply. "Wait, was that her asking me out?"

Doc jumped off his lap and Patrick quickly stood.

"No. There's no way she would. This must be a trick," he muttered and stopped dead in the middle of the room.

Doc turned and started to leave the room. Patrick followed Doc to the kitchen, where the cat sat beside his bowl, obviously hinting that he was hungry.

Patrick rubbed his neck, smiling as he momentarily pushed his own anxieties from his mind and looked down at the black and white cat on the floor cleaning his paw and jested, "Just want me for the food, don't ya?"

Still laughing, he headed to a kitchen cupboard and pulled out a can of tuna. Doc meowed loudly, circling near his bowl. As Patrick bent to empty the can in the impatient cat's bowl, he sighed.

"It's just food. I'm overthinking this way too much, aren't I, Doc?" He let out a loud groan.

"She was more interested in you than anything," he murmured, throwing the can into the recycling. Doc was chowing down on his dinner, not taking the slightest bit of notice what Patrick was saying.

Leaning against the kitchen side and scrolling through the images of Doc, he told himself that she would just want to know more about Doc and to see more pictures. She saw Doc's picture on his phone and wanted to see more, so it was safe to assume she likes cats. Plus, she has all that cat stuff all over her desk at work…

He puts his phone away and heads out of the kitchen, calling out to Doc as he goes. "I'm gonna have a shower and think more. Enjoy your dinner, Doc."

Patrick took a long, steaming shower. Lost in thought, tried to organise the events of the day in his head. By the time he had finished showering and stood in front of the mirror above his sink, wiping away the steam with his hand, he looked at himself and realised that he had bags under his eyes. He was pale—he'd always thought he had the look of a skeleton. *Why would a girl like that ever be interested in a guy like me?*

The next morning, Patrick woke up to his alarm and noticed he was in a surprisingly good mood. He made Doc's breakfast as usual and left slightly earlier than he normally would because he didn't have to make lunch today. It was a strange feeling.

As he got closer and closer to work, his chest tightened. He was going to lunch with someone today. Why did he agree to this? This wasn't him. He was the loner in the corner of the office, keeping out of the way and having lunch at his desk. Why would he risk his comfort zone… What was it about this woman that was making him willing to step out of it like this?

He arrived at the office first and decided to clear his mind as best he could and focus on work. People started to roll into the office in no time, but Patrick didn't look up once. Yet, every time the door opened, his heart pounded, and his chest grew tight.

The morning passed too quickly for Patrick's liking, and he started thinking of different ways to cancel the lunch. What if he accidentally deleted all his work? He would have to stay behind to catch up, right? He thought about it but couldn't bring himself to throw away a morning's worth of work.

There was no escaping it. He became very fidgety, and his leg started to bounce under his table. Even though he was focused on his work, he couldn't hide his anxiety and chewed on the side of his cheek. A few times, one colleague or another approached his desk to ask for some reports but, instead, saw how he was and left him alone.

Far too soon, the clock hit noon. It was lunch. He carried on working, keeping his head down. Perhaps she will have forgotten. In the background, he heard people leaving for lunch and, for a moment, there was silence. It strangely put Patrick at ease and his heart seemed to slow. Relief washed over his body.

"So," he heard and froze. "Uh, are you hungry?"

Patrick's heart stopped. Then, the strong scent of perfume hits him, its scent sweet and alluring. He slowly raises her head and sees her standing over his desk, looking shy but pretty as she waited for an answer.

Patrick let out a breath, realising he couldn't just sit there looking at her. "Y—yes," he said—too loudly.

Isabelle jumped and laughed. "Well, we best get some food in you. Hopefully, it'll help with your volume control," Isabelle giggled.

Patrick nervously laughed, rubbing the back of his head as he began picking up his phone and wallet.

She smiled and started to walk away from his desk and towards the door. "So, I was thinking we should go to *Rachael's*…"

Chapter 8

ISABELLE

Aside from the counter, just four small tables filled the small, rustic, homely space. There were two members of staff; the owner, Nick, and his wife Rachael, who the café was named after. *Rachael's* café had been open for 25 years and, due to its proximity to the office, had become the local haunt of the few staff who worked there.

The owners were both in their 60s but still memorised the orders of their regular customers by heart. The pleasant aroma of fresh coffee, the relaxing sounds of soft jazz and the inviting ambience make this café the perfect spot to take a break and enjoy lunch.

Isabelle opened the door to the café and was greeted warmly by the owner.

"Mind if we sit anywhere?" she asked, looking around and realising that no one from the office was there.

"Ah, yes, Miss Isabelle. We don't have anyone in today—just a lot of takeaway orders, Who's your friend? Will he be joining you?"

Isabelle was about to nod, turning to spot that Patrick was hovering in the doorframe uncomfortably. "This is Patrick," she told the older man. "He works with us and yeah, he's joining me today," she smiled, heading over to the table at the back of the room.

Patrick sheepishly followed.

"Alright, Miss Isabelle, what will your friend be having?" the owner enquired as they took their seats and got two mugs ready to make the coffee. Behind him, his wife started buttering bread to make Isabelle's regular sandwich order.

Patrick sat opposite Isabelle and clasped his hands awkwardly before him, just staring at the table between them. She decided to take the initiative and looked towards the owner. “He’ll have my order today if that’s ok? Please and thank you!” she said with a smile.

“Not a problem—give me a mo and I’ll bring your coffee over,” the man said before puttering away.

Patrick looked up from the table, thankfully, and into Isabelle’s eyes. “Thank you for that.”

Isabelle smiled. His eyes were laser-focused on hers in a way she had only seen before from a distance while looking over at his desk every day at work. It was as though nothing in the world could possibly distract him when his eyes were like this. She looked deeply into his beautiful eyes, starting to feel a little embarrassed from the level of focus he had trained on her, but she didn’t want him to look away.

They both waited for their coffees in companiable silence. Isabelle flicked her hair over her shoulders as she spotted the owner heading over to their table with the two lattes.

“Enjoy! My wife will be over shortly with your sandwiches.” He turned to leave, and the pair murmured soft *thank you*-s to which he gave a half smile.

“Isn’t this latte to die for?” Isabelle said with her eyes shut, enjoying the strong flavour. She opened her eyes to Patrick tentatively sipping the hot coffee, drinking a mouthful and nodding.

The conversation was not flowing, and she pursed her lips. “So, your cat's name is Doc, right?”

Suddenly, it was as though Patrick snapped back into the room. “Yeah, that’s right. I guessed you’d want to see some pictures of him.”

She stopped him as he went to pull his phone from his pocket. “Oh, show me later,” she said with a gentle smile while clutching the warm coffee with both hands. “I want to know more about you!”

Her expression was sincere. “To be honest, I'm not sure there’s anything that interesting about me,” he said, looking down at his coffee once more. “I live alone with my cat and enjoy a quiet life. I go to work, come home and spend time with Doc.”

Isabelle smiled brightly. “That’s so cute, you must love Doc! He's gotta be one special cat… I don’t think that sounds uninteresting at all.” She couldn't understand why he was speaking so negatively about himself. It sounded to her like he was a sweet guy who kept to himself—what was so bad about that?

Patrick’s head bounced up to meet her eyes.

Chapter 9

PATRICK

Who is this woman? Patrick thought.

He took some more time to study Isabelle's face as she started talking about how hungry she was and the amazing sandwiches coming their way. She was beautiful—really—with dark, sincere eyes and silky, bouncy hair. The more he looked, the more he saw and momentarily found himself mesmerised by her full, dark red lips. He tried to recall the last time he saw a woman like this but couldn't, so just sat and listened to her speak more about how good the sandwiches here were.

She suddenly stopped mid-sentence. "Am I talking too much?" she asked. "People tell me I can talk too much sometimes."

Patrick snapped out of whatever spell he had been under and finally spoke. "I'm sorry, I just like to hear you talk," he told her quietly. "You're different to anyone I've spoken to in a long time."

Isabelle jolted her head back and pulled her hair over her shoulders. "Thanks, I think!" she laughed.

The older woman suddenly approached their table, two sandwiches in hand. She placed them down with a short, "Enjoy, lovelies," and Isabelle's face lit up.

"Oh my God, thank you!" she called as the woman walked away. She then turned back to Patrick. "This is literally my favourite sandwich ever—you're gonna love it, Patrick!" She quickly bit down on the sandwich with joy.

Patrick joined her—finding that, while it was not a bad sandwich, it was just a BLT—yet Isabelle ate like it was the best thing ever made. Patrick smiled as she mentioned how good it was again, happy to be around someone who seemed to love life and enjoyed the small things.

"I told you, right? One of the best sandwiches you've ever had?"

Patrick smirked and nodded.

She looked away with a grin, trying to hide the rosiness that was invading her cheeks.

"Thank you for inviting me to lunch, Isabelle. I've not had a lunch like this…" his chest felt like a boulder was placed on his chest and his whole demeanour changed. He placed his empty mug onto the now crumb-filled plate and stood to leave.

"Hold up," she scrambled for her still-full mug. "You've barely finished eating! Wait for me, we can walk back together." She was surprised he wanted to leave so quickly and chugged the rest of her coffee before grabbing her things and following suit.

Her voice snapped him out of the fog that was descending over his mind. He looked back and saw her downing the rest of her coffee before scrambling to gather her things.

"Yeah… okay. Let me just pay." He turned and headed over to the counter where the shop owner was waiting with a coy smile.

"How much do I owe you?" he asked then added in a hushed tone, "I'd like to pay for my friend's as well."

The shop owner put out a hand. "Don't you worry, young man. Mrs Julia came in and paid for both of your lunches. I hope to see you and Miss Isabelle again soon."

Patrick was stunned, *why did Julia pay for our lunch? How did I not see her?*

Patrick stepped outside to wait for Isabelle, trying to figure out why Julia had done that. *Was it a mistake?* He wondered. *I'll pay her back after work.*

Shortly after, Isabelle joined him outside.

Chapter 10

PATRICK

"Oh my God, the owner just told me that Julia paid for our lunch! Isn't she just amazing? She's like Batman, I didn't even see her!" Isabelle laughed.

Patrick just nodded and started to walk ahead, leaving Isabelle to a small jog to catch up with him. The walk back to the office felt awkward and quiet, the sounds of their shoes tapping the pavement the only noise between them.

"Why don't you join us for lunch more often, Patrick?" Isabelle asked softly. "I had a fun time with you, and I think everyone else would enjoy having you around, too." She stopped just outside the office door, in the same spot where they talked yesterday.

Patrick froze in place and slowly turned around, giving her a questioning look.

"I mean, you said yes to coming out to lunch with me. Would it be so bad to go with everyone else?" she prodded.

Patrick's face dropped to the ground and a cold shiver ran down his spine. "I'm sorry, Isabelle, I can't. Going to lunch with people sounds easy but it's a lot harder for me. There's good reason I like to be alone."

Isabelle was confused, "But… but don't you get lonely?"

"No, not really. I have Doc," he replied, tone shifting to something more sombre.

Isabelle walked around him to face him. "I'm sorry, but you can't shut everyone out like that. It's not good for you."

Patrick attempted to walk past Isabelle but still wouldn't look at her.

"That's not for you to decide," he muttered as he passed.

Isabelle realised that she might have overstepped and reached out a hand to grab the back of his suit.

"Patrick, please just wait a moment."

He halted instantly, back still facing her and head still drooped to the ground.

"Look," she continued. "I'm sorry if I said too much or asked too much of you—but did you enjoy having lunch today?" While apologetic, she almost pleaded for him to continue the conversation.

Patrick's response came quickly. "I did."

Isabelle jumped in before he could say more. "Well, how about we go for lunch again next week? Just the two of us," she added quickly. "We can just talk some more."

He turned to see Isabelle's face and was ashamed when it looked different to how it usually did. She looked uneasy.

His shoulders dropped; had he made her feel like that?

"Plus, I need to see pictures, the ones of Doc." She forced a smile despite her eyes indicating that she felt otherwise.

"Please smile normally," he said without thinking. "I like your smile. Yes, I'll go to lunch with you next week."

Everything inside him screamed not to agree but he did so anyway and would do it again just to see that pained look disappear from her eyes.

Isabelle's face changed until she looked ecstatic. "I can't wait! Here, take my number and I can message you over the weekend and we can find somewhere to go."

Before he knew what was happening, Isabelle was putting her number into his phone.

"Right, let's get back to work before we're late."

Patrick didn't get very much work done the rest of the day. He was still bewildered by what had happened outside the office at lunch and, by the time everyone was due to go home for the weekend, Patrick was ready to get back to Doc and rest. He was exhausted.

He started packing his things. Everyone had already left early, and he'd overheard they were going to a bar for drinks.

"Patrick?" He heard Julia call from her office. "Can you come in and see me before you leave?"

Patrick groaned under his breath. All he wanted to do was go home—but he remembered he needed to pay Julia back for lunch.

He entered the office, spotting a picture of Julia and her wife on their wedding day on the desk. Julia looked a lot younger in that photo than she did now, but she seemed happier than Patrick had seen her.

Julia was sat behind her desk writing something on her computer. He knew from experience that she wouldn't speak until she finished, so he sat in the seat opposite and waited. Once done, she took off her glasses and looked up at Patrick. "Did you have a good lunch?"

Patrick was surprised that Julia's question was so blunt. "Erm, yes. It was nice, I think," he replied, confused.

"Oh, I'm glad. Try your best, Patrick. I'll see you on Monday." She watched through narrowed eyes as he reached a hand to his pocket. "Don't even think about it," she said. "Off with you." With that, she ushered him towards her door with her hand, put her glasses back on and continued writing.

Patrick stood, dumbfounded, a frown tight on his forehead. Julia simply waved her hand once more towards the door until he turned, leaving with a somewhat confused, "See you Monday."

On his walk home, Patrick mulled over what Julia had said. *Try your best.* What did she mean by that?

He thought it over like a detective trying to decipher a mystery at his corkboard. What was he missing? What should he try his best at?

He was so lost in thought that he ended up walking ten minutes out of his way past his flat but, once he was finally home, he stepped through the threshold of his flat and felt like a giant weight had fallen from his back. Doc came running to rub his body and head across Patrick's leg like usual and Patrick bent down. Picking the cat up and looking him in the eyes he exclaimed, "It's the weekend, buddy! We can finally relax together."

In response, Doc nuzzled his head into Patrick's cheek. Patrick kicked his shoes off and carried Doc to the living room, where he flicked on the light, slumped onto the sofa and let out the deep breath he had been holding in all day.

With a purring Doc on his lap, Patrick's mind began to ease. Within minutes, he was asleep; a week of stress and overthinking had exhausted him, and he had nothing left in the tank.

During this sleep, he had a dream unlike any he'd experienced for a long time. He was in the café facing Isabelle, watching her laugh and getting excited about her sandwich. It felt natural to him. She looked like a vision—like someone out of a fairy tale.

For the rest of the weekend, Patrick took some time to just laze around with Doc and clean his flat. To him, it was usually the perfect weekend. He could recharge, have time with his cat and shut his mind off to the outside world. It was how Patrick had always been most content. But this weekend had felt slightly different. He couldn't stop thinking about her.

Why could he not just put her in the mental box where he placed the rest of his colleagues and seal them away at weekends? It was starting to frustrate him and, as Sunday approached, he was feeling down. He wasn't enjoying his weekend like he usually did. Why did she have this effect on him? Why couldn't he get her out of his head? It was annoying. Derailing. He knew, deep down, that this wasn't really her fault, but it was annoying all the same. He wanted things to go back to how they had always been.

On Sunday evening, as he ate dinner with Doc in the kitchen, he heard his phone beep with an alert. Patrick paused, hand halfway to his mouth, and looked over to Doc. He never received messages.

He placed his fork on his plate and walked into the living room, where he'd left his phone. As he got closer, however, two more message notifications pinged. This wasn't the norm, and he frowned, reaching for his phone. The screen showed three new text messages from an unknown number.

"Three? How are there three?" He gingerly picked up his phone and unlocked it. "Isabelle?"

Excuse me, you were supposed to be sending me pictures of Doc!

You promised.

I'm looking forward to lunch tomorrow x.o

Patrick paused and realised he must have forgotten to take her number, just giving her his but he knew from just the opening messages that they could only be from one person.

He grinned from ear to ear and sent off a few pictures of Doc before putting the phone down and heading back to his dinner.

His weekend no longer felt gloomy.

Chapter 11

PATRICK

The next few weeks were a blur. Patrick joined Isabelle for lunch on Monday. Then again on Tuesday. Not even one week later, and it was as though the pair were joined at the hip. Patrick had stopped making lunches entirely. And, after each lunch—before he'd even gotten back to his desk—he received a text from Isabelle, each usually along the lines of: *I had fun! Same time tomorrow?*

At the start, even though he liked receiving her messages, it felt a little overwhelming. He wasn't used to someone messaging him as much as she did. Over time, however, he looked forward to each morning and Isabelle's excited messages, wishing him a good day. Even if they did usually end by telling him her coffee order for the morning.

"How did this become the norm?" Patrick laughed as he read through her increasingly detailed coffee orders. He laid in bed stroking Doc's head wondering what a pumpkin-spiced latte tasted like.

Like clockwork every morning, the excited, happy message from Isabelle pinged.

He didn't understand how the routine had fallen into place. It was almost like Isabelle had willed it into existence and he'd fully accepted it.

He stopped off at *Rachael's* for this morning's order. As he picked up her pumpkin-spiced latte, the old woman behind the counter asked, "Will we be seeing you at lunch?"

Patrick nodded and smiled before he turned to leave.

Behind him, the old lady let out a hearty laugh and Patrick left, slightly embarrassed.

Patrick was starting to look forward to work. Not because of the work, itself, but more because he liked being around Isabelle. He'd never felt anything like it before, like someone had lit a fire and melted the icy shell he had unwittingly developed over the years. He was even starting to feel more rested. Normally, his sleep would be disturbed by the haunting memories of his past but, ever since he had met Isabelle, she had taken over his sleeping thoughts.

He started to learn more about what kind of person Isabelle was. He liked hearing how close she was with her family and often asked to hear stories of them. A lot of the time, when they went to lunch together, all he wanted was to listen to whatever she had to say. He liked that she usually said aloud whatever was on her mind at the time.

Every now and then, he would catch himself staring at her too long. In those moments, Isabelle gave him what looked to be an uncomfortable glance, and he'd make himself turn away, quickly going back to sipping his coffee kicking himself internally.

They started to take a slightly longer route to get to the office on their way back from *Rachael's*—and looped the green which had a path around the edge and trees either side. A few times, Isabelle looped her arm through his and, while Patrick wasn't usually a huge fan of this sort of thing, he was growing used to it. The first time she'd done it, he'd jolted away from her like a cat who had been sprayed with water. He apologized and she didn't do it again until a few days later, where she looped her arm around his without thinking. That time, Patrick let it happen. There was comfort in how she was around him, which he wasn't used to.

Patrick knew the office was gossiping about them. He looked past his monitors and saw Iris talking to Albie and Freya. He caught Freya's eyes by accident, and Freya smiled at him; he hadn't seen a smile like it from her before, which spooked him.

"Good morning, Patrick," Isabelle sang as she dropped beside him.

Patrick's head immediately dropped, cheeks tinging in pink. He didn't like how she would bring attention to him in the office like this.

"Please, Isabelle," he said, still looking at the ground. "It's early." He attempted to pass the coffee over to the now-stationary, heavily breathing Isabelle, who stood before his desk.

He had become so comfortable around her but still wasn't a fan of how she shone a light on him.

"Let me catch my breath!" She was holding onto her hip, looking to the sky.

Patrick couldn't help but laugh. "Why did you run like that?"

Isabelle grabbed the coffee from his hands. "Well… I've gotta get the steps in, haven't I?" She seemed embarrassed even as she pointed to her smartwatch.

Patrick laughed again.

"Hey… God, you are so mean to me, aren't you?" She slapped his arm playfully.

He snorted.

Isabelle was suddenly blocking the exit of his desk, by holding her arms out wide. "Did Doc play with the bird-on-a-string toy you got him last night?" she asked.

One thing Isabelle had gotten quickly into was buying toys for Doc. Then, she would demand to see pictures and videos *of* him with those cute toys with him. Then, if she learned that Patrick had bought him a new toy, she'd demand to see those, too.

"You're only allowed to leave your desk if you confirm you took a video of him playing with it," she demanded.

Patrick sighed, "Of course I did; I knew you would kill me if I didn't."

He was reaching for his phone when he heard a voice behind Isabelle. "Come on, you two! Whatever this is, it can wait till lunch," Julia called.

Isabelle dropped her arms, standing to attention and dropping her voice an octave. "Sorry boss lady! I'll sort this out at lunch."

Julia just shook her head and kept walking. "Get to work, you two. It's a busy day."

Patrick was horrified and started to tap away at his keyboard.

Isabelle laughed and mouthed "This isn't over, you know?" as she walked to her desk.

She looked so menacing that Patrick made a mental note to not ever cross her when it comes to cats.

Chapter 12

ISABELLE

Within minutes of Isabelle sitting down, Julia stood at the front of their small office and said, "Hold back before you run off to lunch today, will you? I need to make an announcement." Julia's voice could sound so severe at times that Isabelle found her intimidating.

She had been working at the company for a month by that point and knew everyone fairly well. She and Freya regularly went out for drinks and dinner and messaged each other constantly.

Ahead of her work, she began to search online for a wine tasting she'd heard about for the team. As she prepared to book a slot for them at the weekend, she caught herself hovering over how many people the booking was for and frowned. She looked up at Patrick… *would he come?*

Having her desk positioned opposite Patrick's meant that she could glance over at him every now and then and, each time she did, she could see his intense eyes thoroughly engrossed in his work.

There was something about him, she'd realised. She couldn't pinpoint what it was—but she wanted to be around him.

"Right," Julia's commanding tone snapped Isabelle from her thoughts. "It's coming to lunch so, please, if everyone could gather round."

Isabelle bounced up from her desk and headed over to Julia, everyone else quickly joining her. Patrick made it over after everyone else, and Isabelle giggled.

"I wanted to catch you all before you head to lunch. I'm pleased to announce that Isabelle has passed her probation period and is now officially part of the team." Julia started to clap as she finished her statement.

Everyone quickly followed suit and began to clap and congratulate her. She did not know how to feel. She hadn't realised she was on probation.

This was only supposed to be temporary. I told myself this was just a pit stop, nothing more.

Her thoughts were swimming as she thanked Julia.

Do I want to be here?

This thought crept into her mind as she thought about the goals, she had set for herself. Did she want to be working here?

"Drinks tonight then! Ya'll are coming!" Albie stood in front of everyone, pointing towards them. "We gots to celebrate the newbie, ain't we?" He guffawed in his Santa-like way that Isabelle had immediately loved the first day she met him.

Everyone agreed with Albie and Isabelle finally said, "Well, it *is* a Friday night!" she laughed and looked around as everyone began to talk about where they would go. Then stilled.

Where was Patrick?

Distantly, she listened as everyone decided to go to a bar after work and headed out to lunch while Isabelle walked back to her desk, her head on a swivel as she looked for Patrick.

Checking her phone, she had one new message:

I'll be at Rachael's. Don't worry if you're busy with everyone.

Isabelle was confused. Had he left without her?

She made her way to the café in record time. She was vexed—she did not understand what was happening and why Patrick would leave without her; he had never done it before!

Why now?

Opening the door, she saw Patrick sitting alone at their usual table, looking nothing like his usual self. His expression reminded her of when they first came here.

On the table was their regular order, untouched, and Isabelle's frustrations quickly began to subside as she made her way over to the table where Patrick looked down at his hands, zoned out. He hadn't noticed her enter.

She took her seat—the same one as always—which must have startled him, as he jumped.

"Oh, sorry! I didn't mean to make you jump. Is everything okay, Patrick?" Her concern only grew when she saw his face.

He picked up the coffee in front of him for what she assumed was the first time and, when she followed suit, it was lukewarm.

They sat in silence for a moment before Patrick finally spoke, looking down at his hands. “I won’t be coming tonight.”

Chapter 13

PATRICK

You could cut the tension with a knife. Patrick felt claustrophobic; all he wanted to do was breathe, but he couldn't. So, he simply sat, staring down at the table and looking at his hands. He didn't want to see her face.

"Isabelle, I love coming here and having lunch with you but I'm just not like that." He wished he were at home, snug on the sofa with Doc right then. He hated the thought of letting her down like this.

Isabelle surprised him; she did not sound annoyed or angry when she spoke. Instead, her tone was flat. "Can I ask why?"

"I don't like going out like that." His hands were getting sweaty as he clutched his trousers. He knew this was going to happen at some point. *Of course, she was going to find out how boring and broken I am at some point. I guess this will be the last time we'll have lunch together like this.*

He couldn't escape the thoughts. They had taken over his mind like a virus.

He waited for a response for a moment before looking up, eyes widening when he did.

Isabelle sat, silently stuffing her sandwich into her mouth one bite at a time.

What the hell? His face screamed his confusion.

"Oh…" she murmured sheepishly around a mouthful of bread, her words claggy and hard to understand. "I was… *mmhm*—starving."

Patrick blinked, then realised he was also hungry. He picked up his sandwich and followed suit.

As Isabelle finished her sandwich, she slumped back in her chair. "God, I needed that!" She looked at him, smiled and pointed a finger pseudo-aggressively. "Hey, don't be sitting there judging me for being hungry!"

Patrick held up his hands as though at gunpoint. "I would never."

They both laughed and Isabelle stood up. "Right, we best head back, *eh*?"

Patrick downed the rest of his now-cold coffee before thanking the old man behind the counter and following her out the door.

As they returned to work, Patrick ensured he was walking slower than her to keep some distance. *Why had she not said anything about going out tonight?*

Isabelle slowed down without Patrick noticing and started walking by his side.

"You know I don't care about that, right? It's not like I'd stop talking to you if you don't come out for drinks. You're a bit of a silly goose sometimes, aren't you?" Isabelle's voice was different. Instead of sounding jovial or blunt, it had grown soft and caring. He'd never heard her like this.

He stopped and looked at her as she continued to walk. He was utterly smitten.

Before he could respond, she spun around in front of him, arms spread wide. "Stop where you are right now, criminal."

Patrick was still trying to process what had happened. "Criminal?"

Isabelle nodded confidently. "Yes, you criminally kept a cute video of Doc from me—thus, you are a criminal and may go no further until you cough up the goods."

Patrick couldn't stop laughing. Standing before him was the most petite, intimidating woman, acting fierce so she could see a cat video.

"Okay, okay," he laughed again. "I'm going to reach into my pocket and get my phone. Don't shoot!" He lowered his hands and grabbed his phone from his pocket, pulling up the video he had taken the night previous. Before he got the chance to turn his screen around, Isabelle clutched his arm and peered over his shoulder.

Patrick's heart began to race as her expression filled with excitement as she waited for the video to start. *She's beautiful*, was the only thought in his mind as he played the video. Isabelle let out an excited squeal.

"Oh my God, I knew he would love that one! I saw it and *had* to buy it! You're sending this to me later, yes?" Patrick knew he couldn't say and nodded. She unclasped her hands and looked him in the eye, warningly. "You better!"

As Patrick laughed, a cold chill ran down his spine. Iris was behind him, watching them.

"Come on guys, I'm gonna be late if you don't get out of the way," she said with an exasperated tone that suggested she expected immediate action.

Isabelle passed Patrick and headed over to Iris. "Oh, Iris! How are you? You coming out later? Will be amazing to have you there."

Patrick knew this was his opportunity to escape an awkward situation, so he headed inside and made a beeline for his desk, slipping into his chair and finally letting out a deep breath.

It wasn't that he had anything against Iris, really, but he just *knew* she hated him and likely thought he was weird.

Shortly after he sat down, Iris and Isabelle back inside. As Isabelle passed his desk, she whispered a short, "You're welcome," under her breath before heading to her desk where she threw him a crafty smile that caused his cheeks to turn crimson.

Chapter 14

ISABELLE

The day ticked by with Isabelle looking forward to letting down her hair that evening. Yet, she felt out of sorts and couldn't figure out what was wrong, ultimately spending the rest of the day feeling blue.

As the day wrapped up, she collected her things and joined everyone who were preparing to head to the bar. She looked over and saw Patrick was still at his desk, tidying up.

"I'll see you Monday, Patrick."

Patrick looked up and Isabelle's heart sank. He looked like a said puppy. She wished he would come with them.

But all he did was nod.

They said their goodbyes and she headed to the bar with everyone. In the taxi, however, her phone buzzed.

Giving Freya and Albie a quick glance—happy to see they were preoccupied by bickering with one another—she sat and pulled out her phone, spotting a message from Patrick.

Have a fun time. I'm looking forward to lunch on Monday.

The car started moving and, Isabelle felt a bit emotional. She wouldn't usually have expected a message like that to make her sad. She needed to snap out of it—she was looking forward to hanging out with everyone from work, plus she was excited to see what Albie and Freya would be like after a few drinks. She had her suspicions that something was going on between them.

Isabelle snapped out of it as they arrived at the bar and went inside with everyone else. She was looking forward to having a few drinks.

Julia brought a round and then sharply left—Isabelle got the impression that it wasn't really her scene. Then, Albie took complete control of the night, making sure everyone had a drink in hand and getting people up to dance seemingly putting him in his element. It wasn't long before Isabelle started to knock drinks back, having a great time. Even Iris came out of her shell and cracked a few jokes, encouraging everyone to have another drink. Isabelle wouldn't have thought it, but drunk Iris turned out to be her favourite Iris!

The night turned into a blur of drinking, laughing and dancing but soon ended with Freya and Isabelle holding Iris' hair back as she threw up in the bathroom. When they finally returned to their table, Albie stood up with a smile. "Come on then, girls. Time for us to bin this off and head home." As he said this, he passed each girl their belongings. "I've called my mate, and the taxi is on its way now so chop, chop! Let's get a move on."

Albie herded the girls to the front of the bar, which took longer than it should have after Freya broke away, claiming she had to dance to one last song before leaving. Albie swiftly headed into the throng, intent on throwing her over his shoulder.

Isabelle leaned against the wall of the bar to steady herself, Iris close by, and pulled her phone out of her bag.

I hope you had a great night. Congratulations on passing your probation.

The biggest smile filled Isabelle's face; she hadn't expected to get a message from Patrick so late. Freya spotted her and grinned.

They headed from the bar and, when the taxi pulled up, Albie piled the girls in the back before circling and entering the passenger seat.

The taxi pulled away and started heading to Iris' house as it was closest. "Night babes, make sure you drink some water," Freya shouted out the window as Iris stumbled to her door.

"Right, next up is you." Albie turned back and pointed at Isabelle. "So, you have a good night darlin'?"

Freya slapped the arm he pointed with down. "What have I told you about that!"

Isabelle couldn't stop herself from laughing and Freya turned to her, tutted loudly, and called Albie an idiot under her breath.

"So, babes, you're stuck with us now," she said after a beat. "You have fun?"

Isabelle nodded but looked down at her phone. "Yeah, I had a good time! But can I ask you guys for a favour?" Isabelle asked sheepishly.

"Course, babes! Hit us." Freya gently rubbed Isabelle's forearm encouragingly.

"I was wondering if you two were busy Monday lunchtime?"

Chapter 15

PATRICK

When Monday morning rolled around, Patrick cracked open an eye and had that gut-sinking feeling that he was late. *Really* late. With barely enough time to grab a slice of toast and a sip of coffee, he bolted out of the door and sprinted all the way to the office.

He sped around the corner. He could make it to work on time if he kept his pace up. As he drew closer, however, he saw someone waiting outside. His heart sank; he hated it when Julia scolded him for being late.

He succumbed to his fate, slowing his jog to a sulking walk and adjusting his tie as he walked Julia hated it when he turned up to the office looking unkempt and he didn't want to give her any more ammo than she already had.

But, as he got closer, he saw that it wasn't Julia who was waiting for him but Isabelle—holding two coffees in a holder with one hand on her hip. Patrick's fears subsided, replaced by a feeling he wasn't sure of yet put him at ease.

"Erm, have you not looked at your phone?" Isabelle was looking at him in a way she hadn't before; eyebrows raised, head cocked. "I messaged you, like, a bunch this morning."

She was being sassy, which made Patrick let out an unexpected snigger. "Sorry, sorry. I overslept."

Isabelle sighed and shook her head as she held out the coffee, offering him one. "You're lucky. I wasn't going to get you one for breaking tradition."

Patrick thankfully a cup labelled cappuccino, seeing the other was her favourite latte.

"Don't worry, I forgive you," Isabelle said before sticking her tongue out, spinning around and heading for the door.

Patrick took a big sip of the cappuccino with a slight grin before following her.

“Patrick? You’re this close to being late again.” Julia held up her hand, two fingers pinched together, and Patrick sighed.

“I'm sorry, Julia. It won’t happen again.” Patrick’s head lowered as he skulked his way to his desk. He hated letting Julia down, she was always good to him when they were alone but, when they were in the main office, she seemed to hold him to a higher account than the others and he didn’t understand why.

As he sat, Isabelle approached and stood over his desk like she had ever since her first day.

“Are you still annoyed?” Patrick asked.

Confused, Isabelle frowned. “What are you talking about? I was going to tell you to meet me at *Rachael's* at lunch.”

Patrick was pleasantly surprised. “Oh—yeah, sure! I’ll meet you there.”

Isabelle nodded. “Good.”

Patrick started working but his brain still felt half asleep. After a while, he paused.

Meet her there? Does she not want to go together?

Questions started speeding through his mind. He tried to shake them off by working but couldn't. Why would she not want to walk over together? Patrick’s mood took a dip the rest of the morning, his work below his usual standards.

Fifteen minutes before lunch, Julia called him into her office. He knocked twice, then entered. Julia was sitting at her desk, waiting for him. "Everything ok, Patrick?” she asked, gesturing him to sit down.

Patrick was slightly surprised but, as he sat, he nodded.

Julia rolled her eyes. “Right, I'm going to pretend that you didn’t just lie.” She turned her computer screen around and showed Patrick his work from the morning. His stomach tightened.

“I'm going to ask one more time,” Julia said, voice calm. “Is everything okay? You haven’t been like this for a while.”

Patrick could immediately see the mistakes in his work and hung his head, thinking of what to say.

“Look, Patrick,” Julia said before he could. “It's okay. You can make up for it after lunch—I just wanted to check in with you.” Julia’s tone was softer than usual, and she seemed genuinely concerned.

Patrick felt awful. He hadn't let anything affect him like this in a long time and was annoyed because he was usually proud of his work. He spoke while looking at his lap. "I… I'm sorry Julia. This won't happen again, I promise you. I'll work through lunch to fix my mistakes."

Julia had had enough. "I'm going to stop you there, Patrick. This isn't me complaining; I am worried about you and want to make sure you're doing okay. You can make it up later. It's nothing you can't handle."

Patrick's brow furrowed as he raised his head in confusion.

"Look," Julia continued, her own brow creasing in contained worry. "I understand you might not want to tell me everything, but just know I'm always here if you want to talk." Julia scribbled down her number on the back of a business card and stood. "Here's my number. Look, if something happens and you need help, advice or even someone to talk to, I'm here." She held out the card and passed it to him. "Now get out of here. You're late for lunch now, right?"

Julia sat back down and pulled out her phone, ushering Patrick out the door as she put the phone to her ear and immediately started talking.

Patrick rose awkwardly and put the card in his pocket. Everyone had already left for lunch, so he walked over to his desk and sat; he wasn't sure if he had it in him to do lunch today. He pulled his phone from his bag and saw three messages from Isabelle.

Are you heading to Rachael's*?*

God, I'm starving. Let me know when you're on your way. Hopefully, Julia won't keep you long.

Where are you?

Without pausing for thought, Patrick got up and left for the café.

Chapter 16

PATRICK

It was a horrible, bleak day; the clouds reflected Patrick's mood after his talk with Julia. He was trying to forget about it, but he hated letting her down. Between that and Isabelle's strange behaviour—wanting to meet him at *Rachael's* instead of walking together—he was mentally exhausted.

He tried to shake himself out of the funk he was in and opened the door to the café. As usual, the old couple that owned the place greeted him and Isabelle sat at the same table they always claimed. Then, Patrick stood frozen. Isabelle wasn't alone.

Freya and Albie sat at the table across from her and panic settled into Patrick's chest, his heart starting to pound and hands growing clammy. Isabelle spotted him standing at the entrance and waved encouragingly.

Patrick sheepishly shuffled over to the table where they all sat, eating sandwiches and drinking coffee. "Alright big man—you took your time!" Albie was the first to greet him with a grin before continuing to stuff his face with a pastry.

"Babes," Freya broke in. "Your coffee got cold, so I ordered you a new one. It should be here in a mo! I hope Julia went easy on you." She smiled, radiating warmth.

Patrick shook his head subconsciously as the old man appeared, a coffee for Patrick in hand.

"Cor, there's a lot of you here today," the man smiled. "I'm glad to see you all!" He placed Patrick's coffee down in front of him and left.

There was an awkward silence for a few moments as Patrick tried to collect himself and the others' conversation trickled to a halt.

"You, okay?" Isabelle quietly asked him. He nodded and sipped his piping hot coffee—it was just what he needed right now. Isabelle gave a small smile and continued, "Well—I thought, seeing as you couldn't make it the other night, it might be nice to celebrate here, with you!"

Before Patrick could reply, Albie jumped in, "Bloody 'ell, did you miss out! I thought this one was gonna pass out against a wall!" Albie pointed at Freya. "Dances like a jellyfish, she does." Albie laughed heartily and Freya slapped his arm.

Patrick had always been intimidated by these two. Albie was built like a wardrobe and was, perhaps, too confident and Freya… Patrick could never figure Freya out. He knew she was incredibly smart, too bright for the job she was doing, but the thing that scared him about her was she had this aura about her, like, if you crossed her, she would dismantle you without breaking a sweat. Everyone in the office knew it.

However, intimidated by them he was, they had never been mean or rude to him. Plus, he appreciated that they let him be and only came to him with work-related matters.

Isabelle burst out laughing as Freya slapped Albie's arm again, the pair grinning good-naturedly. Patrick snapped back to attention as Albie tried to feign injury—to Freya's disdain.

Patrick sat and drank his coffee, watching the abrupt chaos in silence. After a few minutes, Isabelle realised Patrick had not said anything since he'd arrived and looked over with a slight frown.

"Thanks for inviting me," he said with a short but genuine smile.

It was short and sweet but it shocked Albie and Freya.

"You know, I reckon that's the first mumble I've heard from you outta the office," Albie chuckled.

Patrick was embarrassed, and his heart started to pound again. Like an out-of-body experience, his mind began to conjure images of how cruel they might be to him without his permission. His fight-or-flight instincts kicked in and he looked over to the door—a way out.

"Oh babes," Freya gushed. "I'm so glad you are here! I've never had the chance to chat with you, but Isabelle keeps bigging you up when we go out. It's nice to meet the mythical Patrick, she's told us about!" Freya teased.

Like the eye of a tornado, everything went quiet in Patrick's mind. She talks about him? Of the million different things Patrick thought may be said next, that was never one of them.

He unknowingly grinned. Patrick had been holding one of his hands under the table this whole time. He was trying to control his anxiety by rubbing and tapping his legs. Still, after hearing Freya say that he brought his hand above the table; he seemed so much calmer.

Isabelle's cheeks turned a shade of pink. "Oh my God, Freya! Why would you say that!"

Freya looked across the table and took a sip of her coffee, seemingly knowing exactly what she had done and feeling proud of herself.

They all began to eat, chatting the whole time and, while Patrick mostly remained quiet, he occasionally got involved in the conversation. When they were done, Albie refused to let anyone else pay and paid for their lunches, causing Freya to roll her eyes and tell Isabelle how much she hated it when he did that.

As they walked out the door, Albie turned and stopped them all. "Right, you lot. We gotta make this a regular thing."

Freya put her head in her hand, but Patrick piped up. "I—I think that would be nice."

Isabelle's jaw practically hit the ground.

"Good man!" Albie smiled. "That's what I like to hear! We'll have to bookmark the week with a lunch, yeah?"

After that, they met up on Mondays and Fridays as a group. In the coming weeks, Patrick was still very stoic—but that was just how he was in big groups. The more they spent time together, however, the more Patrick started to creep out of his shell. He became more comfortable joining in as the girls ribbed Albie and, in time, even began starting conversations.

Their lunchtime conversations quickly descended into Isabelle, Freya and Albie debating the places they should visit together. This was the moment that Patrick had been dreading; he knew no matter how much fun he had with Isabelle and his other colleagues, there was a fork waiting in the road ahead. Down one lane, the three of them would go without him and he would be left behind. Down the other, he would have to accept being uncomfortable and try to follow them. It wasn't that he didn't want friends—that he didn't sometimes feel a tinge of loneliness that even Doc couldn't help alleviate—but he knew his issues would get in the way. He knew how he would react—what would happen if he went with them—and didn't feel he could, no matter how much he would love to.

One Tuesday, on a rare day when it was just Patrick and Isabelle at Rachael's for lunch, he decided that he had to speak with her. Let her down right then—so much that she wouldn't want to speak to him again.

"Isabelle," he murmured, looking down at his half-eaten sandwich. "I need to talk to you about something. I know you'll be disappointed, and I'm sorry but I'm not going to be able to go anywhere with you guys."

Isabelle, who had been about to take a bite of her sandwich, frowned. Put the sandwich down and placed her hand on top of his, "What's wrong, Patrick? Has something happened? Are you okay?"

The worry in her eyes was clearly genuine but Patrick pulled his hand away from hers. Her eyes widened. "I have a lot of issues, Isabelle," he began, and it was clear from his voice that he was struggling with his words. "You guys—Freya and Albie—keep making all these plans to go out but I'm just not built like that. Just joining you for lunch is the most I've put myself out there for a long, long time, and I don't think I'm ready for more."

Isabelle's brows knitted together, and she gripped his hand a little tighter.

"Don't worry," he said quietly when he noticed her drawn-down expression. "I would completely understand if you wanted nothing more to do with me. I'm only holding you back from having fun and I would just get in the way." In that moment, Patrick hated himself. He'd been happier than he had felt in years, spending time with Isabelle, then Freya and Albie. He liked their company. His lunchtimes had become *fun*.

Something hit Patrick's head. He bolted his neck upright and blinked. In Isabelle's hand was a piece of bread that she had torn from her sandwich.

She'd thrown bread at him. Why?

"Why did you do that?" he asked, confused.

Isabelle threw the remaining piece of bread in response and crossed her arms over her chest. She looked annoyed.

"Well, can I speak now?" she asked with no small amount of sass.

Perplexed, Patrick nodded.

She sighed. "Look, Patrick, do you realise what's happened recently, or do I need to spell it out for you?" Patrick just sat with a gormless look on his face and Isabelle rolled her eyes. "God, we're all *friends*, you idiot." Her aggression shocked Patrick, and he didn't know how to react. "I'm pissed that you think we would do that to you! Do you think we're such horrible people that we'd drop you just like that for such a dumb reason like that?"

Each word hit Patrick with a dose of reality that he had never thought to imagine. So many people would drop him when they didn't need him anymore that he hadn't even considered that these guys wouldn't. He didn't know how to react.

Isabelle paused, her expression loosening. She unfolded her arms and softened her tone. "Patrick, I don't know what you've been through in your life, but not everyone is like that—none of us would force you to do something you didn't want or throw you away like some broken toy. We *like* being around you; you make us laugh, even when you don't mean to," she smiled, "and you listen so attentively to everything we say and never interrupt or talk over us. You're genuinely kind—people want to be around someone like that. Even if it's just for lunch in a little café like this. It doesn't have to be a night out on the town or even travelling around the country together. This is more than enough; *you* are enough." Isabelle's face burned. She started to wave her hands in front of her. "I'm so embarrassed, don't listen to me!"

Patrick's eyes were filled with tears, like a dam ready to overflow. It was the kindest thing anyone had said to him in years. Sitting before him looking like an angel, Isabelle helped fix something inside of Patrick that she hadn't broken. He was mesmerized.

A single tear fell down his cheek, snapping him out of his trance, and he wiped his eyes with his arm.

"Patrick, I'm so sorry!" Isabelle's eyes were so wide that they looked like little saucers. "I didn't mean—"

Patrick interrupted her. "Forget I said anything—and... please don't tell the others."

He shot Isabelle a sad smile and she got up from her chair, charged around the table, threw her arms around Patrick's neck without another thought and hugged him tight. Patrick reciprocated the hug and squeezed her tight; the smell of her perfume filling his nose.

After a few seconds, Isabelle let go. "Right," she laughed, throat thick with emotion. "Back to work we go, mister."

Patrick looked down at his watch, noticed the time and nodded in agreement. Their walk back to the office was quiet. Patrick was stuck in his mind, processing what had just happened. He knew he had to say something before they got to work and made himself pause just outside the office door.

"Thank you, Isabelle," he said quietly. "If you weren't the way you are, I never would have had what I have right now." He smiled. "I have a group of friends. I have you. I promise I'll keep stretching my comfort zone for you."

She returned his small smile.

The Friday after Patrick and Isabelle's talk, a slight change came over Patrick. It wasn't anything obvious but the accumulation of lots of small things. He was excited to go to lunch with Isabelle, Albie and Freya.

He smiled more.

Chapter 17

PATRICK

The heat on Saturday made Patrick and Doc lethargic and dreaming of a cooler time.

He laid face down on his sofa with a fan, on full blast, directed at him. "Doc, I need a break. I don't know if I can keep up with her. Don't get me wrong, I love spending time with her; she makes me feel—well, how you make me feel, Doc…"

Doc's head tilts slightly, eyes boring into him.

"You know," Patrick continued, "like… I feel at ease with her; my mind doesn't feel as messy."

Doc jumped onto his back, making Patrick jump. He groans and rolls over causing Doc to jump down to the floor.

"What was that for?" Patrick asks, shocked. Doc turned and sat with his back to Patrick. The behaviour was not like Doc at all. Had Patrick done something wrong?

Patrick's phone buzzed beside his head. It was after breakfast, and he must have dozed off.

He reaches for his phone in a daze, the words on the other end spilling out so fast that he could barely make out what was being said.

"Hey babes, it's Freya. Isabelle wants you to come to the beach with us—so come, yeah? We'll pick you up outside of the office in twenty minutes, so get a shift on!" With that, Freya hung up the phone.

Patrick shot up like a bolt, his face frozen in shock.

"What just happened?" Patrick mumbled to himself, brain still unravelling all that had been said while questions flared through him. How did Freya get his number? The beach? He'd never been to the beach. Twenty minutes was not long enough. He needed to think.

Patrick's breaths grew heavier by the second and his heart began to pound. He grabbed a pillow from the sofa and clutched it tightly as Doc walked purposefully through the room and straight towards Patrick who jumped on his lap and started to nuzzle his neck.

"Doc," Patrick's panicked breaths made his voice ragged. He'd never been in a situation like this before. "I don't know what to do. Freya called me. *She* called *me*! How did she get my number? She said she wants me to go to the beach with them. I only have twenty minutes." The words were a rush of pent-up panic and uncertainty, but Doc's calming presence remained by his side—the calm in Patrick's storm.

Patrick took a moment to collect himself and slow his breathing, stroking Doc's head and focusing on his breathing. One in. One out.

One in.

One out, one in…

He'd recited the words to himself multiple times before and did so now until his breaths came out a little more evenly.

Roughly five minutes had passed since the phone call and Patrick was still processing the turn of events. What should he do? Should he message her back and say he won't be able to make it? Oh, why had she invited him!

He started to replay everything Freya had said in his mind.

Hey babes, it's Freya. Isabelle wants you to come to the beach with us—so come, yeah?

His mind stalled. Isabelle wanted him there?

He hadn't put the words together before. Freya wasn't the one who wanted him there, but Isabelle.

He stood up and looked at the time; he had thirteen minutes to get to work.

"I have to go, Doc." He rushed to the kitchen, put out some food and water for Doc, grabbed his wallet and keys and started walking to work, his decision made.

Once there, he squatted and leaned against a wall before a foreboding sense of panic flared through his mind again. Who else will be there?

What does going to the beach even entail? He'd never been. He looked down at his clothes; he was wearing a white T-shirt, an old pair of jeans and trainers. He didn't look ready for the beach at all.

Should he go home? Was this a dumb idea?

He sat, wracking his brain, when his phone pinged with a message from Isabelle.

Patrick!! I'm so sorry. I said something off the cuff to Freya and she invited you without me even realising what was happening. I'm in the car with Freya and Albie. Please don't force yourself to come if you don't want to—no one will mind at all .x.o.x

Patrick stood and scratched the back of his neck. *Well,* he thought, *she did give me an out.*

A weight fell off Patrick's shoulders and he turned, ready to head home but, as he did, a car pulled up next to him. The passenger door opened, and Freya stuck her head out of the window.

"I knew you would be here!" she called and ran over to him, hooking her arm around his. "Come on, babes, let's hit the road!"

Patrick couldn't get a word out before Freya dragged him to the car, opening the backseat door and practically throwing him in.

Why is she so strong? Or was he weak?

Within seconds of her shutting the door, the car sped off, headed for the beach. Patrick took a second to survey his surroundings; in the driver's seat was Albie, wearing sunglasses and an open, short-sleeved Hawaiian shirt. Beside him sat Freya, who was in a pretty, baby blue sundress and a straw hat with bug-like sunglasses covering her face. Finally, he looked left, where Isabelle was sitting. His eyes lingered on her face, absentmindedly drinking her in.

She's beautiful.

As always, the thought chimed into his head and he smiled as pink stained her cheeks, wearing a pair of high-waisted shorts and a sheer, flowy top. Her hair was up in a ponytail, accentuating her cheekbones.

He had never seen her in her casual clothes before, and the sight blew him away.

Chapter 18

ISABELLE

"So, hey…" Isabelle offered Patrick a small smile before lowering her voice so the others couldn't hear. "I'm so sorry about this," she said and rubbed her hands, trying to hold herself together. When she looked in the mirror, she could see Freya looking back at her with a devilish smile.

Patrick finally piped up, but Isabelle could see he was uncomfortable. "Don't worry," he said, then tacked on, almost as an afterthought, "Thanks for inviting me."

This made Isabelle happy, but she was also confused. She knew this wasn't Patrick's sort of thing and she hadn't really expected him to be here waiting for them. *I mean, look at him,* she thought, *he's wearing jeans to the beach!*

Why would he come? She couldn't figure it out. Suddenly, Albie responded to Patrick before she had the chance. "No worries, big man. Glad to have you along! Would have been outnumbered if you didn't come."

No sooner were the words out of his mouth that he got a slap on the arm from Freya.

"Hey now," he crowed. "I'm trying to drive here! Please tell me that you guys saw that!" he pleaded, but Isabelle and Patrick both laughed. She loved the energy these two had when they were together.

Freya followed up with a, "Don't listen to him, Patrick—he's a moron. Today's gonna be a blast! You didn't dress for the beach though, did you babe? Albie, you have a spare pair of shorts, right?" she asked, her hinting tone thinly veiled.

"Course I do, they're in the boot. I'll grab them for you when we get there. It'll be about an hour and a half before we arrive, though, so get comfy."

Albie let out a hearty chuckle. "What are you like, wearing jeans to the beach? You're a funny one, you!" Albie got another slap on the arm from Freya. "Hey, what's that one for? I'm only messing."

Isabelle jumped to Patrick's defence. "It's not like we gave him much time to get ready. He most likely just came in whatever he was wearing at the time!"

Patrick was amused—he hadn't seen this side of Isabelle before. He laughed, and everyone else in the car quickly joined in.

"Right, let's get some music on." Freya leaned over to the radio, turned it up and started dancing in her seat.

As subtly as he could manage, Patrick leaned over to Isabelle's side of the car and whispered in her ear, "Thank you," before swiftly pulling back.

Isabelle blushed.

Chapter 19

PATRICK

The car journey took longer than they thought but, when they finally reached the beach, Albie parked up and quickly got out of the car to stretch.

"Finally!" he bellowed.

A little more slowly, Freya and Isabelle soon joined him, leaving Patrick alone in the car. They all headed around the car to get out the deck chairs, picnic basket and giant cooler they'd brought along. He realised at that moment that he hadn't contributed at all; his anxiety began to creep its head before he remembered what Isabelle had told him in the café.

They were friends now.

Patrick took a breath before stepping out of the car into the unknown. The sun hit him like a poke to the eye and he quickly covered his eyes to give them time to adjust. Some seconds later, as he pried open his eyes, he was met with one of the most beautiful scenes he had ever seen; golden yellow sand, as far as his eyes could see, waited before colliding with a beautiful, calm ocean.

He had never seen the sea in person before, always assuming it was a terrifying force of nature. Yet, as he gazed out at it, he was filled with awe at the shimmering blue expanse, rolling to and through, before him.

The smell of the salty sea air filled his nostrils, and he found himself closing his eyes once more, as though in an attempt to photograph his experience and never forget it. Lost in his little world for a while, he allowed himself to breathe. He hadn't known how beautiful the world could be.

Then, the smell of Isabelle's sweet perfume filled his nostril's, and he knew she was there before she had the chance to say anything.

"I've never been to the beach before," he murmured. He didn't even look at Isabelle when he said it; he just kept looking out onto the horizon.

Isabelle's voice sounded light. "Well, then I'm even more glad you came."

Patrick turned, opening his eyes to look at Isabelle. She was close, looking up at him. And, suddenly, he felt that they were locked in a moment, just looking into each other's eyes.

The moment was swiftly broken, however, by a bright pair of orange swim shorts which hit Patrick in the back of the head.

"'Ere you go, mate," Albie cut in. "Follow me, you can get changed in the bathroom. I need to go, anyway." Albie gestured towards Patrick to follow him.

"Oh," Patrick murmured, the shock hitting him. He turned to Isabelle. "I'll be back in a bit." He rubbed the back of his head, his cheeks flush.

"Don't worry, Freya and I will find a spot for us on the beach. See you in a mo!" Isabelle giggled as she skipped towards Freya, who was lugging another chair down to the spot they picked out.

Patrick followed Albie to the nearest restroom, unsurprised to find that it was small, with just one stall and two urinals. The stench made Patrick want to vomit as soon as he opened the door.

Patrick reluctantly headed to the stall to get changed and Albie started talking before he even shut the door.

"Thanks for coming, mate," he said, tone uncharacteristically serious. "We were talking to Isabelle about you."

Patrick froze.

Albie continued without waiting for a response. "Yeah, she seems really into you, mate! You guys a thing yet?"

Patrick bit his lip. He didn't know what to say. *What even is a 'thing'?*

He paused for a moment. "What do you mean?" he finally asked, voice sheepish.

"Oh, you know," Albie said. "Are you guys dating? Are you together? Are you fuc—"

"*No*! No… no! We're *not*," Patrick spat, eyes a little wild.

Albie gave a big, hearty laugh. "Well, a bit of advice for you, mate." Patrick was locked still. "Ask her out *before* you miss your chance. A girl like Isabelle ain't gonna be single for long. Trust me." A moment passed where neither spoke, Patrick lost to his thoughts. Eventually, Albie cleared his throat, tone returning to its usual, light-hearted nature. "Right, I'll see you down there, buddy!"

Albie left Patrick to get changed.

Patrick sat down on the disgusting toilet without a thought. It felt like Albie had just punched him in the gut and left.

"She's into me? Why the hell would *she* be into *me*?"

He breathed, trying to ignore his racing heart as he finally got into Albie's shorts. Albie was like a man mountain compared to Patrick, so he was glad he could pull the drawstring tight enough for them to stay up.

"I can't ever ask her out," he muttered and walked out of the stall, to the sink, and started washing his hands. He was unable to look away from his reflection; he looked tired. There was no colour in his face. His body looked skinny, and he lacked the muscles and confidence Albie had. What the hell did someone like Isabelle see in him?

He finished washing his hands and headed back to the car, searching for the group on the beach.

He decided he was just going to ignore it. There was no point in thinking about it anymore. He reached the car and swiftly found the group. Isabelle stood and waved him over.

Chapter 20

PATRICK

"What took you so long, buddy?" Albie laughed and threw a beer towards Patrick. Patrick fumbled with the can and, in the process, fell onto the floor. However, he'd managed to catch the drink and held it up victoriously. "Cor, did you see that!"

The girls cheered and laughed as Patrick picked himself up and joined them.

A vast umbrella, deck chairs and a few towels had already been placed down on the sand. Patrick had only been in the bathroom for five minutes at most, but you'd have thought they'd been there all day.

Freya's dress had disappeared, replaced with a skimpy two-piece. Isabelle's top was also gone, and she was wearing just a bikini top and shorts. The only thing that Patrick wasn't surprised by was the fact that Albie was now shirtless.

Of course, he's built like a boxer.

Patrick knew he wouldn't be taking *his* top off today.

After a while, it seemingly became clear to everyone in the group just how awkward Patrick was feeling, fidgeting with his deck chair and not really joining the conversation unless prompted.

They were drinking canned cocktails and beers. Freya reminded Albie that he could only have the non-alcoholic ones, which was followed by a lot of moaning from him.

"Hey, Freya—could you do my back for me?" Isabelle asked.

"Sorry, babes! Albie's—" Before she could finish, she was in Albies arms with him running down to the seafront.

"So, how long have they been together, do you think?" Isabelle laughed. She got up, moved so she was in front of Patrick, and sat between his legs. She then held out a hand where a bottle of sun cream was held. "Well, are you gonna do my back, then?"

Patrick was immediately flustered. "Erm, sure." he took the bottle and paused.

Okay, you can do this. What Albie said flashed through his mind, but Isabelle bent her head down, facing the ground as she waited for Patrick.

"So, your first time at the beach, huh? Bet you didn't expect this today," she laughed to herself. "You were relaxing with Doc, weren't you?" Patrick squeezed some of the lotion from the bottle and started to put it on Isabelle's back. She flinched.

"Oh, sorry!" Patrick said, almost instantly,

"Oh *shh*! It was just cold," she quipped.

Patrick felt a little more at ease now that they were alone. "Yeah, I was just relaxing with Doc. How did you know?"

Isabelle spun around. "Of course, I know! I know you well enough now to guess what you'd be doing with your weekends." She looked offended that Patrick had even questioned her. "Anyway, I'm sure Doc was okay with you leaving him to relax in the sun without you," she grinned.

"Yeah, you're right. He loves to lay on the windowsill and sunbathe." A big smile flashed across Patrick's face.

Isabelle loved seeing him smile. She thought it was his best feature, but didn't want to make himself self-conscious and didn't say anything. She just jumped to her feet. "Right, you—time to get you in the sea." She reached out a hand.

Patrick looked up at her.

I don't think I've ever been around someone as beautiful inside and out.

He reached out his hand but was quickly met by Isabelle, who grasped it and pulled him towards her. Patrick was propelled and, before he had even let go, she was running down to the sea, pulling him, in a flash. He still clutching her hand.

They moved in what felt like slow motion to Patrick. He couldn't take his eyes off her. She was perfect.

They got to the beachfront in what felt like seconds and played in the water with Freya and Albie. It was like Patrick's mind had been switched off and, for what felt like the first time, he was living in the moment.

"Chicken fight!" Albie yelled as he picked up Freya and put her on his shoulders. Isabelle turned to Patrick.

"We have to beat them." Isabelle said, her expression intense.

Patrick was surprised at how competitive she was but, before he knew it, Isabelle was climbing on his shoulders. It took Patrick a moment to get his balance in the sea with her on top of him but, once he had gained solid footing, Albie yelled, "Fight!"

The shoving match began, and the pair quickly realised it would be tough to win against Albie's tree-trunk thighs. However, Isabelle was stronger than Freya—it all depended on how long Patrick could last.

"Loser has to buy dinner for the group!" Albie laughed.

Is he just making the rules up as he goes? Patrick's focus broke for a moment and Freya took her chance, mustering her strength and pushing as hard as she could.

With a loud splash, the victors were crowned. The momentum of the push toppled Patrick and Isabelle over like dominos. When they emerged from the water, Isabelle was laughing.

"Okay, okay. You win this time." She was soaked and looked over at Patrick, who was equally drenched but lacked her enthusiasm. "What's wrong? Are you alright?"

"I wanted to win," Patrick said softly.

Isabelle waded over to him and put her arm around him. "Oh, we will win. Ready for round two?" She gestured for him to move in closer and he turned to the side of his head was level with her mouth. She whispered a strategy into Patrick's ear and a fire was lit beneath them.

Freya looked down from her vantage on Albie's shoulders and Patrick noticed her grin and gave him a soft kick in the chest.

"Hey! What was that for?" Albie squinted where Freya pointed. "Oi, you," Albie pointed at Patrick and Isabelle. "Double or nothing!" he bellowed.

"What, is he some kind of supervillain?" Patrick muttered. He made Isabelle laugh, though, and they nodded to each other.

Isabelle climbed back onto Patrick's shoulders as Albie got into position in front of them. Freya gestured towards Isabelle to bring it on,

"Fight!" Albie yelled again.

Immediately, Isabelle clutched the back of Freya's bikini.

"Sorry Hun, but it's double or nothing," she whispered in her ear before pulling the thread of her bikini. Freya yelped and instinctively moved to cover herself with her arms while Albie's head shot up to look. With that, Isabelle gave one strong push to knock them both into the water.

Isabelle leapt from Patrick's shoulders and into his arms to celebrate but Patrick wasn't ready, and a slip of his foot had them swiftly joining Freya and Albie in the water.

After some back and forth—where the topic of whether bikini-undoing is cheating was heavily debated—Albie and Freya eventually conceded they'd tied, and they headed back up the beach to dry off in the sun.

"I can't believe you went straight for my bikini! You're evil!" Freya laughed as she scolded Isabelle.

"Hey, I just used Albie's brain against ya." Isabelle smirked and pointedly aimed a finger at Albie's crotch, which made Freya turn bright red.

The girls crash onto their towels and the guys on the deck chairs and the four of them relaxed in the sun, listened to music, had a drink and joked around. Patrick took a moment watching them all laughing together, maybe the unknown he stepped into wasn't as scary as he thought.

When the sun started to set, Albie groaned loudly and stood.

"Right," he said. "We best head off soon."

Freya took objection and started to while but eventually relented. "Before we start packing up, let's take some pictures."

Isabelle jumped up at that and reached for her phone. They took a couple of pictures as a group before Freya said, "Hold on, I wanna get a pic of me and Albie. Isabelle, can you take one for me?"

"Of course, one sec! You two get ready…"

Freya jumped into Albie's arms and kissed him on the cheek.

"And they're not together? *Right…*" Isabelle said under her breath to Patrick which caused him to hide a chuckle.

"Now, you guys! Isabelle, give me your phone!"

Freya held out her hand in a silent demand and Isabelle handed over her phone.

"Right, I want some proper poses from you two…" Freya grinned over the phone. "Get closer to her, Patrick. This isn't some school dance!"

Isabelle wrapped her arm around Patrick's waist, which caused butterflies to swirl in his stomach. He was surprised by how much he liked how close Isabelle was to him and put his arm over her shoulders.

"Perfect, now give me a big smile."

They didn't know that Freya was taking pictures throughout and she passed the camera back to Isabelle, hugging her as she did and whispering into her ear, "Have a look through them." Patrick overheard Freya and was curious to see these photos.

As they started ferrying the beach gear back to the car, there was a moment when Patrick and Freya were left alone, each busily rolling up the towels. "Thank you," he told her softly.

He knew that Freya had invited him for a reason.

"No worries, babes," Freya confidently said back.

Neither looked at each other and, to an outsider, it was like they were talking to themselves. They picked up the last of the beach gear and returned to the car.

Chapter 21

PATRICK

The drive back was quicker than the way there and Patrick only woke when the car stopped, jolting from the un-comfortable position he found himself in.

"Here you go mate," Albie said. "This is your stop."

Patrick was dazed and slowly realised that Albie had parked up outside work.

"Oh, yeah. Thanks for dropping me off."

Albie let out a quiet laugh so as not to disturb the girls who were sound asleep. "No drama, big man. Have a good time?"

Patrick nodded in his direction, eyes widening as he realised, he was still wearing Albie's shorts. He started to say something, but Albie waved him off.

"Oh, you can give me them back on Monday." Albie laughed again.

"Thanks again Albie. I'll see you Monday." Patrick opened the car door and closed it gently Albie pulled away.

Patrick stood in the dark, giving himself a moment to take in what an insane whirlwind of a day that had been. He grinned, taking a final deep breath before starting the walk home. As he turned the corner, however, his brow furrowed in confusion as Isabelle ran up to him.

Isabelle panted, sweat dripping from her forehead. "You—you forgot your jeans." She managed to get out between heavy breaths.

"Oh, thanks," Patrick said, still confused as to why he had felt the need to run after him. "I completely forgot—but, you know you didn't have to bring them back tonight. You could have just given them to me on Monday."

"Keys—" Isabelle panted. "Your keys…" Isabelle was slowly starting to get her composure back.

Patrick's eyes widened as he checked the shorts' pockets; sure enough, he hadn't taken anything out of his jeans at the beach, having been too distracted by Albie talking to him about bluntly Isabelle.

"Oh, God—you're right! You're a lifesaver." Patrick took the jeans from Isabelle and removed his keys, wallet and phone from the pockets.

Isabelle had finally caught her breath and smiled. "Hey, at least now you can get in your flat."

They both shared a laugh before Patrick frowned. "Wait, where's the car? Are they not taking you home?"

Isabelle's expression fell from laughter to pure panic. "Give me your phone, give me your phone," she demanded from Patrick.

"What? Why?" Patrick had already started to get his phone out of his pocket.

"I need to call Freya. My bag is in the car." Her tone was panicked as Patrick quickly switched on and opened his phone, calling the same number Freya had rung him from earlier in the day before passing the phone over to Isabelle.

It rang and rang, then went straight to voicemail. Pacing up and down, Isabelle tried twice more before Patrick's phone flashed to say it was running out of battery.

"You don't think she's still asleep, do you?" Patrick asked.

"Maybe… Let me call Albie instead." She went to open the contacts in Patrick's phone but stilled, looking up at him. "You don't have Albie's number, do you?"

Patrick sighed. "Sorry…"

His phone screen suddenly turned black and Isabelle it back to him.

She was annoyed but Patrick couldn't tell if she was upset with him or the two in the car.

They stood in silence for what felt like an eternity before Patrick finally asked, "Did you want to come to mine and try calling her again when my phone has some—"

"Charge?" Isabelle perked up. "Yes, that's a great idea! They have my bag with my phone and keys. I, I couldn't even walk home now if I wanted to 'cause Wouldn't be able to get in!" She clutched his hands in hers, eyes thankful.

"It's no problem," Patrick murmured as his heart beat faster than he had ever felt it do. His cheeks started to stain with colour.

"Only if that's okay, of course." She bit her lip.

Patrick had never invited anyone to his flat before. The only ones to have ever been inside while he lived there, besides Doc, were delivery men and builders.

"Y—e…yeah, I mean, I have to get home to Doc, anyway."

Isabelle had to cover her mouth to stop herself from screeching. "I'm going to meet *the* famous Doc?" She started to jump up and down. Patrick had never seen anyone so excited to meet a cat before.

"Yeah," he laughed a little. "I guess so. Shall we go?" He started to lead the way but, within seconds of setting off, Isabelle shot past him, grabbed his hand and pulled his arm to get him to walk faster.

"No, not that way—*this* way." Patrick pulled back on her hand and tugged her in the right direction.

Isabelle smirked, finally allowing him to lead the way while looking a bit bashful.

Within ten minutes, they were at Patrick's door, and both of their hearts were pounding. They paused for a second before Patrick coughed. "I'm gonna need both my hands, sorry."

Patrick had only just realised they held hands the entire way there, and he hadn't let go once. Flustered, she quickly released his hand. "Oh, of course. I'm sorry."

Patrick took his keys out of his pocket, opened his door and stepped inside. Like every time he opened his front door, Doc appeared within seconds and started to rub his body and face on Patrick's legs. "Hey, buddy, I hope you don't mind but we have a guest for a little while."

Doc meowed though in approval.

Isabelle stepped inside, a handheld over her mouth while her eyes filled with excitement and admiration for the cat she had only seen in hundreds of photos and videos but never with her own eyes.

The clean scent of cotton was the first thing Isabelle noticed as she looked around. A quick look around told her that it was emanating from a reed infuser which sat on a side table in the hallway. She was pleasantly surprised, she hadn't given much thought to what Patrick's place would be like but now was there, she couldn't help but think it suited what she would have guessed. She was seeing his place! For a moment, anxiety hit her square in the chest but dissipated when Patrick called out to her from the next room, where he'd immediately headed.

"I'll put the phone on charge, won't be long—then you can call Freya," he said.

Isabelle cautiously walked through the entrance to Patrick's living room. It was bright; all the walls were white and a line of spotlights on the ceiling lit up the room from one end to the other. The room was quite bare, though, like he had just moved in. There was a two-seater sofa and a moderately-sized TV on the wall. A small table sat next to the couch, up against the back wall and a large cat tower stood beside it. She hadn't expected it to be quite so empty.

Patrick was standing over the small table, putting his phone on charge. He was facing away from Isabelle when she started to tell him "I sent you some of the photos Freya took, did you see them?" Patrick span to face her, she couldn't help but laugh. "You look like a labrador who's been shown a treat" she was doubling over. Patrick's embarrassment was palpable, but he couldn't help but laugh along.

Chapter 22

PATRICK

"Take a seat while you wait," Patrick said, still looking at his phone.

He was nervous. What was he doing?

He needed a moment alone to freak out.

With that thought, he started to head out of the room, calling an excuse over his shoulder as he went. "Let me grab you a drink while you wait."

In the kitchen, he found Doc on the kitchen side, sitting like he had been waiting there this whole time. Patrick immediately gave him a rub on the head. "I'm sorry about today, bud," he whispered. "Today got away from me—one thing happened, then another, then…" Patrick paused, instead of his mind racing he thought about her beauty with the backdrop of the ocean.

Doc meowed, staring Patrick dead in the eye, bringing him back into the room.

"Patrick rubbed Doc on the head and turned to grab a can of lemonade from the fridge,

"I think you'll like her, so be good," Patrick said but, when he turned back, Doc was gone. Worried, Patrick headed straight to the living room and walked in to see Doc on Isabelle's lap, sniffing her. He had never seen Doc interact with anyone but himself before and didn't know how to feel, so he just kept watching.

"Oh my God. Oh my God, oh my God—he's on my lap!" Isabelle was so excited that her voice had gone up an octave. Patrick stood watching in awe as Doc moved in closer to sniff her outstretched hand.

She heard Patrick enter the room and looked over at him. He was smiling watching her with admiration.

"I love it when you smile like that," she said without thinking, the words slipping out of her mouth without permission.

Instantly, she looked embarrassed and looked away from him.

Patrick hardly heard her. He stood, a can of lemonade in hand, gobsmacked at how Doc was behaving with Isabelle.

Isabelle turned to Patrick, biting her lip and refusing to meet his eye. Patrick looked between her and the cat once more Doc decided that he was cool with Isabelle and curled up on her lap.

Patrick snapped out of his trance and forced himself to walk over and hand Isabelle the can of lemonade.

"I've never seen him like this with anyone but me," Patrick said and sat beside her on the sofa but, after the words left his mouth, an awkward silence hit the room.

Ten seconds passed, neither saying anything.

. He winced, then decided to pretend that he was simply having lunch in the café. He'd grown used to lunch at the café.

In a rare moment of boosted confidence, he turned to Isabelle and opened his mouth but, before he could say anything, she broke the silence.

"Thank you for coming today. I know Freya was the one to ask you, but I'm glad you came." Her tone of voice was suddenly calmer. "I was going to go with them by myself, but I wasn't sure I wanted to. Who likes being a third wheel, right?" she laughed.

"I did want to ask you something, actually," Patrick interrupted her flow. "Why *did* Freya invite me?" He wanted to hear it from her directly.

Isabelle stuttered. "Well, I guess…"

Patrick saw that she didn't want to answer had a moment of panic and interrupted. "Sorry, if I'm being too nosey don't feel you have to answer," he looked up. "The phone has some charge. Feel free to call Freya if you like—I'm gonna put some food down for Doc." Patrick quickly stood and passed her the phone before leaving the room—closely followed by Doc, who heard the word food and knew where to go.

"Why did I do that, Doc?" Patrick had finally lost his cool. He was panicking.

"I shouldn't have asked her," he continued under his breath. "I should have just been grateful for the invite and left it at that!"

He leaned against the countertop, his back to the door. "Why am I like this? Why do I have to ruin every moment with her? She must think I'm an absolute freak."

He scowled as he put the last of Doc's food in his bowl and placed it down in front of him but, unlike usual, he didn't go straight for it. Instead, he walked straight past the bowl and to the door.

Patrick rolled his eyes and gave a small smile. "Oh, I see. Have I upset you now as we—" Patrick turned and saw Isabelle standing at the doorway. He froze.

How much did she hear?

He felt like someone had walked in on him naked.

Doc rubbed his body on Isabelle's leg at the doorway.

She strode into the kitchen with purpose and stood opposite Patrick. "So, can I finish what I was about to say before you ran off?"

Isabelle walked into the kitchen and stood opposite Patrick, "I was talking to Freya about you and how I missed you when you weren't around. If you really have to know." She was speaking so nonchalant, but Patrick's eyes changed and fixated on her.

"What did you say?"

Patrick was giving Isabelle an intense look she couldn't interpret as he interrupted her for the very first time.

"I missed you," she repeated in a breath.

The atmosphere in the kitchen changed, his piercing eyes locking with a laser focus on hers, just as she'd seen them do countless times at work. Her heart skipped a beat. She couldn't help but run her tongue across her lips.

Patrick lunged forward and took Isabelle in his arms.

Isabelle was shocked but didn't resist as Patrick looked deeply into her eyes before closing his and leaning in to kiss her softly. Patrick was holding her so close that she could feel his heart racing in his chest.

It surprised her, how gentle his lips felt against hers, but after a split second of shock, she began passionately kissing him back.

Chapter 23

PATRICK

Usually, Patrick's mind was prone to overthinking every minute moment—every possibility—but his mind was completely clear when Isabelle kissed him back. He was running on pure instinct and ran a hand down Isabelle's back before lifting her off the ground. She instinctively wrapped her legs around his torso, and he pushed her against the kitchen wall, kissing down her neck. Isabelle moaned softly while running her hand through his hair. He smiled before kissing back up her neck.

He pulled away and looked into her eyes. "Is this, okay?" he whispered.

Her face was flush and her breathing heavy. She didn't say anything—just nodded and pulled him back towards her lips breathing heavily into each other while their lips softly teased each other's.

He flashed her a smile before moving them both away from the wall and placing her on the kitchen counter. She didn't unwrap her legs from around him and, instead, grabbed his face, kissing him intensely, like now she had a taste of him she wanted more.

She started to pull Patrick's top up and he stopped kissing her for a moment, pulled away, and helped her take off his top before throwing it to the floor. Isabelle watched this with a small smile and ran a hand down his chest before dancing her hands at the hem of her own top. In a second, it was off and had joined his on the ground.

She leaned in to kiss him again while reaching a hand behind her back to unclasp her bra, pushing Patrick back the next moment. Smiling at him coyly, she made him watch as she finally took off her bra and threw it on the rapidly growing pile of clothes on the floor.

Patrick pulled down his shorts and removed the last of his clothing, until he was fully naked. He looked into her eyes and broke the impassioned silence.

"I want you…" his voice was lower than she had heard before, the tone sent fireworks off in her mind.

Before he could say anything more, Isabelle nodded and pulled him in again, kissing him once before slowly removing the last of her clothes in one swift motion. He couldn't take his eyes off her panting, the passion he was feeling in that moment was unlike any he had experienced before. She slowly opened her legs. Patrick ran a hand down the inside of her thigh causing her to softly moan. His gentle hands were causing her sensitivity to his touch making her bite her lower lip. He could feel how much she wanted him and pulled her towards him gently and slowly sliding himself inside her, which made Isabelle immediately cry out in pleasure as she dug her nails into his back.

As Patrick slowly started to thrust back and forth, Isabelle pulled him deeper using her legs. Her eyes were closed asking him for more. He took her instruction and started to thrust harder, which was met by sounds of approval from Isabelle. She grabbed his face, pulled him in to kiss her, and wrapped her arms around the back of his neck.

He kissed her once more before moving his head to the side of hers. His breathing was steadily getting more intense but could feel Isabelle's smile against the side of his cheek. She whispered into his ears, "Feels so good… I want more".

Her breathing became heavier and heavier and when she no longer had the strength to hold herself up, she fell to the counter, eyes rolling back. The moaning intensified, and her leg started to shake involuntarily. She shot up, wrapped her arms tight around his back and let out a moan of pure ecstasy.

A second later, she gently pulled away from Patrick and kissed him softly and slowly. They paused, looking deeply into each other's eyes. Patrick stroked her cheek before kissing her yet again.

They both collapsed on the floor, breathing heavily in a state of pure ecstasy.

Isabelle swept her hair from her face and looked up at Patrick. When he looked down at her, her smile seemed almost permanent. He couldn't help but smile back at her as he lifted a hand to move more of her hair away from her face.

They each held each other's eyes in their gaze and, as they simply laid there for a few minutes, Patrick slowly stroked her hair. Isabelle looked up at him, her hand on her chest above his still-racing heart.

After a while, Isabelle broke the silence. "Wow…"

They both giggled and Isabelle brought herself to her feet. Patrick couldn't take his eyes off her perfect body.

She headed to the kitchen door and paused. "Well, you coming?"

Patrick's eyes widened and he grinned before he leapt up as quickly as possible and followed her to the bedroom.

Chapter 24

ISABELLE

The sun had caused Isabelle to stir, her face caught looking in the direction of its glow, and she'd slowly opened her eyes from a deep, deep sleep several minutes ago. The morning sun beat down on Patrick's bed, where Isabelle was curled with her head against Patrick's naked chest as he remained fast asleep.

She was warm and comfortable and snuggled further into Patrick's chest before her eyes shot open. She'd almost squealed and jumped out of bed when she'd first woken, nearly scurrying to put on the first thing she could find. Instead, she tentatively padded from bed and pulled Patrick's white T-shirt over her head. She then smiled, got back into bed, and snuggled up to him again.

This woke Patrick up. He seemed startled at first but quickly put his arm around Isabelle and turned towards her. "Good morning," he said.

Isabelle smiled and kissed him.

The two of them lay in a relaxed embrace for a long time before Patrick excused himself and headed to the kitchen, leaving Isabelle lying in his bed, in a happy haze. She hadn't felt this content for a long time, but her haze was broken by Doc jumping on the bed.

"Oh, hey Doc. How are you doing?" she stroked his head. "Sorry for taking your sleeping spot last night," she laughed to herself as Doc meowed at her, jumped off her chest and left the room. Isabelle blinked. Did the cat just respond to her?

Moments later, Patrick appeared with two cups of coffee in hand. "Milk with 2 sugars, just how you have it at work," he said and passed her the mug.

Isabelle was pleasantly surprised. "Wow, you really are interested in me, aren't you?" she jested.

Patrick laughed and got back into bed with his coffee.

Isabelle took a sip. "Wow, this is amazing," she told Patrick.

"That's what they all say," Patrick joked.

"Oh," Isabelle raised a brow, her tone tinged with a hint of jealousy. "They *all* say that do they?"

Patrick looked over and blanched, "No, wait—hold on, I didn't—"

She leaned over and kissed him. "Just keeping you on your toes," she said softly slapping him on the arm and giggling.

They both lay in blissful silence, sipping their coffees and enjoying the sounds of the birds outside the window. Isabelle decided to ask something. "So… last night? Please, be honest with me and let me know—what you are feeling?"

Patrick froze in place and Isabelle could see from the look on his face that he was feeling overwhelmed. He stared directly past her, like she wasn't in the room, and like nothing else existed besides the spot he was fixated on.

As gently as she could, she took his hand in hers and, as soon as she did, his eyes softened until they looked less glazed.

He glanced down at his hand and watched as Isabelle softly stroked the back of it.

"I'm just going to say everything that's on my mind, okay?"

Isabelle nodded even as he looked away from her.

"I tend to keep to myself. Ever since I lost my parents when I was younger… I got to the point where I thought I didn't need anyone else." He paused, looking down. "I felt comfortable in the solitude I surrounded myself with… but that day you stormed over to my desk; you switched up my reality.

"Since then, I've not been able to get you out of my head." He smiled and turned to face her. "I went from talking to and thinking about no one—to only wanting to hear your voice and only ever thinking about you. You bring out parts of me that I didn't know existed. I don't want to mess this up and lose you. I want to keep you to myself."

He finished speaking and there was a pause. Isabelle didn't know what to say. He'd lost his parents when he was young? He wanted to keep her to himself?

He had never been this unabashedly raw and honest about what he felt before. She was slightly overwhelmed but, when she looked over and saw Patrick's whole body drop—his head hanging, his back arched over—he looked so innocent and vulnerable that she climbed onto her knees on the bed and scooted over to him, trying to get closer.

She gently placed her hand under his chin and lifted it to meet his eyes.

In that moment, she saw the pain that was hidden there, screaming about what it had cost him to voice his experiences with her.

"Look at me," she said in a gentle tone and brushed his hair back soothingly. He did. "If you want to keep me, I'm yours," she murmured softly, giving him a tender smile before leaning in to kiss him.

He didn't kiss her back at first but, as she pulled away, she could see what looked like awe on his face and couldn't help but smile sincerely. Before she could do much else, however, Patrick threw himself at her and grabbed her face before kissing her deeply and, while the kisses were passionate, they felt so much more delicate than they had the night before.

Caught by surprise, she couldn't help falling back onto the bed. Patrick followed her momentum but didn't stop kissing her and her body started to feel hot as Patrick's hands crept over her curves. She let out a soft moan as Patrick started to kiss down her neck.

Just then, the loud ring of a phone pierced the air in the worst way she could imagine, making both she and Patrick jump out of their skin.

They tried their best to ignore it but, every time it stopped, it rang again less than a second later.

Patrick groaned and threw himself off the bed before storming into the living room to turn the phone off and Isabelle was left laughing to herself in bed. However, she stopped when Partick sped into the room with a serious look on his face, still holding the phone.

"Hey, what's wrong? Who's been calling?"

He turned the phone around and Isabelle saw that it was Freya, finally calling her back. She quickly grabbed the bed sheet and covered herself.

"Oh, God. I forgot to send her a text when I couldn't get through to her last night. Give me the phone."

Isabelle took a moment to compose herself and Freya called again but, this time, she answered the phone.

"Patrick! Where the bloody hell have you been? Please tell me you have seen Isabelle or know where she is?" Freya's worried tone practically shouted the words down the phone.

Isabelle sucked in a breath. "Hey, Freya…"

"Isabelle? Where the hell have you been!" Freya yelled and continued to shout, having a go at her for not sending a message or explaining she was okay after calling so many times.

Isabelle winced but quietly took the scolding because she knew that she'd worried Freya. She then apologised profusely.

"I'm gonna kick Albie's ass for not waiting for you to come back. What a moron! Did he even think?"

Isabelle tried to defend Albie, but Freya wasn't having any of it.

"That's not the point Isabelle—*hold on.*" Freya's tone of voice changed, and Isabelle could hear the sly grin on her face when she spoke again. "How come you're answering Patrick's phone?"

Isabelle gestured for Patrick to leave the room and shut the door behind him. Alone in Patrick's room, she took a deep breath and sat on the edge of the bed.

"So… I might have stayed at Patrick's last night…"

There was a beat, and then Freya let out a high-pitched screech that had Isabelle pulling the phone away from her ear.

"Calm down, please!" Isabelle pleaded.

"Okay, okay. I'm calm, I'm calm," Isabelle could hear Freya moving around on the other end of the phone. "Tell me everything…"

Isabelle started to relay what happened when she got out of the car, explaining how she had forgotten her bag that had both her phone and keys inside.

"So, he invited you round?" Freya was gobsmacked. "I didn't think he had it in him!"

Isabelle giggled. She felt like a teenager. "It was adorable! We held hands all the way to his door."

Freya was speechless and Isabelle grinned. She hadn't expected to be telling Freya any of this the night before and, before she knew it, the words kept flowing out of her—leading up to her talking to him in the kitchen.

"He wanted to know why he was at the beach," Freya repeated. "But why?"

"I don't know… You know him. He's kinda insecure, so I told him what we talked about yesterday morning."

Freya was surprised. "You told him everything?"

Proudly Isabelle nodded. "Yep."

Freya squealed "Oh my God I'm so proud of you, that couldn't have been easy! I couldn't do that! What happened then?"

Isabelle continued, "Well, I told him that I miss him on the weekends when I know I won't be going for lunch with him… and he kissed me."

Freya screeched "Oh my God, he kissed you! Did you… you know?" she asked.

Chapter 25

PATRICK

In the living room, Patrick peacefully cuddled up beside Doc.

However, that comfort was swiftly broken when he heard excited screams coming from the bedroom, and he started to feel embarrassed.

"I can't believe they are talking about it already," heat crept up his neck. Couldn't she at least wait until she'd gotten home? Doc meowed, making Patrick laugh.

Three-quarters of an hour later, Isabelle emerged from the bedroom. She'd gotten changed during this time, whereas Patrick was still naked since he'd run from the bedroom when the phone rang.

She joined him on the couch and told him that Freya had told her off for not letting her know where she was last night—how she was a good friend, checking up on her and ensuring she was safe.

Yeah, sure—that's all you talked about, Patrick thought but decided to leave it.

They chatted for a while until Isabelle looked at the time and gasped. "Oh, I'm sorry! I need to go soon; Freya's meeting me in front of work with my bag."

Patrick's face dropped. He knew she would have to leave at some point, but he didn't want it to be so soon. "Oh right,' he forced himself to say. "Sure."

"Don't be sad, silly. I'll see you tomorrow at work. Lunch?" she said while gently caressing his shoulder.

Patrick smiled. "Yeah, of course."

They kissed and hugged again, and Patrick walked her to his door. "I'll see you tomorrow, then."

He felt a little awkward and held a pillow in front of his crutch, adding to his discomfort tenfold. It made Isabelle laugh, though, and she kissed. This made him drop the pillow.

"See you tomorrow, sweetie."

She left in a rush, and Patrick was left alone in his flat.

He walked back to the bedroom and threw himself on the bed face first. He was exhausted—not only from the beach but from his night with Isabelle.

As he slept, his dreams weren't as tiring as usual. Instead of the eruption of flames, the overwhelming scent of oil. He dreamt of ocean waves flowing backwards and forwards, the sunset filling the sky with colour, the smell of the sea air and, most importantly, Isabelle standing in front of him with wind flowing through her hair.

***

Doc jumped onto Patrick's bare chest and looked down at him. A smile spread across Patrick's face.

"Morning, buddy. Sorry about yesterday." Patrick stroked Doc's head and was met with a purr from Doc. "You were amazing with Isabelle, yesterday!"

Patrick laughed as he got a meow back from Doc and made himself get up and head to the kitchen. He poured some food for Doc and made a coffee, drinking while leaning against the side, happily watching Doc.

His phone was on the side, where Isabelle had left it yesterday after her call with Freya. Patrick picked it up to see that Isabelle had messaged him late last night. It was short and sweet.

I can't wait to see you tomorrow xxx

He smiled and warmth spread through his chest. He had never experienced such a strong reaction from a text message before and stood, absentmindedly looking at the text for a few minutes before finally messaging her back.

After showering, he headed to work. He was early but wanted to get Isabelle a coffee for when she arrived. He was a few minutes away from work when *déjà vu* hit him, and he saw someone at the end of the path. A few steps closer, he could clearly make out Isabelle waiting and holding two coffee cups.

"You took your time," she said and walked towards him.

Patrick was confused—had they organised to meet before work? She said nothing as she reached him, leaned forward, and kissed him. The worries left Patrick's mind, and his short-lived confusion was replaced by bliss. Proudly, Isabelle thrust a coffee towards him.

"I thought I would treat you this morning, seeing as you brought me one in bed yesterday," she cheekily giggled before taking his free hand into hers.

They slowly walked the rest of the short distance to the office in silence, enjoying their coffee and time together. After a few seconds, Isabelle slipped her hand into his and he smiled but let go before they got to the corner of the building.

"What's wrong?" she asked with a frown.

He moved to one side of the path and called her over with his hand. She hooked her hair behind her ear and followed him.

In a hushed voice, Patrick said, "I don't like people knowing my business. People will talk, and that never ends well."

Isabelle gave him a pensive look and, before he knew it, her hand reached up to stroke his face in a comforting gesture.

"Please don't worry. I mean, Freya already knows, which probably means Albie knows..."

Patrick winced slightly; he hadn't put two and two together. He was clearly pulling a face because, when Isabelle saw him, she leaned in to kiss him. Patrick couldn't resist and kissed her back. As she pulled away, all he could see was warmth and care in her eyes, which drew a smile out of him.

"Do not worry, okay? If anyone makes you feel bad, I'll deal with it."

It was clear she meant what she said, and his mind eased.

In a burst of courage, he grabbed her hand to continue their walk to the office. He still pulled his hand away before they walked through the door—his mind getting the best of him—but, this time, Isabelle laughed.

Patrick was ready for eyes on him. His heart pounded in his chest, and he could feel himself starting to sweat through his shirt while his eyes darted around nervously. In the corner, Iris was speaking to Julia. Freya and Albie were in the kitchen making coffee.

If he could just get to his desk, they would likely leave him alone.

With a small smile aimed his way, Isabelle brushed past him and headed towards Freya; as she passed him, she shot him a smile. "See you at lunch," she said, her voice louder than Patrick would have hoped.

Iris and Julia turned their heads, barely sparing him a glance before continuing their conversation. Patrick rushed towards his desk like he was being chased and sighed as he threw himself into his chair with a sigh. He took some time to take a breather before beginning his work but, not five minutes later, Albie knocked twice on his desk to get his attention. Startled, Patrick's head shot up.

Coffee in hand, Albie shot him a look and slyly smiled before saying, "Told ya, big man," with a wink. As he walked away, Patrick sank below his monitor.

He felt awkward all morning, constantly looking around the office in case someone was looking at him. As soon as he heard someone talking, he turned into a meerkat, craning his neck to see who was talking.

He'd experienced anxiety in the past, but nothing compared to those first few hours. When he spotted Isabelle and Freya talking in the kitchen while grabbing a drink, he immediately worried that they might be talking about or laughing at him. The thoughts started to consume him, and he couldn't stop tapping his hand against his bouncing thigh.

"Patrick," Julia interrupted his racing mind, startling him. "My computer is playing up again. Can you come and sort it out for me, please?" Julia was annoyed; Patrick could tell by her disgruntled voice.

He nodded, thankful for an escape—no matter how short—and quickly followed her to her office.

"This bloody thing is useless…" Julia started ranting about her computer while Patrick got to work. It was the problem thing every time, so Patrick knew precisely how to fix it. She stood behind him, watching every click and button press he made.

"See, I tried… oh. Yeah, I didn't do that."

Patrick smiled slightly, the moment of normality relaxing him.

"What did you get up to this weekend, Patrick?" Julia's question was entirely innocent but, in Patrick's stomach, a well of anxiety opened. He froze briefly before rushing to finish the fix.

Not hearing a response, Julia prompted, "Patrick?"

His defences shot up, and he belligerently asked, "Why?"

Julia was taken aback. Patrick had never spoken to her like that before and now he was acting like an annoyed teenager.

Her eyes sharpened and her tone was equally cutting as she said, "Go back to your desk, I'll take it from here."

Like a dog who'd been reprimanded, Patrick left her office with his tail between his legs. He knew he'd messed up and, as he got to his desk, he slumped into his chair.

All he wanted was for the ground to swallow him whole. He sat staring at it, feeling numb.

Chapter 26

PATRICK

"Hey, you! Ready for lunch?"

The chirpy voice broke through Patrick's stillness and, when he looked up, Isabelle was approaching with a beautiful smile on her face.

Patrick nodded, grabbed his things, and followed her out the door. However, on the walk to *Rachael's*, he was his old stoic self. Not saying a word, looking more at the ground than anything.

Once they made it to the café, they were greeted by the old man as usual, who started preparing their usual order without needing to be asked. They headed over to their table and sat down.

Within seconds, Isabelle asked, "So, what's going on?"

Patrick sighed. He could tell she was worried and started to tell her about his morning—the anxiety, the stressful feelings and, most importantly, what had happened with Julia.

By the time he finished, their food had arrived. Patrick expected Isabelle to respond after the food and coffee had been placed on the table but, to his surprise, she dove into her sandwich without a word.

He couldn't help but chuckle.

"God, that hit the spot. I was starving!" she exclaimed, still chewing the rest of her mouthful. She wiped the crumbs from her mouth and sipped her coffee. "Well, you've been a bit of a dummy, haven't you?" she said like it was obvious and placed her cup back on the table.

Patrick was blown back. "Dummy?" he repeated, eyebrows raised.

"Yep," she laughed. "A giant dummy!"

"Go on..." Patrick encouraged.

"Well, let's break this down, shall we?" Isabelle sat back and Patrick steeled himself some hard truths. "First off, are you a mind reader?" she asked, and he shook his head 'no'. "Well, then—you'll never know what people think about you unless they tell you. Also, people talk; it's not the first time and won't be the last."

Patrick attempted to interject, but Isabelle continued her monologue, "Freya and I were actually talking about something that's nothing to do with you. It's a little bit egotistical to think we focused on you, isn't it?" Patrick didn't respond, but he knew she was right. "And what on earth made you talk to Julia like that? That one's all you."

By the end of her speech, Patrick was pressed back in his chair like he'd been forced back by her words alone.

"I dunno. I was wound tight, I guess. She's never asked me what I've done at the weekend before and I just snapped…"

He frowned, guilt churning in his stomach.

"See, this is why you're being a dummy." She pulled out her phone, took a quick photo of him, and turned it around to show him before he even knew what was happening. "You caught the sun! Of course, she would ask what you got up to!"

Patrick's face heated and couldn't believe his stupidity.

"Oh…" He rubbed his forehead.

"You can get used to that now we're together…" Isabelle stopped short.

Patrick didn't blink. "You're probably not wrong there," he replied nonchalantly before tucking into his lunch, feeling better after all she'd told him.

Her eyes immediately softened, and her mouth turned to a smile.

Now we're together…

He smiled, gingerly asking, "Isabelle, are we together?"

Her face scrunched up. "Do you not remember me telling you I'm yours?"

With a quick shake of his head, he said, "Of course I do, I'd never forget that."

Isabelle's face softened again. "Good, well that's that isn't it?" she says with a cute smile that gave Patrick a sense of relief he wasn't used to.

He smiled to himself and finished his coffee.

After paying up and leaving *Rachael's*, Patrick took hold of Isabelle's hand, feeling warm and fluffy inside as soon as he did.

“Well, I'm sure you don’t need me to tell you what you need to do now, huh?” Isabelle prodded as they reached the office door.

“I’ll talk to her later,” he acknowledged, and Isabelle smiled, lifted onto her tiptoes, and kissed him quickly.

“Shall I come round after work?” she asked.

Patrick nodded without hesitation.

“Okay, I’ll wait for you out here,” she smiled. “See you later.”

He watched as she walked through the door and took a moment to himself. Closing his eyes and taking a deep breath, he prepared to walk through the door but was interrupted.

Julia waited impatiently behind him. “Excuse me, can I get through?”

After his lunch with Isabelle, Patrick felt full of vigour. “Can I speak with you after work?” he asked confidently.

Julia sketched a brow but nodded slowly. “Yes, come see me after work,” she said as she blew past him.

Patrick followed her into the office with slight confidence for the first time in a long time.

***

The rest of the day flew by and, as it did, the confidence boost he received from Isabelle slowly faded away. Every tick of the clock meant a second closer to his conversation with Julia. In no time, the office started to empty. Isabelle was the last to leave, and she mouthed *good luck* before heading outside.

It was just Patrick and Julia, and she was getting ready to leave. It was now or never. Julia spotted him as he approached her office and sat back in her chair.

“Excuse me, is it okay to have that talk now?” Patrick sheepishly asked.

Julia nodded slightly and invited him to sit down, “Well?” Patrick sat down and looked at the floor. “Come on, Patrick,” Julia coaxed, a slight sense of jest lightening her tone. “It’s not a conversation with the floor you’re having.”

He took a deep breath and looked up. He’d expected to see an angry expression lighting her face but… she looked warm. Seeing her eyes look so kind helped him break through his nerves. “I'm sorry, Julia, I shouldn’t have spoken to you like that seeing as you are my boss…” His tone was genuine, but Julia put her hand up to stop him.

“Patrick, thank you for apologising but I don’t think you understand why I was so upset with you.” She spoke softly. “I was upset with you because the way you spoke to me felt like a slap in the face. It wasn't just what you said but it's how you acted with me from the moment you stepped into my office; like a conversation with me was beneath you. I like to think we have a good working relationship, and I always try to help you however I can—only to have you throw it back to me like that. It was rude."

Julia seemed upset, but not in the way that Patrick had expected.

He hated the idea of letting Julia down and of having offended her. His back bolted straight, eyes meeting hers in an attentive way that was like a recruit with command.

He blurted out, "I was with Isabelle at the beach. She came back to mine and we're together now."

Silence blanketed the room and Julia smiled at Patrick and stood up.

Walking past him, she put a hand on his shoulder and squeezed it. "I'll see you tomorrow, Patrick. Someone is waiting for you outside."

Patrick's face turned scarlet as he turned to see Julia leave the office.

"H—how did you…?" he stuttered.

Julia simply held up a hand and waved goodbye. "Just remember, Patrick, I know you better than I think you realise. Have a good night."

Chapter 27

PATRICK

Isabelle and Patrick's relationship seemed to grow stronger every day after that and, before they knew it, the next few months had flown by. They were crazy about each other, everyone in the office knew it. They were so obviously infatuated with one another that Julia eventually had to warn Patrick about watching Isabelle work, rather than working himself.

Isabelle stayed with Patrick and Doc almost every night, using her place once a week at most. She preferred to be in the comfort of Patrick's place, plus Doc and Isabelle formed a quick friendship; she always brought him snacks and toys and, to Patrick's surprise, a new cat bed for when she stayed over and took his place in Patrick's bed. Doc fell in love with the attention and treats Isabelle bestowed on him and she was now the person Doc greeted first at the door. It vexed Patrick at first but seeing Isabelle and Doc giving each other so much love had him treasuring these moments.

After a long day of work, Isabelle told Patrick, she craved cuddling on the couch with him and relaxing with Doc. He enjoyed how peaceful it could be with her staying at his place. He never felt awkward with her, he felt at ease. He hoped she felt the same. It was like they had been together for a few years, not a few weeks.

Patrick was worried. Things had been so relaxed that he thought Isabelle might get bored, just spending time around his flat. He'd never actually taken Isabelle on a date or anything.

After spending time with these thoughts he came to the conclusion that he needed some help, as he didn't want to disappoint her He had never turned to someone for advice before, let alone relationship advice, and spent a morning at work trying to think of who he could ask. Freya, despite always being excellent to Patrick, intimidated him. He couldn't approach her.

Then he remembered that time at the beach in the toilets with Albie. Patrick never really had any feelings towards Albie but, in that moment in the bathroom, he realised that Albie was a genuinely good person. He'd ask Albie for advice, he decided. He just needed to wait for the right moment.

Mid-afternoon, he looked up and noticed that Albie was alone in the kitchen, making a coffee and taking his afternoon protein shake from the refrigerator.

This was his chance.

He remained rooted for a moment, clutching at the arms of his desk chair before shaking himself. This is for Isabelle. He had to do it.

He forced himself from his chair and tried to subtly move towards Albie. It was rare for him to be in the kitchen alone; he usually would be accompanied by Freya, but she was on a call.

"Erm, hi Albie," Patrick awkwardly stood beside him and took a glass from the cupboard, getting himself a glass of water.

"'Ello, mate 'ow you doin?" Albie shot him a beaming smile.

"I'm okay, thanks." Patrick poured his water.

"Good to hear, big man. Did you need that email? I'm so backed up right now."

This surprised Patrick and he realised Albie must think he needed something from him because he had only spoken to him about work when in the office. "Now?" Patrick asked. "No. No, don't worry about that." He paused. "I was going to ask you for some advice… if that's okay?" he still hadn't looked at Albie but was standing next to him.

Albie laughed heartily. "Mate, I am full of good ideas, me! Hit me." He leaned against the kitchen side and took a gulp of his shake.

"Well, it's about Isabelle—" Albie cut him off before he could finish.

"Ah, love-life advice? You came to the right man!" Albie put his arm around Patrick's shoulders and pulled him in closer.

"Yeah, I guess." Patrick felt so uncomfortable and badly wanted to break away from Albie's massive arms and return to his desk.

"Trouble in the bedroom, is it?" Albies whispered in his ear and Patrick pushed away.

He was shocked Albie would ask such a personal question with such ease. "What? No! I was going to ask for date ideas!"

Albie laughed. "Oh, I see. Hey, I had to ask! *Hmm*, date ideas, *eh*?" He scrunched his face and looked towards the ceiling. "Well, I don't wanna tell you all my secrets, so how about this? Why don't you think about what Isabelle likes and go from there?"

Patrick was surprised. He'd expected Albie to spam him with date ideas, not give solid advice. He nodded slowly. "…Yeah, I guess that makes sense. Thank you."

"Hey, I'm not just a pretty face over here!" Albie chuckled. Patrick was lost in his thoughts. "Righty, I've gotta head back or Julia will kill me. Good luck, big man, you'll smash it." Albie gave Patrick a big slap on the back, grabbed his shake, and headed to his desk.

Still lost in thought, Patrick muttered, "Thanks, mate."

Patrick slumped into his desk chair and started to form a plan.

Chapter 28

ISABELLE

It's finally the weekend, Isabelle thought, it had been an intense week and all she wanted to do was crash on the sofa with Patric at his flat, she headed to Patrick's place after grabbing some clothes from her flat to see her through the weekend.

She knocked on the door when she got to Patrick's and, when he opened it, Doc was on her like a bee to honey, like usual.

"There you are, gorgeous!" Isabelle picked up Doc, holding him out before resting him against her chest. Doc nuzzled into her neck before jumping away and heading into the living room.

"Hey, you." Isabelle finally greeted Patrick and leaned in to kiss him. He kissed her back tentatively before pulling her in to kiss her more passionately, causing Isabelle to drop her bag and wrap her arms around his neck.

Isabelle went to pull his t-shirt off, but he stopped her, placing his hands on hers. "No… no, not right now."

Isabelle felt utterly insulted. "You what?" She folded her arms across her chest, irritated.

Patrick looked at his watch. "Damn, we're gonna be late."

With that, he walked off and grabbed his wallet and keys from their usual spot in the kitchen and, as Isabelle watched, her anger turned into befuddlement. "What do you mean we're gonna be late?"

Patrick walked past her, opened the door, and held it open for her. "Leave your bag there. We need to go," he said.

Isabelle was surprised by Patrick's attitude; she had never seen him like this, but she was also intrigued to see what was happening and followed Patrick out of the flat, who took off at pace.

Patrick held Isabelle's hand while constantly looking at his phone, following directions with the other.

As they headed into town, Isabelle kept asking him, "Where are we going?"

His response every time was, "You'll see when you get there."

Isabelle didn't know what was happening, but she could tell he was nervous from the sweat lining his hand.

After a twenty-minute walk, Patrick suddenly stopped and turned. Isabelle's jaw dropped.

"Oh my God!"

She covered her mouth and screamed in joy before starting to jump up and down excitedly.

Patrick had brought her to a place she constantly talked about a month ago*, Missy Fantastico's Cat Café*.

"Yeah, I booked us a slot."

Isabelle jumped into Patrick's arms. "Oh my God, thank you so much!" She started to leave quick kisses all over Patrick's face before jumping out of his arms. "Can we go in?"

Isabelle bolted to the door. "Come on!"

The café was bright pink inside and there were cats everywhere, lining the several shallow tables on the floor where cushions were waiting in place of seats.

They sat down and Isabelle couldn't help herself from looking around and letting out a quiet squeal now and then. They ordered some drinks, and she very suddenly became surrounded by cats. Not a single cat approached Patrick, but he didn't appear to care, smiling over every time Isabelle *cooed*.

She barely spoke to Patrick apart from repeatedly saying *thank you*, a little too sporadically. She also barely touched her drink, opting instead to just sit and stroke every cat she could while feeding them the treats she kept making Patrick get up and buy at the counter.

Their hour in the café flew past and, when the owner approached them to let them know, Isabelle's face dropped. "Is there no way we can have longer?" she asked Patrick.

The owner apologized, but they had a booking coming in shortly. Isabelle quickly gave a hug to every cat she could while Patrick got up from the floor and stood near the exit.

"Come on, Isabelle," he said, "time to go."

Isabelle pouted at him but slowly got up and headed towards the door, thanking the owner as Patrick left the shop. Isabelle had a short talk with the owner before joining Patrick outside and, as soon as she stepped out, she burst into tears.

Patrick rushed to hug her. "What's wrong? Are you okay?"

Isabelle sobbed in his arms, thanking him over and over. "Thank you… this was the best thing ever. I can't believe you took me to *Miss Kitty Fantastico's*!"

Patrick t continued hugging her before kissing her on the head. "I wanted to take you on a date, and I knew you wanted to go here; you kept talking about it and looking at their social media."

She grabbed his face, pulled him down, and kissed him softly. After, he looked into her eyes, full of tears, but happy. She was still holding his face. "Patrick, this was the greatest date ever, thank you."

The sincerity in her voice caused Patrick to turn a brilliant shade of red. She let go of his face and grabbed his hand. "Come with me right now, I'm going to thank you properly when we get to yours."

Patrick's eyes widened and he increased his pace, overtaking her and almost running back to his flat.

Chapter 29

ISABELLE

Patrick and Isabelle started to interchange nights spent at home and trips out, organising dates and days away. Once a week, they did this. Patrick's anxiety sometimes overwhelmed him, occasionally causing their dates to end earlier than usual, and he always overly apologised to Isabelle when it did. This slowly began to annoy Isabelle, who always reminded him that she didn't mind one bit.

"I don't care if we cut date night short, silly. We could sit and have a movie marathon in your living room for all I care, all I want to do is spend time with you."

This reassurance always helped bring Patrick a sense of calm and, though Isabelle wasn't used to being around someone with social anxieties, she took it in her stride. It could be challenging at times and frustrating beyond belief, but she cared about Patrick more than she had anyone else before; she could deal with whatever issues he might have.

At work, Isabelle arrived slightly late an irritated look was plastered on her face, that Freya immediately noticed.

Freya followed her to the kitchen, "No Patrick today, lovely?"

Isabelle shot around to Freya; she was fuming.

"I have no idea! No calls, no texts—nothing! He just didn't turn up at the place we always meet the morning after I sleep at mine. He'd better have a good reason, I tell you—"

Freya cut off Isabelle mid-rant, "Woah, woah babes! He's properly just overslept or something. Have you missed your morning coffee or something?"

Isabelle sighed. She knew Freya was right. "Yeah, I need coffee."

Freya laughed and poured her a cup. "Thought so." She passed Isabelle the coffee. "Just go sit down. He'll be here soon."

Isabelle agreed. She knew it was stupid but, for the longest time, they had met there every morning.

An hour passed, but no Patrick. Isabelle was starting to get worried. She sent Patrick a few texts but didn't receive a response. She sat, tapping on her desk, leg bouncing up and down beneath it. Her impatience eventually had her shooting out of her chair and storming into Julia's office.

"Julia?" She asked as she entered. "Do you have any idea where Patrick is?"

Julia put down her pen, looked up at Isabelle, and saw how uneasy she was. "Good morning to you too Isabelle," Julia sketched a brow. "Yes, I have spoken to Patrick this morning; he is taking a couple of days off."

Isabelle was perplexed. "Huh?" She said thinking she'd perhaps heard wrong. "He's taking a couple of days off. Why?" Julia picked up her pen and looked back down at her work.

"I'm not at liberty to tell you that, Isabelle—you know that."

Isabelle nodded slowly. "Yeah—I'm sorry, Julia. I know I shouldn't have asked; I'm just worried."

Julia pursed her lips and gave her a small, encouraging smile. "Come on now, get your work done. I recommend seeing him later; I'm sure he needs it."

Isabelle spent the rest of the day half working and half looking at her phone, waiting for a text that never appeared. She was partially worried about him, partially pissed off at him. Why would he just disappear on her without a word?

As soon as the day ended, she rushed out the door and headed straight to Patrick's flat where she knocked but received no response.

Her knocking became more and more forceful until, eventually, she heard the door unlock with a click, but it wasn't opened. Isabelle frowned.

Slowly, she pushed the door open and was immediately met with a pitch-black flat.

She was starting to feel slightly scared. "Patrick?" she walked into the darkness and softly shut the door. "Are you okay?" To each question, there was no response. Even Doc didn't come to greet her.

Biting her lip, she shut the door behind her and headed to the living room. There was nothing.

"Are you in the bedroom?" There was still no response. She ran to the bedroom to see Doc curled up at the foot of the bed and Patrick curled up in a ball under his duvet, facing away from the door.

Isabelle had no idea what was happening or what she was supposed to do. "Patrick?"

She entered the bedroom and walked around the bed to the side Patrick was facing and was stunned by what she saw. Patrick's eyes were sunken, his mouth flat and almost every feature on his face looked hollow.

"What's happened? Are you okay?" There was still no response. Isabelle went to put her hand on Patrick's side. "Patrick?"

"Leave me alone," he grunted before rolling over to face the other way.

Isabelle's temper flared. "What the fuck, Patrick? Talk to me, would you? Why did you bother letting me in if you aren't talking to me?"

There was no response and, as the silence stretched out, Isabelle's anger reached meltdown territory.

"What the actual fuck is going on, Patrick!" she yelled at him. She had never raised her voice at him before, but she was at her limit. No response. "Fine."

She stormed out of the room and headed to the living room, where she flung open the curtains and threw herself onto the sofa. From there, she yelled, "I'm going to wait right here until you come and talk to me." Then, she folded her arms, crossed her legs and waited.

An hour passed and no sound came from the bedroom. There was no sign of Doc, either.

Isabelle couldn't wrap her head around what was happening; she had never experienced this. Suddenly, she finally heard a noise coming from the bedroom. Sobs.

It took her a second to process what she was hearing, but then she was off the sofa and popping her head around the door. Patrick was still in his curled-up state, crying his eyes out. Isabelle rushed to his side.

Her anger dissipated immediately. "Oh, Patrick, baby. What's wrong?"

Patrick turned over yet again, mid-sob, and continued to cry. This time, Isabelle wasn't angry and felt a weight of sadness wash over her. She climbed into the bed, shuffled over to Patrick and moulded her body around his, holding him tight.

This caused Patrick to cry even more than before, but Isabelle laid there, hugging him, never saying a word.

After ten or twenty minutes, Patrick's sobs slowed to a whimper and

Isabelle gently stroked his hair. She could feel him slowly calming and eventually drifting off to sleep.

Isabelle stayed by his side the rest of the night.

She woke up before Patrick. He was out cold, and the cold light of morning filtered through the slats in the blinds. She got up and headed to the kitchen to make some coffee and have some toast. Shortly after she poured her coffee, she was joined by Doc, who entered the kitchen and rubbed his head against Isabelle's legs before jumping onto his usual spot on the kitchen counter where he waited for his breakfast.

"Oh, you've finally come to say hello, have you?" Isabelle stroked Doc's head before emptying some of his food into his bowl.

Isabelle had work today, and she only had a couple of hours before she had to leave. She took a shower and put the clothes from the previous day back on. She wanted to stay with Patrick and talk to him so badly but didn't want to wake him, so walked back to the kitchen to finish her toast. By the time she took her last bite, a figure appeared in the door frame. She looked up to see Patrick, a duvet draped over his shoulders and his hands tightly wrapped around him.

"Are you okay?" Isabelle asked.

Patrick stood for a moment before he finally spoke. "I'm sorry…"

Isabelle rushed over and threw her arms around him. "I was so worried about you! What's happening? *Did* something happen?"

Patrick gestured with his head towards the living room and they both sat on the sofa. The duvet was still wrapped around Patrick.

"Come on, Patrick. Talk to me; what's happening?" Isabelle pleaded.

Patrick was staring at the floor. "I'm not doing good."

Isabelle replied, a teasing lilt of sarcasm in her tone. "Well, I guessed that silly. Why are you not doing good? Did something happen?"

Patrick took a deep breath, looking down at his knees and speaking softly. "Yesterday was the anniversary of my parent's car accident." His voice was so low that she almost missed his added, "They died when I was ten."

Isabelle was lost for words and the room was silent until Patrick broke it. "Everything is too much for me around the anniversary. It's like I'm getting crushed by the pressure of just existing. Acting like a human is hard. I just need to take myself away from it."

Isabelle stroked his leg. "Is that why you were crying?" she asked softly.

Patrick slowly shook his head and let out a shuddering breath before answering, "No, I was crying because you saw me like that. I felt like a waste of space. I could hear you getting angry, and it was like you hated me."

Isabelle stopped him. "I would never hate you, don't ever think that." She pulled him over, hugged him and rested his head on her chest where Patrick began to cry into her. She sat, stroking his hair and comforting him as best she could. "It's okay," she murmured, let it out."

She noticed him slowly calming to the sound of her beating heart and her softly stroking his hair.

"I'm sorry, I can't help it," he whimpered.

Isabelle pressed a soothing kiss to his forehead. "It's okay, I know."

After some time, Patrick finally sat up and looked at Isabelle. She had holding back tears of her own. All of this was so overwhelming, and the tears began to slowly roll down her face before she could stop them. She wiped the tears away using her sleeve.

"This is just part of my life; my brain becomes broken. I normally just shut down and replay everything that happened that day. The only one that's ever seen me like this is Doc. He stays with me—looks after me."

Isabelle shuffled over to him. "Have you not had any help? Like from a doctor or therapist?" she asked, stroking the back of his head.

Patrick pulled away from Isabelle for the first time, his eyebrows drawn.

"I'm sorry, baby. I was just asking. I didn't mean to push you."

Guilt was once again plastered on Patrick's face. "I'm sorry—I didn't mean to." He shook his head. "I don't want to talk to anyone about it."

Isabelle pulled him into her arms again. It's okay. We don't need to talk about it. Just know I'm here now, and I'm not going anywhere."

They sat in a comforting embrace for a while before the alarm on Isabelle's phone started to go off. She bit her lip as she looked at the time on the screen. "Shall I call in and take a day?" she asked.

Patrick shook his head. "No, you should go in."

He sounded so heartfelt that Isabelle couldn't refuse him. "Okay, will you be alright by yourself?"

Patrick nodded. "I was alone for a long time before I met you, I'm used to it."

Isabelle didn't know how to respond to that—she was completely shell-shocked by that sentence—but the silence was again interrupted by her backup alarm.

"I'm going to come back later, okay? Just message me if you need me." She got up and kissed him on the forehead. "I'll see you in a bit, okay?"

Patrick just nodded and she grabbed her bag and left for work.

The day went slowly. Isabelle felt withdrawn from the rest of the office, struggling to process what Patrick had told her that morning.

At lunch, she went to her place and finally got changed, packing a bag with enough clothes for the rest of the week before she left and returned to work.

Iris saw her walk in with her bulging overnight bag and raised her brows. "*Ooh*," she cooed. "You going away somewhere nice?"

"No," Isabelle sharply replied.

Iris opened and closed her mouth. "Well, *I'm* sorry." She stormed off back to her desk.

Isabelle did the same, feeling guilty for snapping at Iris like that. The rest of the day dragged on without a single text from Patrick. She just wanted to go to him.

Isabelle zoned out for a while and didn't notice Freya and Albie leaving. Iris was getting her things together, also about to go when Isabelle got up and headed over to her desk.

Iris spotted her and rolled her eyes. "What do you want?"

"I'm sorry, Iris. I shouldn't have snapped at you."

Iris still looked annoyed. "What did I do? I just asked a question."

And, without any warning, Isabelle started to cry. Iris' eyes widened as Isabelle momentarily stood crying, letting out all the emotion that had overwhelmed her last night. After a few uncomfortable moments, Iris approached her and awkwardly stroked her back. Isabelle pulled her in and hugged her, sobbing into her shoulder while Iris tensed, clearly confused about what was happening.

Eventually, Isabelle slowly stopped crying and released Iris from the awkward embrace.

"I'm sorry, Iris. I didn't mean to be like that with you. Patrick's not very well, and I'm going to stay with him for a few days."

Iris was surprised. "Oh, really? Well… I hope he feels better soon."

Isabelle smiled. "Thank you, Iris, you're the best."

Isabelle stayed with Patrick for the next few days and his mood slowly improved over time—with just a few blips where he would regress into the state, she found him in. She was glad he was doing better but, after a week of basically living with him, she was exhausted.

The toll soon started to become visible to those around her and, at work, she had practically become a zombie.

By the end of the week, Freya stormed over to Isabelle's desk and said, "Right, you—just go home and rest, already." Her tone was like a concerned sister's. "You can't keep doing this to yourself."

Isabelle pursed her lips but silently agreed with her. Deep inside, however, she knew that she wouldn't be able to stop acting how she was until Patrick returned to his old self. She was too worried about him. "I can't, Freya—he's not well. I need to look after him."

Freya had enough and grabbed Isabelle's bag from under her desk. "He's big enough to look after himself for a few hours; you're going home right now."

Isabelle tried to protest. "I can't—Julia will be mad."

Isabelle's protests fell on deaf ears. "Let me deal with Julia."

Freya pulled Isabelle out of her chair and marched her to the door. "How can you look after him if you can't look after yourself?" Freya's voice softened. "Now, I want you to go home, order a takeaway, and sleep—okay?"

Isabelle nodded.

"Okay then, babes. I'll text you later." Freya leaned in and kissed her on the cheek.

Isabelle hugged her. "Thank you, Freya."

Freya hugged her back. "It's okay, babes. You know I've got you."

As soon as Isabelle got to her flat, she collapsed on her bed and slept for six hours before her phone rang. It was Freya checking up on her and Isabelle's chest warmed—she knew she was lucky to have a friend like Freya and the sleep was precisely what she had needed.

She took a long shower before heading back to Patrick's.

A week passed, and over time, Patrick started to become his old self again. Isabelle stayed with him and went to work each day, and, thanks to Freya's big sister energy, she was doing better at looking after herself.

After an exceptionally long day at work, Isabelle headed back to Patrick's flat. As she opened the door, a wave of flavour filled her nose. Curry—one of her favourites.

She dropped her bag, picked up Doc and hugged him tight to her chest—their own welcome ritual—and headed to the kitchen where Patrick was wearing an apron, cooking and listening to music.

Isabelle leaned against the door frame for a moment and watched him with a smile as he hummed along to the music and stirred the sauce. She then sneaked up and wrapping her arms around him from behind.

"Oh, hey! You back already?" Patrick asked in the way Isabelle hadn't heard for a long time.

"I've missed you."

Chapter 30

PATRICK

Three months had passed since the anniversary of his parents' deaths. Patrick had come back to work, and things had slowly been returning to normal. Isabelle had gone back to staying at her place every night to get some extra rest.

Patrick felt guilty for how much he'd let Isabelle in—how much he'd let her see—and that part of him was thankful that she was there, at arm's length. The other part of him—the part that missed her—wished she had never seen him in that state and had never needed to put some distance back between them. He'd never shown anyone that side of him before, and the experience left him feeling naked.

He knew he had to make it up to Isabelle somehow, so started buying flowers for her on a regular basis and surprising her with presents a couple of times a week. When he first started treating her, she loved it but he'd noticed that, the more he did it, her reactions grew less and less.

"Do you not like it?" Patrick asked, holding out a cute pink cat mug he'd spotted at the shops.

"Of course, I do… but, come on, Patrick. This is getting silly now. I love that you're thinking of me, but you don't have to do this." She took the cup from Patrick and held his hands as she stared deep into his eyes.

"I'm sorry," he said, feeling flustered. "I didn't mean to—" Before Patrick could finish his sentence, Isabelle put a finger on his lips.

"I know—a few months back—I was there for you when you needed me, but that's just what a girlfriend does. Yeah?" Isabelle smiled softly.

"Yeah, I guess so," Patrick mumbled, lips pressing against her finger that was still on his lips.

"Good. No more presents, then, okay?" Isabelle quickly replaced her finger with her lips and kissed him easily.

Patrick took her in his arms, gently squeezing her and kissing the top of her head. Isabelle squeezed him back and looked up at him through her lashes. "I love you; ya know?" Her eyes began to water.

Patrick picked her up and she instinctively wrapped her legs around his waist. His hands clung to her back as he looked into her eyes.

"I've loved you since the first time you grabbed hold of my arm and demanded to see pictures of Doc. Every time you look at me—in that way, only you do—I know that I would give anything to see you look at me like that every day for the rest of my life. You mean everything to me."

Isabelle's eyes started to stream, causing Patrick's eyes started to water in turn. He knew, then, that he would do anything for the woman he was holding in his arms. He would be anyone she needed him to be and do anything she needed him to do.

Isabelle softly stroked his face and started to kiss every inch.

"I love you, Patrick."

Before Isabelle could say more, Patrick turned and carried her to the bedroom. Kissing her along the way.

***

For the next few weeks, the pair were in an incredibly loved-up state and the whole office could feel it. Patrick started to come out of his shell completely, slowly at first—then almost entirely—joining Isabelle at a dinner party with Albie and Freya and organising dates that he knew Isabelle would enjoy. Isabelle's love unlocked a part of Patrick he never knew existed and, for the first time, he was purely happy.

His anxiety never left, though, but he was constantly pushing himself outside his comfort zone. Anything to make her smile. It was worth it.

He did notice the toll it was starting to take on him, though, and felt exhausted most evenings. He went to work and came home to Doc. Went to beaches, on dates and attended dinners. He did his best to ignore the exhaustion and push through.

One rare Saturday, he spent a day resting and relaxing with Doc while Isabelle was out with Freya for the day. He laid on the sofa with the small cat laying sleeping on his chest, listening to music, and felt at peace—completely relaxed. That serenity was, however, suddenly disturbed when he heard a knock at the door.

His eyes flared open and he begrudgingly rose from the sofa. This annoyed Doc, who scrambled to the top of his cat tree as Patrick lumbered over to the door. He was still slowly opening it when Isabelle burst through.

She kissed him and rushed through to the living room. "Oh my God, Patrick," she said. "You're not going to believe this." Isabelle bounced in place, so obviously excited about something that Patrick gave a slight smile.

He followed into the living room and sat down on the sofa. "Believe what?" he asked, trying his best to rouse himself to attention.

"So, Freya and I were walking around town, and I saw a leaflet for a funfair! Then Freya told me she had never been to one—can you believe it?" Isabelle slapped the side of her forehead in amazement.

"I mean, I've never been to one, either. Is it that surprising?" Patrick asked, confused.

"Well, well, well," Isabelle grinned. "It's a good job I brought us all tickets to go tonight, then, isn't it?" Isabelle proudly whipped 4 tickets out of her purse.

Patrick couldn't hide his groan and covered his eyes while rubbing his brow.

"Oh," Isabelle's smile dropped. "Don't you wanna come?" She seemed surprised by his reaction.

Patrick realised what he had done and jumped back up from the sofa. "No, no," he hastened to say. "Of course, I wanna come." He waved a hand in protest.

Isabelle put the tickets back in her purse. "Look, Patrick, if you don't want to come you don't have to—you know?"

Patrick panicked. He didn't want it to come across the way it did. The disappointment on Isabelle's face was clear. "I was just waking up. Of course I want to come!" He walked over to her and hugged her tight.

Isabelle hugged him back, but he could sense her hesitation. "You know you don't have to come if you wanna chill out tonight, right? I'm not forcing you…"

Patrick kissed her on the forehead and shook his head. "I can't wait."

He took a shower and got ready for the funfair but, while standing there, all he could think of was how much he wanted to stay home. Shortly after, however, they were picked up by Albie and Freya and drove to the fun fair.

As soon as Patrick got out of the car, he was hit by the sound of loud music. Hundreds of people walked around loudly, talking or screaming, and the lights were so blindingly bright that he had to cover his eyes to help himself adjust. Isabelle approached him, rubbing his arm, and asked if he was feeling okay, so he put a smile on to help p at ease.

As they walked around the fairground, Patrick only grew more and more overwhelmed. People bumped past, yelling at him to try their obviously rigged games. His breaths began to stumble out of his mouth. The lights flared, the sounds were too loud and there were so many sounds—it was quickly becoming too much. He was numbly walking around, spending so much of his effort on just standing up and not huddling in the corner.

Isabelle was off playing some basketball game with Freya, leaving him and Albie alone as they waited for them. He wasn't making a sound—descending more and more into being completely withdrawn as he struggled through. Albie tried to make conversation with him—but to no avail. Isabelle and Freya walked back to them, jumping up and down in joy while each clutching a blue, fluffy cat they had just won.

As Isabelle turned to face them, her pace slowed, and her face quickly dropped. Patrick was sure he looked like a beaten man, standing by pure will alone, and he wasn't sure what he could do to help the situation. His eyes were glazed over. He felt trapped inside his own head.

Isabelle approached slowly and placed a hand on his cheek. "Patrick, baby," she said quietly, speaking gently like she was afraid to startle him. "Are you okay?"

Patrick snapped back into his body and threw on a smile. "Oh, did you win?"

Isabelle dropped her hand immediately, the corner of her mouth twisting down as her jaw ticked. "Do you even want to be here, Patrick? You've not joined in at all!"

Patrick knew that he should be honest, but he really didn't want to let her down. He forced himself to smile. "I'm just tired," he said, believing it would be enough to calm the situation.

Isabelle threw her hands up in the air. "I told you at your place, you didn't have to come! Why didn't you just bloody tell me rather than wandering around like a husk?" Isabelle was angrier than Patrick had ever seen. He wasn't sure what to do. "Just fuck off back home, Patrick. For God's sake, there's no point in coming if you're just going to ruin the fun for everyone."

With that, she stormed off. Freya quickly followed, trying to calm her down, and Patrick was left standing with Albie. His brain felt fuzzy. Everything felt like a bad dream.

"Fancy a lift home, big man?"

Patrick nodded, resigning himself to leaving early. He moved methodically, one step in from of the other, until they got into Albie's car where Albie told him to buckle. They sped off and Patrick was surprised by how fast Albie was driving—but he didn't hate it. It felt freeing, in a way. They were parked up outside his flat before he even knew it.

Albie turned in his seat to face Patrick. "Look, mate. Do you know why Isabelle blew up like that?"

Patrick felt slightly intimidated and sat up straight. "I'm guessing 'cause I wasn't having fun?"

Albie unironically slapped his forehead. "Bloody 'ell, Patrick. You muppet! She was annoyed 'cause you didn't talk to her. Didn't communicate. If you're tired and don't fancy it, you don't have to come. You could have just told her."

Patrick sat stunned, and Albie put a giant hand on Patrick's shoulder. "Mate, just talk to her. She's not exactly some monster that's gonna chew your ear off for being tired, is she?"

Patrick was starting to realise how much he messed up and cast a desperate look at Albie before asking, "What do you think I should do?"

Albie let out a bellowing laugh. "Patrick, mate, go inside and wait for her. You'll know what to do. I'm not gonna sit and give you all the answers." He gestured with his head towards Patrick's flat. "Go on with ya. I'll meet back up with the girls and drop her back round yours a bit later, okay? Gimme your phone a sec—I'll give you my number and message you when I'm on my way back."

Patrick nodded and handed Albie his phone, and they exchanged numbers. Albie gave him a slap on the back and Patrick turned to open the car door.

"Good luck, mate." Albie grinned and revved his engine.

As Patrick stepped out, he looked at the huge man revving his engine like a teenager and felt slightly silly as he sincerely said, "Thank you, Albie."

Albie gave Patrick a wink and sped off, leaving Patrick standing alone in the cool night air.

Chapter 31

PATRICK

As Patrick opened his front door, he was met by Doc as usual and made his way to the living room. He planned to sit and think about everything but, as soon as his head hit the back of the sofa, he was out like a light. He was so exhausted that it completely took over and a few hours passed before his phone started to buzz in his pocket, making him jolt upright.

Albie had messaged.

On the way.

Patrick jumped up and rushed to the kitchen. He'd meant to have some dinner cooked and ready for Isabelle by the time she got there so he could apologise over dinner. He rushed around his kitchen, pulling out pots before filling one with water and setting it to boil. He started to pace up and down his kitchen, begging the water to boil faster so he could fill it with pasta.

Finally, the water started to bubble, and he poured some twisty pasta into the pot. As he did, there was a soft knock at the door.

Patrick's eyes widened as he gingerly walked to the door and opened it slowly. Isabelle stood, a light blush on her cheeks as she nervously twisted the fur of the large, stuffed, fluffy cat that was held under her arm.

"Can I come in?" she sheepishly asked, looking down at her shoes.

Patrick stood, holding the door and smiling to himself. She looked so cute, holding that stuffed toy. "Yeah, yeah. Of course." He held the door open as Isabelle scooted past him. As he turned and shut it, however, he heard the water boiling over the pot and onto the hob beneath it. "Shit, the pasta!" he cursed and moved as quickly as he could to the kitchen, practically breezing past Isabelle, who followed him into the kitchen as he rifled through drawers for a spoon.

Isabelle watched him and couldn't help but laugh, "Patrick, what are you doing?" she giggled.

Patrick stopped; a wooden spoon held in hand. She walked over to the cooker and turned down the heat. "The heat was just too high," she laughed. "What are you even doing?"

Patrick rubbed the back of his head, slightly embarrassed. "Well, I wanted to cook you your favourite meal…"

Isabelle's eyes softened. "I'm so sorry, Patrick. I didn't mean to shout at you like that. I'm so sorry."

Patrick could feel her tears leaking through his shirt. He didn't understand why *she* was apologising to *him*. He pulled her away from his chest so he could see her distraught face.

"Please don't cry. I'm so sorry. I should have just told you I was tired—I didn't mean to upset you. I'm so sorry."

Isabelle looked up as tears slowly rolled down her cheeks. Patrick took his hand and wiped away a tear from each of her eyes. "I promise, I'll try to be more honest when I just need some rest, okay?"

Isabelle simply nodded, looking up at him while leaning to kiss him. They held each other for a while before Patrick suddenly jumped into action.

"I forgot the beef mince!" he yelled, running to the fridge.

He pulled out the mince beef and turned to see Isabelle putting on an apron and tying her hair back into a ponytail.

"Well," she said, "we best get cooking, *eh*?"

The panic he'd felt earlier felt like a distant memory as the tension fell from Patrick's face. He smiled.

They spent the next hour having fun making a sauce and cooking spaghetti together. Before sitting down to eat, Isabelle walked over to Patrick and hugged him again.

"Please," she implored. "Just talk to me next time. I don't ever want to fight like that again." Her vice-like grip around his chest was tight but felt like love. Patrick kissed the top of her head and softly squeezed her back.

"I love you," he reminded her. "Let's eat."

Chapter 32

ISABELLE

The months began to blur together, rapidly unfolding like the pages of a book and before Isabelle knew it, she and Patrick were approaching their first anniversary as a couple. The months began to blur together, rapidly unfolding like the pages of a book and before Isabelle knew it, she and Patrick were approaching their first anniversary as a couple. Everything felt natural between them. They would get lunch together at work, go on dates and she would spend long periods of time at Patrick's. They were happy in each other's company.

Isabelle woke to Patrick's hand on her arm. It was a Saturday, and he placed a card on her chest.

"What's this?" she groggily asked, opening the card. It was an anniversary card. She furrowed her brow and laughed. "Patrick, our anniversary isn't until next week. You're a bit early here."

"Oh, *shh.* Just read it." Patrick waved a finger towards the card.

Isabelle examined the card; the front had two cute cats with their tails curved together in the shape of a heart. She grinned and flipped the card open, and a stack of money fell out.

"*Whoa*! What is this?" She was still waking up and her tired brain was struggling to catch up.

"Just read the card," Patrick said with a laugh.

Her eyes flicked over the written note.

My Dearest Isabelle,

The past year has been the best year of my life. You mean the world to me, and I can't imagine my life without you.

I've booked a night at Tree House Hotel with a dinner at their restaurant to celebrate our anniversary.

You best go out and buy something to wear.
Always yours
Patrick

"Come here, you silly…" Isabelle got on her knees and shuffled towards Patrick on the bed with open arms.

After a long hug, Patrick told her, "You best get a move on. Our reservation is at 7 pm."

She immediately jumped out of bed, grabbed her phone and called Freya. "Please tell me you're free for some shopping today!"

Isabelle wasted no time and booked it to the local shopping centre. While shopping, Freya accidentally let slip that she had been taken there not long ago and Isabelle teased her—she knew Albie must have taken her, but she still couldn't get Freya to admit they were together. Isabelle wasn't upset by it, though. Teasing them was her favourite thing to do. She was glad Patrick had gone to Albie to ensure he picked somewhere nice and fancy.

Isabelle bought a stunning, silky white dress and a pair of red accent heels. Freya insisted she buy a dress that showed off her figure and, though Isabelle momentarily protested, Freya's ability to fill her with confidence won her over.

When she arrived back at the flat, Patrick was waiting in his suit. Even though she had seen him wearing it countless times at work, to her, it was his best look. She dropped her bags, moving quickly to straddle him on the sofa and kiss him passionately. He tried to pull away to tell her something but couldn't resist.

"I was not expecting that," Patrick said, trying to catch his breath.

They both shared a moment of laughter before Patrick's eyes widened. "God, what's the time?" he asked, scrambling to check his phone before showing it to her. It was 5 pm. They had an hour before the taxi arrived. "Isabelle, we need to shower, get changed and finish packing within the hour!"

Chapter 33

PATRICK

A mad rush getting ready and a taxi ride later, they finally arrived at the hotel on time and checked in. The restaurant, attached to the Treehouse Hotel, was a Michelin-star Restaurant, and was, without a doubt, the fanciest place Patrick had ever been. They were shown to their table, ordered a bottle of wine and sat, enjoying the ambience of the beautiful restaurant. In the middle of the room, a pianist played beautiful music on a piano.

They decided to order for each other as a bit of fun and made a bet about who would get the worst dish. They were having the time of their life.

"I'm going to powder my nose—don't you dare steal my wine, Mr! I know how much I have left!" Isabelle tried to be as severe as she could but wore a big smile.

"Go on, I won't, don't worry," Patrick tutted but, after she'd left, he decided that pouring some into his glass would be funny.

He waited for her to come back with restrained humour. Five minutes passed. He started to grow concerned. After ten minutes, he'd go look for her. What was taking her so long?

He asked a female staff member to check on her in the toilets, but they told him she wasn't there. This left Patrick feeling very worried, and he started wandering around the hotel, trying to find her. He decided to check the bar area in case she got lost.

As he neared the bar, he froze; Isabelle was talking to a guy, twirling under his arm as he held her hand. A rage he hadn't felt before built inside him as he watched. Isabelle kept touching the guy, feeling his clothes and laughing in a way that had Patrick's hackles rising.

Isabelle then grabbed the man's hand and started to drag him towards the restaurant. Pulling him behind her, she turned and finally spotted Patrick standing in the hallway.

"Oh, hey you! I was just about to come and find you!" she exclaimed before noticing the foul face Patrick was pulling as he stood with his fists clenched.

The man stood awkwardly behind her and asked, "Everything okay hun?"

Isabelle frowned like she wasn't sure what was happening.

The guy behind her picked up on the vibe and said, "I'm gonna leave you be, lovely. I'll catch you later." He then leaned in, kissed her on each cheek, and left.

Isabelle headed over to Patrick. Now they were alone, he finally asked, "Who the hell was that?"

Isabelle seemed thrown by his anger. "What is wrong with you? It was just a friend I went to university with." Isabelle matched his rage.

"Oh, just a friend, is it? I saw you all over him at the bar."

Isabelle was stunned. "Are you actually acting like this right now? Tonight, of all nights?" Her face contorted with rage.

"I caught you red-handed, Isabelle; you can't deny it! So, tell me, is he the only guy?" Isabelle's jaw dropped. "Are you fucking kidding me? I'm so fucking done. I'm leaving." She turned and headed towards the exit.

"Where are you going? This isn't done," Patrick yelled after her.

He quickly ran to the restaurant and paid. He knew he could catch up with her. After paying, he jogged towards the exit. To his surprise, Isabelle was pacing up and down outside the front of the hotel.

"Don't get any ideas! Stay away from me. I don't even want to see you right now." She pointed towards him using her clutch bag.

"You're the one waiting outside the hotel for me," Patrick said, heading towards her.

"Oh, shut up, you self-obsessed prick. I'm waiting for a taxi."

Hearing how angry she was only enraged him more.

"I can't believe you, Patrick," Isabelle continued. "On our anniversary dinner, you really think I'm cheating on you?"

Patrick clapped his hands together. "Ah, see, you're bringing up cheating."

Isabelle turned around and started walking. "Oh, grow up Patrick. You're being pathetic."

Patrick started to walk to catch up to her, and as he got close, he stretched his arm out and took her hand in his.

"What the hell are you doing? Get the fuck off me." Patrick turned her around to face him and she swatted his arm away. "Honestly, Patrick, this jealousy is an ugly look on you. You're being pathetic over—what, this? The guy you're so adamant I'm cheating on you with is someone I went to university with. He's here with his husband, for goodness' sake and I was excited to introduce him to you!"

Patrick's heart compressed as a sinking feeling washed over him. He felt less than dirt. She'd told him about her friend from university before. She used to love going to clubs with him because he would look after her while they were out. Guilt pulsed through his chest.

Isabelle continued dressing Patrick down with her eyes. "Oh, feeling like a bloody idiot now, are you? *Good.* I can't believe you would doubt me like that after everything! I'm so done with you, Patrick. I'm *done*!" With that, she charged across the road to get away from Patrick.

What had he done? He needed to fix this. The only thing running through Patrick's mind was that he had to find some way to salvage what was between them and he turned to see where Isabelle had gone, finding her across the road. His heart pounded.

Is this it? Have I ruined everything?

All the air escaped his lungs. He was a man floating in space with no air and no ground to stand on. He threw his hands on his head and started to pace. She was walking further and further away from him. His world was imploding right here, and it was all his fault.

Why did I say anything? She was completely innocent, and I accused her without evidence…

He was speeding through all the mistakes he'd made in the last ten minutes. Who could blame her for being angry and leaving? He was an idiot. The king of idiots.

And he was going to lose the best thing that had ever happened to him because he'd been so dumb.

Patrick's mind kicked into overdrive as he thought about everything, he'd done wrong, everything he had lost and how much he despised himself.

"No," he muttered to himself, internally filling with resolve. "No, I can fix this! I can make things better. I can't lose her like this. I refuse."

Without another second to think, he turned to cross the road to catch up with her.

Chapter 34

ISABELLE

The loud screech of tyres filled the night air, making Isabelle jump out of her skin. The sound paused the barrage of thoughts running through her mind.

She turned on a dime and, from down the street, she watched as the red brake lights of a stationary car in the middle of the road flickered. Isabelle frowned and looked around for Patrick. Her eyes scanned the street and around the restaurant, but he wasn't there. Had he already left?

A slight hint of relief washed over Isabelle, and she took a deep breath.

Then, she heard the tyres screech once more and the car accelerated away with speed. She turned again and saw something left in the road.

"Oh, my God, did they hit a dog?"

Isabelle took off at a brisk walk towards the scene of the accident. She couldn't believe they'd just drive away like that without checking on the poor creature.

As she got closer, however, she realised whatever was on the road right now wasn't a dog at all. It was bigger, for one. In a sudden burst of speed, her brisk walk became a run and she took off as fast as she possibly could. She dropped her heels at some point, sprinting towards the body left in the road, as a growing sense of panic gnawed at her.

"Patrick!"

Isabelle stumbled as she tried to slow down. She felt as though she were trapped in a nightmare.

Patrick's limp and unconscious body lay in the middle of the road. She was less than a foot away and could see the blood that was starting to fall from his nose. A small pool of blood was seeping from behind his hair.

Isabelle froze.

Nothing. She had nothing for this moment; not a breath, a thought or anything at all. She was locked in time, looking down at Patrick.

People from the restaurant started to pour from the door to investigate what had happened and someone shrieked. It took Isabelle a moment to realise it was her. The sound was one of ultimate despair and the cries continued to leak from her mouth as she dropped to the floor.

The scream bounced off every building in the street. She didn't think it would stop reverberating.

People started to pull out their phones to call an ambulance, rushing over to where Isabelle huddled.

"There's been an accident." She could hear them say in some distant way. The murmurs layered until they were one in her mind.

"We need an ambulance right now."

"There's been a hit and run."

As people approached, something inside of Isabelle snapped, turning feral. She arched her body over Patrick's torso and warned, "Don't any of you fucking touch him!" Her face twisted in fury, ready to rip the hand off anyone who tried to touch him like a wild animal protecting what was hers. "You back the fuck off, right now," she scowled.

The restaurant manager held his arms wide to stop anyone getting closer and looked at her pleadingly. "Miss, please. We've called an ambulance and need to check if he has a pulse." He gently bent down and stretched his arm to feel Patrick's neck, but Isabelle smacked his hand out of the way before it even got close.

"You're not going to touch him!"

The restaurant manager backed off slightly. "Okay, Miss. I understand but please can you see if he has a pulse?"

Isabelle knew what he was saying made sense and some withdrawn part of her reared its head. Her dress getting damp, and she looked down to find her white dress, stained crimson red.

She felt like she wasn't breathing.

Without thinking, she threw her ear down to Patrick's chest. "Please be there, please be there," she chanted and listened intently. A cold shiver crept up her body; she couldn't hear anything.

She shot up and put her ear to his mouth, "Breathe, Patrick. Breathe, God dammit, you stubborn idiot. For once, do something I tell you to," she shouted, rubbing her hand over his chest.

People were watching with bated breath. Some of their heads dropped.

"I can't feel anything!" she screamed at the restaurant owner. "Don't be dead, Patrick. Don't be dead."

It was all that she could think of.

"Miss, please listen to me. Let me check his neck for a pulse."

Isabelle conceded out of fear, moving out of the way to sit beside Patrick's head, and started stroking his face. "Please, baby. *Please.* I'm sorry, I'm so sorry—please don't leave me."

The restaurant owner knelt and held two fingers to Patrick's neck, looking for his pulse.

Isabelle's hands were covered in Patrick's blood, but she didn't notice or care as she sat stroking his face, pleading for him not to be dead. She looked up at the restaurant owner, her eyes begging him to tell her any good news.

"I've got a pulse. He's alive!" The restaurant owner shot up and pointed to one of his employees. "Get that ambulance here now," he bellowed.

Isabelle cried out, filling the night air. She kept repeating, "Don't leave me, please don't leave me."

His blood was everywhere; in her hair, on her dress and coating her skin. The restaurant owner started to push people back, asking for space.

Seconds later, blue lights filled her vision as an ambulance and two police cars pulled up alongside the scene. Everything seemed to be happening in slow motion to Isabelle. Two paramedics leapt out of the ambulance, one toting a medical bag and both dragging a stretcher between them. They ran towards Patrick and Isabelle, shortly followed by some officers, who got the crowd to back up and give the paramedics room.

"Miss, step away, please. Let us get to him; what happened?"

The paramedics easily moved Isabelle away from Patrick's body to examine him, but she was so distraught she couldn't comprehend what they were asking.

"Don't leave me, Patrick. Don't leave me," she muttered, eyes wild, hovering nearby and slightly in the way.

A female police officer clocked Isabelle, who was still covered in blood. The paramedics were still trying to examine Patrick, but she was making it hard. The police officer jumped into action, taking her outer jacket off and throwing it over Isabelle's shoulders before tucking an arm around her and leading her further away.

"Please let them do their jobs." She spoke softly. "They're helping him; if you want him to be okay, you just have to let them do their jobs."

Isabelle finally realised the police officer was there and turned to look at her, eyes glassy.

"Why don't you come sit on the kerb with me over there." She pointed less than two feet away from where they were now.

Her face was warm and trusting and Isabelle looked at her for a few seconds before nodding. Before she knew it, she was being guided to the curb by the police officer.

The officer sat Isabelle beside her with an arm still around her shoulders. She was trying to comfort her in any way possible yet, at the same time, keep her away from the paramedics. "Why don't you tell me what happened? You're not hurt, are you?"

Isabelle couldn't stop crying; she was laser-focused on Patrick. Like a hawk, she watched every move the paramedics took, every facial expression. Close by, the restaurant manager spoke to the police, explaining to the officer that he'd heard the loud screech of tyres and had seen a stationary car outside his restaurant. When he'd looked out the window while heading to the door, finding a man on the floor, the car had sped off, leaving the person behind. Leaving *Patrick* behind.

He went on to mention that, before anyone else could reach him, the woman sitting on the curb had and was first on the scene. She'd been at dinner with the man shortly before he was hit, he said.

The police officer sitting with Isabelle overheard everything. "So, Patrick is your boyfriend?"

Isabelle blinked. "Yes, he's mine," she snapped but her tone didn't match the look on her face; she was petrified.

"Okay, I understand," the officer nodded. "What's your name, Miss?"

Isabelle went back to staring at the paramedics. "Isabelle," she whispered.

"Okay, Isabelle, my name is Betty. Just sit here with me, and we can wait together, yeah?"

Isabelle nodded. They sat together on the curb for some time, Betty rubbing her shoulders and trying to comfort her. It felt like hours passed but perhaps it was only minutes. The paramedics were working fast; one ran to the ambulance to get a neck brace while the other delivered oxygen.

Before Isabelle could gather what was happening, they had Patrick on the stretcher, lifting him and carefully heading to the ambulance. Isabelle shot up, sprinting towards them like a horse out of the gates, but ran into an imposing man who stopped her. He was quickly followed by Betty.

"Isabelle, stop! Please stop and listen to me!" Betty's tone became more assertive.

Isabelle turned around and looked at her. "This is my partner, Don. If you come with us, we can follow the ambulance to the hospital with you, alright?"

Isabelle nodded sheepishly. "Okay, Miss, please follow me." Don directed her to his car, and she was escorted by both Betty and Don. "Don't worry, Miss; we'll look after you and get you there as quickly as possible." Don's voice was very masculine but genuinely kind.

Together, they got into the car. Betty got into the back with Isabelle and held her hand. They sped off to the hospital, closely following the ambulance.

"This is all my fault," Isabelle finally said. "This is all my fault." Her head was in her hands. She was sobbing.

Betty rubbed her shoulder. "What do you mean it was your fault, Isabelle?" Isabelle didn't respond and Betty's voice took on that same authoritative tone she'd used with her before. "Isabelle, you need to talk to us and tell us what happened."

Isabelle wiped away her tears as best she could and explained to Don and Betty that they'd had a fight. She told them how she'd shouted at him and left him in the street—and how, the next thing she knew, he was on the floor in the road.

Her face was covered in streaked makeup, blood and tears. Betty pulled a packet of tissues from her pocket and started to wipe as much as she could from Isabelle's cheeks.

"Can I be completely frank with you, Isabelle?"

Isabelle nodded and slowly calmed.

"I can tell by your eyes how much you love this man. No little bicker in the street would stop that, would it?" Betty passed Isabelle a tissue.

From the front seat, Don took over. "Miss, this wasn't your fault, not one bit. It was just an accident. You have done nothing wrong."

Isabelle dabbed at her eyes with the tissue and nodded in acknowledgement but didn't necessarily feel it.

Betty continued, "Let's just get you to the hospital so you can be with him, shall we?" She offered Isabelle a genuinely warm smile.

"Okay," Isabelle agreed. "Thank you for everything."

Betty and Don, in sync, responded, "Just doing our job."

They arrived at the hospital seconds after the ambulance and the paramedics were unloading Patrick from the ambulance, on a stretcher, as they pulled up.

Isabelle tried to leap out of the car and yanked at the door handle. "Please—let me out, please," she begged them.

Don got out and headed to her door.

"Isabelle, look at me," Isabelle reluctantly turned to look at Betty. "You have to stay with us, okay?"

Isabelle nodded.

Inside the hospital, Don headed for the desk and explained everything. They were then shown to an empty waiting room. The room was small, with a few chairs and a low coffee table with generic magazines scattered across it.

"Isabelle, please just wait here with Don for a moment; I need to make a report but will be back in a minute."

Isabelle sat down on one of the chairs and Don sat one away from her. They waited in silence for a few minutes—Isabelle's first moment of silence in what seemed like hours.

Shortly after, Betty came back and held a pile of clothes in her hand. "Isabelle, why don't you come with me and get cleaned up."

Isabelle was confused at first and looked down at her dress, realising what she looked like. Her dress was covered in Patrick's blood and dirt from the road. She was speechless, eyes filled with horror.

"Come on, Miss," Don gently helped her up from her seat. Up we get." They escorted her to the closet bathroom.

The bathroom had a shower, and Betty put the clothes onto the sink, waiting for her.

"Hop in here for a bit," she directed Isabelle to the shower. "We can get rid of them clothes, yeah?" Betty said softly as she held out a medical waste bag. Isabelle nodded, unzipped her dress, and put it in the bag. "Lovely, I'll be sitting outside the door; take as long as you want and shout if you need me." Betty left the room and closed the door behind her.

Isabelle stood momentarily before taking her underwear off and stepping into the hot shower. As soon as she did, the water running off her and down the drain was red. She stood under the shower for a while, just looking down at the plug and watching the blood-filled water circle down the drain; she felt numb.

"What is happening? Is this a nightmare?"

She stayed under the shower until the water turned clear. She got out and dried herself off before putting the scrubs Betty left on the sink.

She stood and looked at herself in the mirror. For a good thirty seconds, she simply looked deeply at her reflection before collapsing on the floor sobbing. Like a flash, Betty flew through the door and lifted Isabelle off the floor. She was okay; she was just exhausted.

They laid her down on a couple of the chairs and told her to try to sleep and that they could be there for a while. Isabelle didn’t respond. She just lay staring at the door.

“Is there anyone we should call? Patrick’s family?”

Isabelle finally spoke. She pulled her phone from her bag, unlocked it, and passed it to Betty. “Julia.”

Chapter 35

ISABELLE

An hour passed and Isabelle, lying on the seats and staring at the door, was still with Don and Betty. It was quiet enough to hear a pin drop and the only sound was the clock on the wall as it ticked away.

Isabelle was still wholly numb; in the hour she had laid there, it was like her brain had switched off from exhaustion but there was irritatingly enough energy left to keep her awake.

The door swung open, and Isabelle bolted to attention. Julia stepped into the room and, before she could say anything, Isabelle threw herself at Julia, who clutched her as she wailed into the older woman's shoulder.

"Julia," she cried. "I'm so sorry."

Julia let Isabelle cry on her shoulder and stroked her hair while squeezing her tight.

Don and Betty stood and collected their jackets. "Thanks for coming; I was wondering if you have a contact detail for Patrick's family?"

Julia continued to hug Isabelle. "I'm sorry, officers. His family passed away when he was young, but I am listed as his emergency contact."

Don put his jacket on as Betty filled Julia in on the situation. Isabelle didn't let go of Julia the entire time she did.

"Well, thanks very much, officers. I'll take over here now. Thanks for looking after her until I arrived—you have my details if you need to get in touch with either Patrick or Isabelle."

Isabelle was starting to calm down and finally pulled away from Julia, turning instead to the officers. "Thank you so much, both of you. I don't know what I would have done without you."

Don and Betty, in unison, said, "Just doing our jobs." They smiled before leaving Julia and Isabelle alone.

Julia and Isabelle sat beside each other, "What is he like, eh? A man his age should know to check both ways. I'll yell at him about that, what do you think?"

Isabelle didn't expect to laugh, but Julia's no-nonsense attitude, even in such a situation, made her chuckle.

Julia took Isabelle's hand—Isabelle hadn't expected the comforting gesture but was glad of it. "Don't you worry about him, he's too stubborn to leave us yet." Julia squeezed Isabelle's hand tight.

It didn't show, but Isabelle could tell she was hurting inside, too.

Julia had only been there for ten minutes when a knock sounded on the door. A doctor came through and Isabelle tried to jump up, but Julia held her down, holding tight to her hand.

"Hi there," the doctor said. "Is this Patrick's family?" Julia nodded, which surprised Isabelle, but she didn't interject. She just wanted to know about Patrick.

The doctor pulled out a chair and sat before the two agitated women. "So, there's good news and bad news." Isabelle audibly gasped. "Good news first, then," the doctor swiftly said and continued without pause. "He's stable and we have him in a medically induced coma."

Isabelle broke, then, and started to sob again. Julia still didn't let go of her hand.

"Don't worry, it's not bad; we're just letting him sleep to give his brain a chance to recuperate."

Beside Isabelle, Julia was stoic. She was yet to make a noise or move. Isabelle, on the other hand, felt like she'd been punched by this news and couldn't help the tears that noisily choked her on their way out.

The doctor frowned and hovered for a moment. "Shall I tell you the other news separately?" they asked Julia.

Julia shook her head. "No, tell us both."

The doctor nodded. "Right, well, Patrick's suffered a bad head injury, and we had to do some emergency surgery to relieve the pressure. He's also suffering from multiple broken ribs. Luckily, none of them have caused any damage to his lungs."

Julia gasped and covered her mouth.

"I'm sorry," the doctor continued. "We don't know how these injuries will affect him. We'll only be able to tell once we take him out of the coma."

"Can we see him?" Julia asked, momentarily catching Isabelle off-guard. Her sobs paused.

"Well, he has been moved to the intensive care unit but, tomorrow afternoon, you should be able to speak to the doctor in charge there and visit him. They can give you more information on what happens next."

Julia finally let go of Isabelle's hand and stood up. Facing the Doctor, she firmly held her hand out. "Thank you for your fine efforts, we couldn't have wished for a better emergency doctor."

Somewhat surprised, the doctor held out their hand and shook her hand. "Thanks. You're welcome—I need to go now, though." They apologised before leaving the room and closed the door behind him.

Isabelle was an empty shell at this point. Her tears hadn't stopped falling since the doctor first spoke and her eyes were sore from the amount she had cried in one evening. She couldn't comprehend everything the doctor had said.

"Right, Isabelle," Julia said. "Now we get to work." Isabelle looked up at Julia, frowning. "He's done his hard work, it's on us now. So, stand up. We need to get some coffee—it's going to be a long day."

Isabelle tried to wipe the tears from her face as she stood but she was still confused. "But... but what can we do?"

Julia scoffed. "Well—first, we need to get you some proper clothes. We must tell work we won't be in for a few days. One of us needs to go feed Doc and we need to get some home comforts for Patrick's room. You need to get some rest—and that's just the start."

For some reason, this was precisely what Isabelle needed to hear and her spine straightened as Julia narrowed her eyes at her. She took a moment to compose herself and collect her belongings.

"Right, Julia," she said, voice stronger than before. "Let's go find that coffee."

Patrick was in a medically induced coma for 2 months, but the doctors had said they would be waking him up soon. Isabelle had been by his side the whole time and took leave from work until he was awake. Every day, she arrived at the hospital looking more and more dishevelled than the one before.

Barely eating, she was losing weight rapidly due to her already-petite figure. A few of the intensive care nurses started to notice and took to offering her food and drinks while she was there, but she rejected everything. Instead, she sat beside Patrick's bed every day in the uncomfortable hospital chair, lost in her own mind.

Every other day, Julia came to visit Patrick. Each time, these visits ended in Isabelle crying in her arms and Julia reassuring her that he would be fine and would wake soon. It got so bad that Julia even mentioned she'd reached out to Isabelle's parents but, due to their travels, they wouldn't be back in the country for months more. They thanked and pleaded with Julia to be there for her and help her if Isabelle needed it which Julia was happy to oblige.

The room was getting to Isabelle; every day, it felt like it was becoming bigger and bigger, and she was shrinking. The clock on the wall was getting louder and louder. *Is this hell?* she wondered to herself.

Trapped in a room with someone she cared deeply for who didn't know she was there, feeling smaller and smaller as the room expanded, Isabelle felt insignificant, useless and guilty. Was this her penance?

Chapter 36

JULIA

Two days before Patrick was due to be woken up, Julia went to the hospital to check up on him. She said hello to the nurses—who, by this point, had become familiar faces—and signed in. However, when saw Isabelle's name already on the list, she sighed and wondered what state she would be in today.

She walked down the hospital hallway carrying her bag and a small bunch of flowers she'd taken from her garden to replace the ones she put in last week. Julia had always thought it was important to add some life to the room.

As she approached the door to Patrick's room, she was shocked into a stunned pause after a heart-breaking cry broke out. She knew it was Isabelle.

Right... enough is enough.

She burst through the door and Isabelle seemed taken aback. "J—Julia?" She leapt up and wiped away the tears from her face.

Isabelle could not hide the apprehension on her face. Julia turned, shut the door, and sternly said, "Sit down". The tone Julia was using reminded her of the scoldings her parents would give her as a child.

Julia didn't say a thing. She strode over to the vase, dumped the dying flowers out and into the bin and took the vase to the sink where she washed it out. She then put the new flowers inside and added fresh water before placing it on Patrick's bedside table.

Julia reached over and stroked his hair "Afternoon Patrick."

Isabelle couldn't take her eyes off Julia, who'd entered the room with such fury yet now seemed like a mother checking on her sleeping child. Julia's eyes caught Isabelle's. "Look at you..." her tone changed back to the commanding voice she'd entered with.

Isabelle's back shot straight; she had been slouching this whole time.

"Who even are you?" Julia's eyes were piercing and furious. "You're not Isabelle. I don't know who you are… but you're not the Isabelle I know."

Isabelle didn't respond for a moment, a somewhat confused glint in her still-damp eyes.

"I want you to stand up and look in that mirror. Go on; look." Julia pointed to the mirror above the sink and Isabelle slowly lurched over and looked into her own eyes.

She stared at her reflection in silence and Julia could tell when she saw what she had seen all along. Her hair was mangled and unkempt, her skin dry and blotchy. The bags under her eyes practically had bags and her eyes, themselves, looked void of life. Even her lips looked chafed like she had been wandering a desert.

A tear slowly rolled down Isabelle's cheek.

Julia appeared behind her, looking at her through the mirror. Her face and tone were much softer than before as she said, "Isabelle has such hope and love behind her eyes that she infects everyone around her—and makes people's hearts lift even when she doesn't mean to. Her smiles fill a room and talking to her causes you to smile even when you're telling her off." Julia started to stroke Isabelle's hair. "The Isabelle I knew made a man that had given up on people believe again. But the Isabelle I see right now mirrors what she pulled him out of."

With that, Isabelle turned and wrapped her arms around Julia. "You don't understand, Julia," she whimpered and began to sob in earnest, tears streaming down her face. "This is all my fault."

Julia pulled Isabelle away from her and asked, "What do you mean? A car hit him, Isabelle. You weren't at fault. Catch your breath and talk to me."

Julia let Isabelle catch her breath before pulling out a seat so they could talk. Isabelle sat sheepishly.

"Right. I haven't asked you about what happened yet because I thought you needed time but now, I think you must tell me." Julia rubbed Isabelle's knee and looked into her eyes.

Isabelle took a breath and explained to Julia what happened after their dinner and the argument that led to Patrick getting hit by a car. Julia allowed her to say everything she needed and did not interrupt her once. As Isabelle explained, she simply held her hand and comforted her.

"Oh, Isabelle, that doesn't make it your fault." Julia's heart clenched as she pulled Isabelle towards her, hugging her tightly. She was shocked every time she saw Julia; she was the one who had initiated the hug. Julia never did this. She felt a tear hit her shoulder.

"Is this why you've let yourself get in such a way?" Isabelle nodded. "Oh, you silly girl, I wish you had spoken to someone! Everyone has been so worried about you!"

They sat embraced for a few minutes before Julia stood up.

"Right, I'm gonna tell you what's going to happen now, okay?" Isabelle wiped her face and nodded again. "You are going to go home right now, and, on the way, you are going to stop at the supermarket and buy food. Then, you're going to make that food and eat it—*then* you are going to sleep. You are going to sleep for as long as you need and rest. *No* alarms, you hear me?"

Isabelle nodded and Julia sighed.

"Then," she continued, "tomorrow, you're not coming here; I'm going to tell the nurses you're not allowed in tomorrow."

Isabelle opened her mouth to protest but was quickly shot down by Julia. "I don't care what you have to say; I'm not gonna sugar coat this, Isabelle—you look worse than he does," Julia pointed over to Patrick. "You need to spend a day recouping and resting. I'm not going to take any excuse. I will send Freya around after she finishes work tomorrow and she's going to stay around yours with you. I've already spoken to her, and she said, 'yes' before I could even get the words out of my mouth."

Isabelle looked at the ground, pink teasing the apples of her cheeks. She nodded to show Julia she was listening.

"So, you're not coming here tomorrow? You're gonna look after yourself.... yes? Look at me and tell me." Julia recognised her mother's voice coming from her again.

Isabelle raised her head and looked at Julia, whose eyes were filled with care, concern and tears.

"Okay," she finally agreed. "I won't come tomorrow—and I'll rest, promise." Isabelle smiled softly at Julia.

"There we go, that's the smile that I've missed." Isabelle gave an embarrassed look and laughed. "Right, now, off with you. Go and buy yourself some food."

Isabelle stood and collected her things. As she picked up her bag, she paused and turned to Julia. "What about Patrick?"

Julia had already taken her seat and had pulled out a book, put on her reading glasses and started reading while Isabelle was getting ready. She peered at Isabelle over the top of her book. "Tonight—and tomorrow—Patrick is my responsibility. Now, go home," Julia sternly barked before pulling her book up again and continuing to read.

Before she left, Isabelle took a breath, crossed the room and planted a small kiss on the top of Patrick's head before whispering, "I miss you."

After Isabelle left, and it was just Julia in the room with Patrick, she took off her glasses and placed her book on his bedside. It felt like it was her child that was laying on that bed. She cared about Patrick more than he would ever know.

Her heart felt heavy as she clutched his hand. "Rest up my boy, I'll be here until you wake." A tear rolled down her cheek which she quickly made sure to wipe away.

"I hope you're a fan of Stephan Fry, because I'll be reading his book to you for the next two days."

She smiled, picked up her glasses and book and began reading aloud.

Chapter 37

ISABELLE

Today was it. They were going to wake Patrick.

Isabelle was starting to feel more like herself again after spending the night with Freya. They talked over a bottle of wine all night, cried, laughed—and cried some more. She'd missed Freya's say-it-how-you-see-it attitude, sure, but she missed her friend more than anything.

At that moment, Freya was still asleep in Isabelle's bed while she was up and making breakfast. Isabelle stood with a coffee in hand in her kitchen, lost in thought.

Before she knew it, Freya stumbled into the kitchen wearing a giant, baggy T-shirt.

"Hold on," Isabelle mumbled sleepily, the connections whirring in her head. "I recognise that T-shirt... That's Albie's!"

Freya groaned. "Please—no shouting. It's too early."

Isabelle couldn't help but laugh and handed Freya her coffee. "So, I wonder how you got hold of that then?" Isabelle sniggered.

"Hey, don't judge me," Freya sighed. "I guess, over the years, he's worn me down. We've been dating for a while now." She looked deep into her coffee as red crept up her neck.

"Obviously."

Freya's head shot up as Isabelle laughed into her coffee.

Isabelle waved a hand in the air. "I've known you guys for ages now—I've been waiting for you to tell me about him from pretty much the day I met you."

Freya's face flamed. "Oh, shut up!"

They both laughed and spoke more about Albie and how Freya was *obviously* madly in love with him, even though she didn't show it around other people.

Freya looked at her phone and remembered what day it was. "So, Patrick wakes up today, right?" she asked hesitantly.

Isabelle didn't say anything but nodded.

"Right," Freya said with a nod. "Let's make you look drop-dead gorgeous, then, so he has a vision to wake up to, yeah?" Freya stood and held out her hand.

A million thoughts had flowed through Isabelle's head about today, yet none of them had involved how she looked. Still, Freya's positivity couldn't be ignored and Isabelle agreed with a small smile.

"Right," Freya said. "Let's sort out that smell first. "

Isabelle took a long hot shower and tried her best to clear her mind. She didn't want Patrick to worry about her when he saw her.

When she got out of the shower, Freya was sitting on her bed with Isabelle's hairdryer, curler and a collection of sprays next to her. "Right, time to sort that mop out," she said while pointing at Isabelle's head.

They both started to laugh, and Isabelle simply told her, "Good luck," before sitting with her back to Freya.

After drying her hair, Freya curled it and asked, "So, what are you going to wear today?" But Isabelle barely heard her. She was lost inside her mind, images of Patrick's unmoving fragile body in the hospital bed. "I was thinking of one of your cute sundresses as it's such a gorgeous day outside."

Isabelle nodded noncommittally.

"Hey, you… none of this moping today, okay? Today is a happy day! You're gonna see him awake and he's going to be fine! And, let's be honest, with you looking this good, he's gonna be crawling back to you in no time!" Freya said very matter-of-factly.

Isabelle shook her head. Freya was right. This was a good day! She *would* finally get to see him. She turned and looked at Freya, hope surging within her.

Freya smiled, "There you are."

After finishing her hair, Freya started to rifle through Isabelle's wardrobe and threw dress after dress onto the bed until Isabelle stopped her.

"That one." Isabelle pointed at a blue sundress covered in white flowers.

Freya nodded with a grin, grabbing the dress. "Any reason?" she asked curiously, examining the dress.

"It's one of his favourites," Isabelle replied, as quiet as a mouse.

"Perfect!" Freya sang and held the dress up to a still-towel-wrapped Isabelle. "You can wear this and some sandals. Once you've put it on, let me know and I'll do your make-up."

Less than an hour later, Isabelle felt ready to see Patrick again.

"Okay, babes," Freya said, walking up to Isabelle. "I'd best be off. I've got to head to work now. Good luck—I hope everything goes alright! Message me as soon as you know how he is." Freya kissed Isabelle once on her cheek and hugged her hard.

With her gone, Isabelle was left to sit and wait for the phone call. She didn't know what to do with herself. After forty-five minutes of waiting and a couple of coffees later, her phone suddenly rang.

It was Julia and Isabelle answered with shaky fingers.

"Hello, Isabelle? Patrick is awake and talking…"

Isabelle started to cry from the sheer relief those words brought her.

"Is he okay?" she managed to choke out.

Julia's delivery was blunt, "Patrick suffered some nerve damage. We don't know the extent of the damage yet but there's a chance he may never walk again."

The room turned black. All air was sucked from Isabelle's vicinity. She couldn't breathe—just stood in a void, hearing nothing, seeing nothing.

"Isabelle? *Isabelle*? Can you hear me?" Julia's voice sounded worried, and Isabelle realised she hadn't answered.

Still, she let a few moments of complete silence pass.

"Isabelle," Julia was hesitant, and Isabelle's eyes flared with resolve. "I've spoken to Patrick..."

"What did he say? Is he okay?" She immediately demanded, her tone panicked as she started to collect her things, ready to leave. She continued without waiting for a response, "Tell him I'm on my way. I'll be there—"

Julia interrupted her before she could finish and, after they'd said their goodbyes, Isabelle slid to the ground and cried.

Chapter 38

PATRICK

Patrick… Patrick… can you hear us?

There was a bright light flashing across his eyes.

"Mrs, can you please say something reassuring?"

"It's about time you woke up," a voice said, gently. Patrick recognised that voice. "You've been late for work for weeks now," the woman laughed.

Patrick's vision was slowly becoming less blurry.

Is that Julia?

He turned his head to see his boss sitting in a chair next to him with a big smile on her face, holding his hand. He blinked.

Looking around more, he realised that he didn't recognise where he was; everything looked strange to him but, after a moment, he realised that he was in a hospital room.

"Hi there, Patrick, I'm your doctor. Call me Jan."

Patrick looked to the opposite side of Julia and saw an older woman with a short grey bob and glasses staring at him with a big smile on her face.

"W—water." He managed. His mouth and throat were dry.

"I've got it right here for you." Jan stood, warmth radiating from her, and held a small plastic cup with a straw. He drained the cup.

"So, Patrick, I have a couple of questions to ask you. Do you think you can answer them for me?"

Patrick nodded.

"So where are you right now?" she asked.

"I'm in the hospital." It was a lot harder to respond than Patrick had realised. He hinted at the water cup, and Jan poured more for him.

"Good. now, question two: do you remember why you're here?" Patrick paused momentarily until he looked towards Julia, his panic evident.

"Isabelle!"

Julia squeezed his hand. "She's fine, Patrick, now answer the doctor."

Patrick looked towards the ceiling, and light flashed before his eyes. "Isabelle broke up with me…" he heard himself say, "then I stepped into the road to go get her. A car hit me… that's all I can remember." He took a moment.

"Thank you, Patrick. I'll leave the questions at that today."

Patrick was glad it was over, taking a deep breath as he looked over to Julia. Why was she here with him?

"I just need to check one more thing and then I will leave you to rest, yeah?" Jan asked politely, always with a smile on her face. "Right, there we go. We thought as much."

Patrick was confused. "What do you mean?" He turned to Julia.

"I'm so sorry, Patrick." A tear rolled down Julia's cheek. Patrick had never seen her like this before—she had always been so stoic.

Panic twisted his gut as he turned back to the doctor. "What's going on?" Patrick asked, almost shouting the words as he struggled to get them out.

"Now, now, Patrick," Julia said, her voice back to its typical, stern tone. "Lower your voice. You're in a hospital."

The doctor took over, "When you were hit by the car, you suffered some major head injuries, and we had to operate. We suspected you may have suffered some nerve damage in your left leg and, now you're awake, I ran a piece of metal down your left foot as we talked. You had no reaction to this at all."

Patrick sank into the bed, his heart palpitating so much that the machine he was hooked up to began to beep at an alarming rate.

"I'm afraid until we know the extent of the damage, we will not be able to operate again or try and fix the issue. It's going to take some time. So, unfortunately, until then, you will have trouble walking."

No one said a word for almost five minutes after that and Patrick tried to digest all the information. Eventually, Jan told Julia, "I'll give you some time, please come and get me if you need anything."

Julia nodded in her direction, and the doctor left.

Patrick had not moved, spoken or even made noise. In his mind, he was alone. There was no one in the world but him and it seemed the world was empty. *He* was empty.

The silence was broken by Julia, "I'm just gonna call Isabelle to let her know you're awake and that she should come down to—"

"*No*!" Patrick snapped at Julia and even the loud beeps of the machine couldn't distract Julia from the fear in his eyes.

He could tell she was shocked. She had never heard Patrick raise his voice like this before. "Patrick, don't you dare raise your voice at me again! Under any circumstances!" Without even raising her voice, she'd swiftly shot Patrick down and made him feel infant. "Now… wanna try that again?" she asked calmly.

"I just… I *can't* see her." Patrick turned his head away before continuing quietly. "I don't want to see her."

Julia said nothing for a few seconds, just took a breath. "Okay," she said finally. "I'll let her know you don't want her to come. I won't say any more than that."

With that, she left the room.

Patrick was alone, staring at the ceiling. Was this karma? Should he have just stayed in his lane? Did this happen because he opened himself up to the world?

Patrick was consumed in thought. No outside stimulant fazed him. Julia came back in for a while but left him due to the time. Nothing. He felt nothing. All he did was stare at the ceiling.

The minutes turned to hours and before Patrick even realised it, it was dark outside. Nurses had been in throughout the day checking on him but Patrick hadn't even registered that they were there; he was a man who was broken to the core, his life changed forever and all he could wonder was why had he let the world in?

If he'd stayed in his comfort zone and kept away from people, he would have been safe. Just him and Doc in his flat enjoying each other's company. It wasn't an exciting life, but it was enough; it kept him going.

"Why did she have to come into my life…" he muttered before falling asleep.

***

Patrick was in the hospital for a month. In that time, they got him used to using a wheelchair and helped teach him how to live his life. He would have to use the chair day-to-day until they could operate again, however far in the future that may be.

The hospital offered him all kinds of counselling and therapy to help him work through everything that happened and the changes to his life he faced but Patrick shunned every suggestion of help. He didn't care about what they had to say. It was like what happened to his parents all over again—doctors trying to make him talk about how he felt. He couldn't understand why he would want that. It wouldn't bring his parents back—now it wouldn't bring his ability to walk back.

He just wanted to go home to Doc and hide away from the world.

Doc was being looked after by Julia and her wife while he was in the hospital and, for some reason, it was winding Patrick up. He knew they were just helping, but it was *his* cat, not theirs.

Every time Julia showed him a picture, he would grow visibly mad. He was the one who should be feeding him, talking to him and getting hugs—not Julia and her wife.

Jealousy once again crept into Patrick's heart. *Why do people take away everything I love?*

It was his last day in hospital and Julia was picking Patrick up to take him home. The hospital had supplied him with a wheelchair to use and it was cheap and uncomfortable, but it did the job.

Julia had bought him a speciality cushion to make him more comfortable and Patrick couldn't believe his luck when she had.

His clothes and belongings were packed into a duffle bag by the doctor. She didn't have to do this, but they'd become close while he was in the hospital. Since he woke, she'd taken to spending her breaks with him and would bring him coffee as they chatted. Patrick liked Jan but kept her at arm's length; he didn't want to let anyone else in.

Jan finished packing Patrick's belongings and sat in the chair beside his wheelchair. "Patrick, I wanted to chat with you before you go," she said, very matter-of-fact.

Patrick nodded his head and waited for her to speak. "I've spent some time around you the last couple of weeks and I've enjoyed talking to you, even though you haven't said much. I want you to listen very carefully to what I'm about to tell you."

Patrick nodded his head again, but this wasn't enough for Jan who cupped her hand to her ear, indicating she wanted an audible answer.

"I'm listening,", Patrick muttered, resenting the prompt.

"Good." Jan lowered her hand and looked straight into Patrick's eyes. "I don't want you to give up..." she paused and looked into his eyes for a few seconds. “I think I’ve picked up an understanding of what you're like and, after speaking to Isabelle—” Patrick looked away as soon as Jan said her name, but she but didn’t stop “—while you were in your coma, it sounds like you’re likely to shut yourself away from the world again now. She told me about how much more outgoing you’d started to become… relative to your starting point, of course.”

Tears were starting to well in Patrick’s eyes, but he didn’t want to release them.

“So,” Jan continued, “you need to try and scrape that back. Don’t let all this progress go to waste; you will only let yourself down if you don’t at least try.”

At this, he couldn’t prevent his tears, and a single drop rolled down his face as he started to think about his time with Isabelle and getting closer to his workmates like Freya and Albie. He didn’t want to think of them right now, but their faces were all he could see.

“There’s a lot of people that care about you. I know this because I was here when they came to see you. Please don’t throw all of that away.”

Jan’s words hit Patrick like a truck but, still, he said nothing—made no noise as his eyes streamed.

“I’m sorry if I said too much or overstepped my mark. I just want the best for you and, right now, you need to lean on the people you have around you.”

Jan sighed and jumped to her feet “Right, I'm going to stop lecturing you now.” Her whole persona had changed, and she was once again her bubbly self—like every other time Patrick had seen her. She pulled a card from her white coat and popped it onto Patrick’s lap.

“Look, if you need anything or things start to get too much for you, feel free to call me.” She shot him a wide grin and started to leave the room. “It was a pleasure meeting you, Patrick. You look after yourself and, please, have a think about what I just said.”

As she opened the door, Patrick finally spoke, his words soft. “Thank you, Jan.”

She paused for a moment, smiled, and kept walking.

Chapter 39

PATRICK

Julia was the one to help Patrick into his flat. Luckily, he lived on the ground floor, so it wasn't too much of an issue. Plus, she'd already made sure he had everything he needed, had done a food shop for anything he'd need and moved his furniture around, so it was easier for him to move around in his chair.

Twenty minutes later, Julia's wife arrived with Doc in tow—safely away in his carry case. Patrick couldn't help but erupt in tears as Doc got out of the case, ran and jumped onto his lap; he couldn't control it anymore. It was like the last stick out of a beaver dam before the water came gushing through.

Julia and her wife decided to leave them be and left a note on his fridge with both of their numbers before silently letting themselves out.

On the way to the car, Julia started to get emotional. She hesitated to leave him alone, worrying whether it might be the last time she sees him. Her wife gently consoled her offering reassurance before taking her to the car and driving away.

Patrick sat, still in his chair, and sobbed with Doc on his chest, nestling into him. They hadn't been together for so long that the reunion was emotional for them both. After a while, Doc jumped down and started sniffing around the wheelchair.

"Yeah, it's strange, right buddy?" Patrick sniffled.

Doc meowed, which caused Patrick to break down in tears again. "I'm sorry, it's been so long since I've seen you, Doc. Talking to you again feels like I can finally breathe."

Doc jumped back on Patrick's lap, laid down, and licked at his paws. After some time, Patrick fell asleep; it was the best sleep he'd had since waking from his coma, even though he was in an uncomfortable wheelchair. Doc calmed his mind.

A few hours later, he woke up with Doc still asleep on his lap and, as he looked around his flat, he truly noticed the efforts Julia had gone to in moving the furniture around. She also must have come in and cleaned before he arrived because everything was spotless. She'd done way more than she needed to, but he was thankful—he wasn't sure what he'd have done if she hadn't.

"I guess this is my life now." Patrick rolled around his flat and looked around. Everything was as he remembered but somehow more depressing, and he sighed.

He'd had enough for the day. He put a mound of biscuits into a bowl for Doc and rolled his chair to his bed. It wasn't easy, someone had always helped him to move from his wheelchair to his bed when he was in hospital, and it was much more challenging than he'd imagined. Rolling on the carpet, was challenging enough and it took almost all his strength to just get himself into his room.

He grabbed the mattress and started to pull himself onto it, just about managing to pull himself onto the bed face first. Utterly spent, he laid there, face stuffed against the mattress and screamed. Every emotion was expelled from his body, and he knew, if Julia could hear him, he would break her heart.

He remained there for a while before shifting himself to lay on the bed. Shortly after, Doc jumped up and joined him. He was home and, with that, Patrick fell asleep—exhausted from both his emotional outburst and the realisation that this was truly his new world.

Over the next few days, Patrick spent most of his time in bed, his time there only broken up by Doc's meows as he asked for food. These where the only times Patrick would get into his wheelchair, pour another heap of biscuits into Doc's bowl—so much so it overfilled—and some water into his bowl. He'd found it was easier for him to use bottled water, as he couldn't reach the tap. A whole week of this passed.

Patrick resorted to buying an automated feeding bowl on his phone and a much larger water bowl to avoid getting out of bed as much. He had given up.

He was numb, his mind was no longer racing—just numb and empty. No worrying, no hoping… nothing. It was like his life was already over and the only thing that gave him a passing dose of happiness was Doc, but even that faded.

Eventually, he even stopped talking to Doc—something he never thought would happen. From Patrick's perspective, he was in complete darkness. Still, once or twice a day, a blink of light flickered through the room before fading away as swiftly as it had come, and he was back to slowly drowning in the dark abyss.

A fortnight after Patrick was released from the hospital, he'd had so many people knock on his door that he'd taken to ignoring them and pretending he couldn't hear the people calling his name.

He'd barely eaten, and his stomach was starting to hurt. He knew he'd have to get up and eat something at some point, but he waited another few hours until his stomach hurt again.

He dragged himself out of bed, to his chair and slowly rolled himself to the kitchen. Today was one of the more difficult days.

He opened the fridge under the counter to grab something to eat, but it was empty, so he slammed the door shut and cursed the air, only looking down when he noticed Doc staring at him.

"Go away, I don't want to look at you right now," he yelled and Doc, startled, ran from the room.

I hate myself.

The thought came so quickly but rang so true in his mind that Patrick burst into tears and started to punch his numb leg, softly at first, then harder and harder. He felt nothing.

The tears turned to wails as he punched harder and harder, only broken by a knock at the door.

Patrick didn't want to see anyone, so he ignored it and slowly rolled back to his bed. When he was in the hallway, however, he heard the lock click and watched in mute horror as it started to open. Patrick froze.

Julia entered his flat, pushing a shopping trolly loaded with a big cardboard box and shopping bags. As soon as Patrick saw who it was, he continued to his bedroom and pulled himself onto his bed.

"Well," Julia sarcastically called. "Hello to you, too."

He heard the door shut behind her and, a moment later, she walked into Patrick's room. It was dark, light barely creeping through the side of the curtains, but it was still enough for Julia to see what a sorry state Patrick was in.

He knew his hair hadn't been washed in a while and was sure it looked unkempt and overgrown—the smell emanating from the room embarrassed him, his facial hair was messy, and he knew he had lost weight.

Julia was angry, he could see it on her face. She charged in and threw the curtains open, letting all the light in. Patrick hid his eyes with a groan.

"What the hell is this?" she yelled but he didn't respond. "I thought if I left you to adjust before I came to see you, we could have talked and see what I could do to help you." She seemed concerned but her tone was harsh. "But no, this is what I come back to—a withered, pathetic-looking man who has given no thought to anyone but himself. I've been worried about you all week, but I presumed you would call me if you needed to. I waited and waited, but nothing—and now I know why."

She looked at him with disgust, yet she seemed so sad at the same time. She stormed out of the bedroom a second later and Patrick was stunned. No one had ever been so brutally honest with him but, after thinking about it, it made sense that Julia would.

He knew he had messed up. He had to talk to her.

Mustering all his energy, Patrick pulled himself into the chair and started to roll himself to the kitchen where Julia was banging around. When he got there, he could see her putting things in the lower cupboards as she slammed the doors and drawers shut.

"Wait for me in the living room," was all she said without sparing him a glance.

He dutifully rolled into the living room, and it stank. He hadn't been there since the first day he was released from the hospital.

"What is that smell?" he said, instantly covering his mouth and nose.

Julia suddenly appeared behind him. "*That* is the smell of a bad pet owner who is too self-obsessed to look after their own cat."

Julia pushed him further inside, walked over to the windows, and opened as many as she could.

Patrick felt like scum.

He looked around for Doc and called for him, but he didn't come.

"He's in the kitchen eating some tuna I got for him."

Patrick looked up and found Julia wearing rubber gloves and carrying a bin bag. She started to empty the overflowing litter tray, scowling at the smell coming from it, before taking the bag outside. She re-entered and slammed the door shut behind her.

"That's disgusting, Patrick. Let me never see or smell that again, you got me? You are responsible for Doc and you're lucky I don't take him off you. I would have never imagined you would be so selfish to treat him so poorly."

He was hollow inside. How could he have not realised his self-hatred was bleeding onto Doc this whole time? She was right. He didn't realise how bad things had gotten.

Patrick watched as Julia sprayed an air freshener and lit candles in the living room to help remove the horrid stench.

"Julia," he said, "I'm sorry, I should—"

"I don't want to hear any forced apologies, Patrick. You can show me you're sorry by your actions, not your words."

She headed to the bedroom to do the same; the musky smell in there was overpowering.

Patrick started to wallow in his own self-pity again. The weight of his own actions was crushing him.

Julia came back into the living room and sighed. "Look at you, have you even washed *once*? Cleaned your teeth?"

Patrick looked at the ground and shook his head. Before he knew it, Julia was pushing him towards the bathroom. "Wait, wait—" he was slightly panicked.

"Oh, shut up, Patrick, you've got nothing I want to see—you're getting in the shower." She pulled him up to the bathroom and told him to strip his clothes then disappeared for a moment with one of the boxes from the trolly in hand. It was a shower seat.

She put the toilet lid down and started assembling it, which took all of thirty seconds to complete. She then got up and put it under the shower.

"Right, come on—you're getting in." She pulled one of Patrick's arms over her shoulder. "Well, come on then, only one of your legs is numb, right? Stand up, I've got you."

Patrick pushed down with his right leg and, shakingly, started to rise with Julia's help. He was standing for the first time since the accident...

He was standing.

Patrick started to smile, and the anger started to dissipate from Julia's eyes.

"Christ, come on, get in the shower. You stink."

With Julia's help, Patrick laughed, got into the shower and sat on the shower seat.

"Right, now I'm going to make you some food. You have 15 minutes to make yourself more respectable." She handed him his electric razor and a hand mirror. "Have a shave while you're at it; you're no Vagrant."

Patrick laughed again and suddenly winced. Julia had turned on the shower.

"Cold, cold, cold!" he squealed.

Julia finally laughed. "That, my dear Patrick, is karma." Then, she turned and headed to the kitchen.

As the water slowly warmed, Patrick allowed it to wash over him. The heat felt good. He looked up towards the showerhead with his eyes shut so the water enveloped him, coating his face.

He took his time washing his hair and used the scrub Julia had left him, starting to feel clean for the first time in a while. He picked up the electric shaver and the hand mirror but paused for a moment, looking at his reflection.

It was, he realised with startling clarity, the first time he had looked into a mirror since the accident. As he stared intently at the man looking back through the glass, no recognition sparked. His hair had grown so long—his facial hair out of control—and his eyes had sunken in his face.

A tear rolled down his cheek.

"Is this me?" he asked. Whimpering into the mirror

Julia burst into the bathroom. "Patrick, what's wrong?"

She grabbed a towel, turned off the shower and wrapped it tightly around him—hugging him as she did so.

"It's okay, Patrick," she soothed. "Let it out."

Patrick embraced Julia, accepting her comfort, and cried into her shoulder. After a few minutes, Julia pulled away. "Do you feel better? What brought this on?"

Patrick didn't say anything, Julia took offence to this. "Hey," she pressed. "I asked you a question, Patrick."

That jolted him enough that he snapped back into the room. "Sorry… I just looked in that." He pointed towards the mirror that he'd dropped to the ground.

"Oh," Julia paused. "I see. Well, do you want to do something about it?"

Patrick nodded.

"Right. Well, you can shave that horrible facial hair off and I'll get some scissors to cut this mane back. Deal?"

She picked the mirror up off the floor and held it out for Patrick to take.

For the first time that day, Patrick looked into Julia's eyes, showing her the pain and despair that lurked. He could see the care in hers, in turn.

He nodded, took the mirror from her, and picked up the razor. Then, Julia came behind him with a pair of old scissors and started to cut his hair. Soon, Patrick was back to being clean, as he preferred.

"There we go, there's the Patrick I remember," Julia laughed, and Patrick couldn't help joining in. Ten minutes later, Julia had finished cutting his hair. "Look, I'm no hairdresser, but this is the best I can manage."

When Patrick looked around the shower floor, it was covered in hair. "Aren't you gonna take a look?"

He lifted the mirror and looked at himself. His reflection was a little like he remembered but he still couldn't recognise himself in the exposed expanse of skin now visible on his jaw. "It looks great. Thanks, Julia."

Julia smiled, got him back into the wheelchair, and helped him get dressed before wheeling him into the living room, which now smelled much better. She helped him onto the sofa—the first time he'd sat there since returning from the hospital—then went to get the food she'd made for him from the kitchen. She sat with him while they both ate, and they sat and watched a trashy mid-week afternoon show.

After finishing their meal, Patrick started to thank Julia but, before he could, she took the plate from him and said, "I think you two need to make up." She nodded her head towards the living room door where Doc was sitting, then got up with a groan and headed to the kitchen. As she left, she said, "Take your time, I'm gonna change your bedding."

She shut the door behind her, and Doc and Patrick were alone. Doc looked at Patrick and decided to climb to the highest point of his cat tower. It was the equivalent of a slap in the face for Patrick, but he knew he deserved it.

"Hey buddy…" he whispered. "I'm sorry."

Looking down at Patrick, Doc laid on the highest perch of his cat tower and blinked.

"I can't believe I treated you that badly," Patrick continued. "I never thought I would leave you in such a state." Patrick stopped looking at Doc and turned to the ground. "No matter what—since I've had you in my life—you've been my one constant. You're not just my cat; you are one of my closest friends. I'm not sure if you'll ever understand how sorry I am."

Patrick started to get emotional and felt such shame and disgust for himself that he began to sob, sputtering, "I'm sorry," every now and then as he stared into his lap. After a while, he lifted his head and opened his eyes to find Doc sitting at the base of his feet, looking up at him.

He wiped his eyes with his arm before reaching his hand down for Doc to smell; he was hesitant at first and sniffed at Patrick's hand before rubbing his face against the back of it. Patrick smiled, happier than he had been since he had woken up from his coma. He lifted his hand to wipe his face once more and, as soon as he raised his hand, Doc jumped onto his lap and sat down.

Patrick softly stroked Doc's fur and, as Doc purred in appreciation, Patrick felt at ease. Nothing calmed Patrick as much as stroking Doc. Well, nothing except…

Before he could finish his thought, Julia opened the door startling both Doc and Patrick.

"Right," she said. "I need to pop out and grab some things; where is your bank card?"

Patrick was confused and pointed over to his wallet, which was on the TV cabinet.

Julia grabbed it and gave Patrick a searching look. "Well, tell me your pin, then."

Patrick told her the pin and attempted to ask her a question before Julia continued, "Right, I'll be gone for about an hour. You gonna be okay watching TV with Doc until I'm back?"

Patrick nodded and, in a flash, Julia had left the flat and was on her way, Patrick's questions still on the tip of his tongue. He knew in his heart that Julia wouldn't take his bank card for no reason, though, and so continued to stroke Doc while he waited.

He was exhausted and yawned, looking at the time on the TV. "She said she would be back in an hour… what do you say, Doc, an afternoon nap like old times?" He looked down at Doc, who was already asleep, and Patrick laughed before following suit.

Chapter 40

PATRICK

Patrick and Doc jolted awake as the door swung open with a thud. "Oops—sorry, Patrick! Don't mind me, back in a second." Julia was back a few seconds later, shutting the door behind her.

She walked into the living room and saw Doc on Patrick's lap and smiled. "Ah, looks like you two are friends again," she laughed before walking over to Patrick, lifting his arm and putting it around her shoulders. "Right, you; back in the chair. I want to show you something."

She helped Patrick into the chair and wheeled him to the hallway, where a big, long box and a smaller, more rectangular package with a laptop in front waited.

Patrick was confused. "A laptop?" he questioned Julia.

"Yeah, that's right. Did you think I would let you off work forever?" she laughed as she walked over to the boxes.

Patrick didn't say anything and just watched her in mute confusion. She slapped the long box. "This—this is a desk we can put over your bed that you can push and pull towards you.

Patrick was amazed yet equally confounded. "Is this why you took my card?" This must have cost a small fortune.

"Oh, yeah, don't worry, you had the money for it. You've been on sick pay since the accident." Julia laughed, picked up the laptop and handed it to Patrick. "Right, the last thing I'll be doing today is building this for you. You're gonna set up the laptop. From Monday, your contract will be part-time; all you have to do is sign the papers in my bag."

Patrick looked like he had just been shocked by a cattle prod. "Did you *really* think I was going to let you get away with not working?" she repeated, laughing her way over to push him into the bedroom.

She helped him onto his bed and put the laptop box beside him. "Right, get to it."

With that, Julia left and started to build the desk in the hallway. Patrick still hadn't fully processed what she'd said but had begun setting up the laptop anyway—which was excellent. Patrick could tell Julia had bought the most expensive one she could find, but he didn't mind. After about an hour and a lot of swearing from the hallway, Julia had finished building the desk and Patrick had set up his laptop. His desk was on wheels and Julia wheeled it into the bedroom, lined it to the bed and slid it underneath. It was a perfect fit.

Proud of what she had accomplished, she quickly left, only to return with a bundle of papers and a pen which she slapped down onto the desk.

"Right now, sign here."

Patrick looked at the paperwork and, reading through it, thought it all seemed up to snuff. He was about to put pen to paper when he paused and looked at Julia. "I'll sign this if you answer one question for me."

Julia crossed her arms. "Go ahead," she huffed.

Patrick paused before asking, "Why are you doing this? Why are you helping me so much?"

Julia was visibly taken aback. "So, I answer this and then you come back?"

Patrick nodded and started to pet Doc's head, who had joined him on the bed.

Julia took a moment. "Why do I do this?" she repeated with a shake of her head. "Simple. I want to and, if I want to do something, nothing will stop me."

Patrick frowned, waiting for the answer to the second part of his question.

Julia sighed. "Look, Patrick. I don't know how much you know about me, but my wife and I tried to have children a long time ago. It never worked out for us. For some reason, the first day I interviewed you, I was hit with this maternal instinct I didn't realise I even had. You were so innocent—sheepish and obviously in pain. I just wanted to protect you from the world and give you a safe space to work and feel better. When I heard about the accident, I forgot to think of you as an employee; I only thought of you as… my surrogate son, I suppose." She turned away from him, seemingly anxious about his response. "As to why I am helping you so much… who wouldn't help their son in their time of need?"

Moments later, Patrick signed the documents and Julia watched until he finished, picked up the contract and glanced over it. She nodded once and looked over to him. "Perfect," praised. "Are you happy with this?"

Patrick nodded and Julia seemed a little awkward that he hadn't said anything in response. "Right, well—I best get this mess cleaned up."

After she'd cleared everything, she returned to Patrick's room with her handbag hooked over her elbow.

"So, I'll be giving you a call next Monday to let you into the system; make sure you are all set up by then. Also, this desk isn't an excuse to stay in bed all the time, I don't ever want to come back to what I did today; you hear me?"

Patrick nodded again and finally asked, "Can you come here for a moment?" He pushed the desk away and turned himself around, so his legs were hanging off the bed.

As Julia approached him, he pulled her towards him, wrapped his arms around her and gently rested his head on her shoulder. "Thank you so much, Julia." His voice was scratchy and soft. "No one has looked after me like this since my mum. I know she would like you."

Julia's face broke and she hugged him back and squeezed him tight, his words affecting her so clearly that he was glad to have said them. After, Julia stood straight and brushed herself down.

"You'll be having someone come and see you next Wednesday, so make sure you answer the door." She was back to being all business but looked emotional at the same time.

Patrick wiped his face and nodded. "Okay, I'll make sure I let them in."

Julia bobbed her head in acknowledgement and turned to leave. "I'll be back this time every Saturday from now on. I'll see you next week."

And, like a passing tornado, Julia left silence in her wake.

Chapter 41

PATRICK

Patrick had just the weekend to rest and prepare for the coming Monday. He wasn't sure if he was ready to go back to work. Had he jumped the gun too early because Julia wanted it? Did *he* want it? He wasn't even sure anymore. He knew he didn't want to let Julia down—especially after all she had done for him—but was he just confusing this feeling with a desire for his old life?

Patrick also wasn't sure how he felt about interacting with the people from the office; it had been so long since he had and he'd never been good at keeping in touch with people, especially if he hadn't talked with them for a long time; he knew it wasn't the smartest way to deal with things.

"Well, Doc, we have a weekend to relax and spend some quality time together."

Doc meowed, jumped off the bed and headed to the kitchen. He was obviously hungry, but it meant something else entirely to Patrick.

"Okay, Doc, okay. I'll get up and wash, then feed you." He pulled himself into his wheelchair and headed to the bathroom; he felt weak and tired. How was he so tired when he'd only just gotten up?

He stripped off and started to wash himself with the supplies Julia had brought him. And, as he washed his body, the full extent of his not eating became clear. "No wonder Julia was so worried," he muttered to himself.

He finished washing and put on some clean, comfortable clothes. He rolled into the kitchen where Doc was waiting on the kitchen side for him and, as soon as he rolled into the kitchen, Doc jumped onto his lap and nuzzled his way into Patrick's chest, almost like he was acknowledging him.

Patrick fed Doc and even made himself breakfast for the first time since he'd gotten back. He sat in his chair and he and Doc ate breakfast together. Patrick was happy, despite everything. And even though he still disliked himself and hated his situation, he found an ounce of normality. They spent the rest of the day cuddling together on the sofa and relaxing in comfort.

On Sunday, Patrick woke and thought, *another day like yesterday would do the treat before Monday* and laid in bed until 11 am. Then, someone knocked on his door.

At first, he panicked and wondered who it could be, but eventually calmed. It wasn't Julia, he pacified himself, as she would have let herself in. He decided to ignore it. The knocking stopped as swiftly as it began, and Patrick slowly sank back into his bed.

Was it *her*? Patrick's heart sank; he hadn't thought about Isabelle for a while. No, he'd pushed her into a box that he kept tightly shut into the dark void of his mind. He liked to visualise that the only bit of light pinging around in his mind was Doc bouncing off all the walls and zipping through, stopping the void from getting enveloped by the darkness. In the centre was a group of boxes locked away, dust-covered and old, unopened for a long time.

Before he had the chance to let his mental gymnastics begin, they knocked again and, this time, he could hear a familiar, booming voice from the other side of the door. "'Ello mate. Let me in, would ya? People are giving me funny looks."

What was Albie doing here? Patrick wasn't sure if he wanted to let him in but, at the same time, he didn't want his neighbours calling the police due to a large, loud and strange man banging on a door. So, he got into his wheelchair and rolled up to the door.

"Stop shouting and give me a second," Patrick snapped and momentarily took a deep breath. He wasn't sure if he was ready for this, but it seemed he had no choice.

As soon as he unlocked the door, Albie barged in. "Bloody hell mate, you took your time…" Albie paused as he took in Patrick's wheelchair.

He wore shorts and a gym vest, as though he's come straight to Patrick's from his morning workout.

"How you doing, big man? Come on, don't stay in the hallway. Let's head inside."

Patrick turned and started to roll into the living room. *What's this all about? I don't want him here.*

He felt cold towards Albie, even though he hadn't done anything. The feelings were sudden and confusing, and he really wanted to be alone to process them.

Patrick parked his chair opposite the couch and Albie perched himself down, dropping his duffle bag onto the floor with a loud thud which startled Doc. The air was awkward. No one said a thing for a while before Albie slapped his knees, got up, entered the kitchen and started clanging around. A minute later, he returned to the living room with two mugs.

"'Ere you go, bud—have a cuppa!"

Patrick took the mug and quietly thanked him.

"Haven't seen you for a hot min', 'eh, big man. You been globetrotting, have you?" Albie laughed but it was awkward and forced—not his usual loud, boisterous laugh.

Patrick's words were clipped as he asked, "So, why are you here?" He took a sip of the tea but didn't look at Albie.

Albie didn't know how to answer that, and it was clear Patrick was annoyed by his presence. Albie took a deep breath. "Cor, someone woke up on the wrong side of the bed, huh?" his laugh was genuine this time. Patrick noticed the difference. "Well, I got a call from the boss lady, and she told me that she had a job for me—that it was something only I can do." He stood proud, bent down and pulled a weight tree with 3 pairs of weights on it.

"Well," he continued, "she told me that my buddy Patrick had little needle arms, and he needed beefing up if he was gonna be wheeling himself round." Patrick didn't have much of a reaction for Albie, but he ploughed on regardless. "So, it's my job to turn them arms into pistons so you can wheel yourself around like it's a walk in the park."

He didn't want to put the extra pressure on the walking stick just yet. Julia had told him how Patrick refused all the physiotherapy and occupational therapy the hospital offered to help him get used to his new body and use the walking stick to get around short distances. He needed to accept the fact he was disabled and that he could be Semi ambulatory if he got strong enough.

Patrick was stoic, what did Albie expect him to do—joyfully jump at the chance to lift weights with him? Did he not understand the situation?

"Plus," Albie continued, seeming not to notice the glower Patrick was shooting at the weights. "I hear you're joining work again soon and I'm sure you don't want to turn up on your first day seeing Isabelle—" Albie cut himself off when he saw the anger plastered over Patrick's face.

Patrick shot him an evil look. "Albie; *leave*."

Albie was stunned. "What do you—"

"*Leave*!" Patrick shouted and turned away in his chair.

Albie was starting to get annoyed now and angrily grabbed his duffle bag, put it on and approached Patrick. "Turns out," he began, voice like nails, "there's no helping an ignorant, selfish asshat who ruined the one good thing he had in his life—who pushed everyone else away because of his own mistakes. You're lucky Isabelle hasn't seen you like this; she would think you're a pathetic waste of space. You never deserved someone as good as her and you broke her; she's not the same as she was before and it's *your* fault. You're a jealous, self-intitled little man."

His sudden burst of vitriol shook Patrick to his core. He'd always known, on some level, that when someone like Albie got angry it would be terrifying—but he'd never thought *he* would be on the receiving end of it.

Albie started to leave but before he shut the door, he loudly said, "The world didn't stop turning just because you shut yourself off from it."

He slammed the door shut.

Chapter 42

PATRICK

Patrick withdrew within himself. He hated how he treated Albie. He hadn't meant to; he just reacted after hearing her name.

More than that, he loathed the way he had treated *her*. He couldn't bear the sound of her name or even think of her without a wave of remorse and self-hate washing over him. He slumped in his wheelchair. In that moment, his self-disgust reached new heights. Secretly, it was simultaneously the worst and greatest feeling he had felt in his life. It was all he had left. What else was there? He felt empty, alone and broken.

Doc rubbed against Patrick's legs. Usually, that would be enough to snap Patrick back into the room, but nothing. His hate consumed him. He knew, that if someone were to see him right then, all they would notice was someone deep in thought. On the inside, however, a riot swirled in Patrick's mind; his darkest thoughts had joined forces and were pushing him closer and closer to the cliff edge in his mind.

He didn't push the thoughts back. He followed them gladly to the edge of that abyss.

Should I even be here anymore? Patrick's thoughts turned even darker, his heart pounding in his chest. *What impact do I have on the world? Not a single person would miss me. They'd remember the arrogant hermit who treated them like shit; nothing else.* A tear rolled down his face.

If I wasn't here, it would make everyone's life easier. All the people I've relied on would suddenly have so much less to worry about.

Albie's words echoed in his mind, cutting deep. *A jealous, self-entitled little man.*

All Patrick could think about was how his life was basically over. It had been ever since the accident… ever since he lost Isabelle.

Albie would talk to Freya and Julia about how Patrick had acted for sure.

Then, Freya would speak to Isabelle—and she would hate him even more than she likely already did. No one would ever talk to him again. No one would ever give him a chance again. It was over; what little life he had and what few people he'd cared for were gone. He was alone.

Time stopped, then.

"Everything he said was right," Patrick muttered to himself. "All I think about is myself, how things affect *me* or how they could affect me."

That darkness was approached quicker and quicker.

Why was he like this? Couldn't he just be normal for once in his life? Why couldn't he treat those people the way they should be treated? Was he broken? Did he get so wrapped up in himself that they didn't matter anymore? And now, when he needed them more than anything, he acted like this… He wanted, wanted, wanted and, yet still pushed them away. He wasn't crying and he wasn't sad—he was emotionless. Somehow, he'd numbed his entire face.

"I'm never going to be anything more than I am now." Those few words were the first thing to break the silence that had taken over the flat.

He was exhausted from thinking, from feeling, from everything.

Patrick punched his leg with all the force he had. Everything he'd ever wanted had been taken away and he was the idiot who made sure it was. His heart raced in anger.

My parents would be disappointed in me.

He started to repeatedly punch his leg over and over, screaming in pain which didn't emanate from his leg. But when he thought of how his mum and dad would react to him attacking himself, it slowly made him stop. What would they think if they could see him do this to himself?

He slowly lowered his fist onto his now bruised leg and thought about the kind of people his parents had been. He knew they would love everyone from the office. He likely would have had to stop Albie from playfully flirting with his mum; she'd been beautiful. The image brought a smile to his face. He imagined bringing them into work with him, introducing them to everyone, knowing that they would have loved the people he surrounded himself with brought him to tears.

The hours slipped away as he sat in his chair, imagining scenarios with his parents and friends. Mostly, they made him happy, but he couldn't help sad.

He looked around for Doc; he wanted some comfort. Like he knew he needed him, Doc wandered into the room and made a beeline for Patrick's lap. Patrick wheeled them to his room and lay on his bed, his mind full of daydreams of his parents and how different things could have been. It was for them he knew he had to keep going.

***

After his setback with Albie, the next few months passed quickly for Patrick. He would wake and feed Doc in the mornings, then head back to bed and work for a while. Once he had finished work, he would get lost in his mind, day after day. Julia was the only change in this routine and every Saturday, without fail, she let herself in and made sure Patrick was looking after himself. Without asking, she would tidy the flat and fill his fridge, taking his card to the supermarket herself.

Conversation became rarer and rarer, and Julia worried she had put too much on Patrick with getting Albie to come around so soon. She wanted to talk to him, he could tell but never did.

This cycle lasted four months. Until one Saturday.

Patrick was expecting Julia any moment. She was late. That had happened a few times so, when his phone started to ring, he was unsurprised to find Julia's name and picked up.

"Good morning, Patrick. Sorry, but I'm not going to be able to come around until tomorrow; my car had to be taken in for some quick repairs and I won't be able to get to you. Will you be okay until tomorrow?"

Patrick's anxiety peaked; he was so used to her coming around on a Saturday that the change threw him through a loop. He didn't know what to do.

"Don't worry," she continued, sensing his hesitation. "I'll be there tomorrow bright and early; you should still have some food for you and Doc… Patrick?"

Patrick finally responded, "Thank you. I'll see you tomorrow."

Julia was glad to get a response. "Good, well, you have a nice day relaxing with Doc, and I'll see you tomorrow."

Patrick said goodbye, then fell back onto his bed.

After sleeping most of the day, Patrick woke up in the evening due to hunger. He pulled himself into his chair and went to the kitchen to get him and Doc some food. He put some food in Doc's bowl but, when he looked around, he was nowhere to be seen; this was a first. Patrick started to roll around the house and finally found him lying on the bathroom floor, his breathing heavy and slow. Beside him was a pile of vomit.

"Doc!" Patrick screamed and practically threw himself on the floor to get a closer look at him. He pet him, called his name and begged for him to move, but nothing. He grabbed his phone in a rush of panic.

"I'll call Julia—don't worry, Doc." But like a punch to the gut, Patrick remembered that Julia didn't have her car that day.

"No," he said, horror filling his gaze. "No, no, no, no—why today! I'm so sorry, Doc, I don't know who to call."

Patrick, panicked and filled with dread, scrolled through the contacts in his phone, his tears falling on the screen as he did. He paused on her name, then pressed dial.

Chapter 43

ISABELLE

7 MONTHS AGO

Isabelle was emotionless and stood stun-locked in the kitchen; she had hung up the phone from Julia without a word.

"Patrick doesn't want to see you." Julia's words played over and over in her head.

Too numb to process what she was doing, she put her phone on the kitchen side and quickly got out of her dress, threw it in the kitchen bin and got straight into her bed. She just wanted to sleep. When she woke up, all of this would have been a dream.

"This can't be real," she whispered.

She rolled on her side and forced herself to sleep and managed to for a few hours but woke up dazed. When her mind dinged with alertness, she jumped out of bed and ran to her phone—but there were no messages or missed calls from him, only a message from Freya asking how he was.

Isabelle placed her phone on the table and gently turned to pull a glass from the kitchen side but knocked it on the floor where it shattered. She stood, staring at the broken mug on the floor and tears began to fall, hitting the broken pieces. She fell to her knees and started to pick up the shards.

Her tears blurred her vision, but she didn't want to let the emotions overtake her and forced herself to clean each broken piece from the floor. Then, she sat at the table.

An email notification popped up on her phone, lighting up her screen and displaying the picture of her and Patrick that Freya had taken at the beach. She'd set it as her background. Her lip trembled and, in an instant, she picked up the phone and launched it to the other side of the room.

Finally, after fighting it for as long as she could, all her bottled emotions came spilling out. She was sobbing; it was like the world was reminding her that her heart was broken but she didn't want to notice it; there was nowhere she could hide from the fact that Patrick didn't want her.

"I told him to leave. I told him to leave me before he got hit—it's my fault." Her voice was muffled from behind her hands, covering her face.

The night of the accident played back in her mind—the argument, the anger then the utter shock and despair after she found Patrick lying on the road.

Patrick doesn't want to see you.

She thought of him lying on the hospital bed—going to see him every day, putting his needs over hers yet again. *Patrick doesn't want to see you.*

Her sadness shattered and twisted until anger sparked her heart.

"He doesn't want to see me? Doesn't he know all I've done for him—what he meant to me? He was the one who ruined everything. Not me!" She screamed the words into her hands as she shook but the anger was fleeting and quickly reverted to sorrow.

She tried to shower but only cried more. She wished she could go back—she'd take everything back, so she didn't have to lose anything. Getting out of the shower, she wrapped a towel around her waist and wiped the condensation from the bathroom mirror, finding her eyes puffy and red. She looked into her own eyes for a moment; her heart was shattered to pieces. All she wanted was to be by his side.

She could hear her phone ringing in the other room and ran but couldn't see where she had thrown it. She threw the pillows from her bed in her search but, eventually, it stopped ringing.

"Please, no," she begged, her search turning frantic. "Please call me back, Patrick!"

She slumped on her bed in her towel, still wet from the shower. The phone started to ring again and, this time, she jumped up and found it under her wardrobe.

Full of hope, she smiled but that smile faded quickly when she saw it was Freya, not Patrick calling. She was breathless, so took a second to compose herself. She wasn't sure if she was ready to talk to anyone yet. She sat back on her bed and finally answered.

"Hey babes, everything okay? I haven't heard from you."

It was the sound of her voice that did it. Isabelle burst into tears.

"I'm coming over," Freya said in an instant, no context needed. "I'm gonna stay on the phone and drive over now, okay?"

Isabelle mumbled a wet, "Okay," before laying back on her bed, listening as Freya got into her car, swore at some slow drivers and made her way to her flat.

Within minutes, she arrived. Though they had been on the phone the whole journey, Freya sometimes forgot that she was on a call with Isabelle and started calling Patrick all the names under the sun before she realised what she was doing and made herself stop. She blamed it on another driver who cut her up on the road. Then, Freya parked up, told Isabelle she would be there in a moment and hung up.

Isabelle opened the door before she could knock and stepped out to meet Freya. Isabelle looked tired; her eyes were puffy, her hair unkempt. Freya dropped her bag and wrapped her arms around her; Isabelle fell into her arms, buried her head in Freya's shoulder, and started to sob. "Let it out babe, I'm here."

They headed into her flat and, within seconds of Freya putting her bag on the kitchen side, she pulled two bottles of wine out of her bag. "Get two glasses," she instructed, and Isabelle let out a faint laugh before fetching the glasses from her kitchen cupboard.

Freya took the glasses, opened a bottle and poured.

"Right, sit down and explain what happened." Freya pushed the glass of wine towards Isabelle, who sat opposite her.

"I don't know where to start, Freya. I really don't." Isabelle hung her head.

Freya wasn't having it. "Lift that head up right now!"

Isabelle was shocked by the authority in Freya's voice and threw her head up, looking directly at her friend.

"Pick up that glass and neck it."

Isabelle looked at the glass—it was half full—but, as instructed, Isabelle picked up the glass and downed it.

"Good girl, now pass me your glass." Isabelle wiped her lips and passed the glass over. "Right, now we're gonna talk about this slowly and, if it takes all night, it takes all night—yeah?" Freya said calmly and filled Isabelle's glass once more.

Isabelle smiled as she took it.

It takes an hour, the rest of the bottle of wine and a lot of tears but, eventually, Isabelle manages to tell Freya all about the call from Julia. Somehow, Freya managed to keep her cool and not explode. She just consoled her.

"Is there anything I can do for you?" she asked repeatedly, her helplessness clear.

Isabelle cried more and Freya hugged her. "Let me nip to the loo and we can open this other bottle, yeah?" Freya softly said.

When Freya returned, she didn't talk to Isabelle about Patrick, so put on some music. Then, she attempted to get Isabelle to try on different outfits for her whilst they both polished off the second bottle of wine.

When Freya attempted to pour more into Isabelle's glass, but nothing came out. "No," she whined, drawing out the '*o*' sound.

"The wine's gone!" Isabelle exclaimed—they were both clearly tipsy by that point.

"What the hell? He should have been here by now!" Freya grumpily grabbed her phone, hammered a message out and threw it back down.

Isabelle was confused. "He should be here?" she asked quizzically.

Before Freya could reply, her phone started to ring and she lunged, grabbed her phone and ran from Isabelle's flat, leaving Isabelle completely confused, sitting at the foot of her bed in a dark green cocktail dress. She looked at herself in her mirror. *What am I doing?*

Concern for Freya eventually had Isabelle getting up to look for her. She found her fairly quickly, though; in the kitchen, Freya stood waiting for her looking like the Statue of Liberty. One arm was bent, holding her waist, where a large leather satchel hung with bottles of wine poking out the top. In the other hand, which was lofted in the air, she held a giant pizza.

"Guess who has a drop-dead gorgeous housemate for the rest of the week?"

Isabelle couldn't help her burst of laughter before taking a picture on her phone and sending it to Albie.

Chapter 44

ISABELLE

Both girls woke up in pain the next morning; they'd drank too much wine. Freya stumbled into the kitchen before Isabelle had a chance to fully wake and turned the kettle on. Isabelle watched with one eye squinted. When Freya returned, two coffees in hand.

"Here you go, babe. Time to wake up."

Isabelle roused herself slowly, mutely taking her coffee. Finally, Isabelle broke the silence,

"Thank you."

Freya turned to see the pain and sadness which hadn't ebbed from her eyes and put her arm around her. "It's okay, babes; I'm gonna make sure you forget about that clown this week. I promise you that."

Isabelle pulled away from Freya. "Forget him? I don't want to forget him." Her sadness morphed into fury. "I can still get him back, Freya!"

"Hey, calm down—I thought *you* broke up with *him* before the accident, now he doesn't want to see you? Doesn't give you much of a chance to get him back, right?" Freya gestured defensively.

Isabelle burst into tears and Freya instinctively hugged her. "I—I know Freya…" she whimpered. She shouldn't have lashed out.

Freya squeezed Isabelle's arm. "It's okay but, sometimes, these things need to be said."

After a while, Isabelle calmed down enough to have breakfast and both girls were quiet, with just the radio playing in the background.

"I'm sorry, Freya, I shouldn't have snapped at you like that. You were just trying to be there for me—"

"So, I'm thinking today we go shopping and then tonight… we go dancing!"

Isabelle was confused. "I dunno, Freya. I'm not sure if I'm ready for that."

Freya headed for Isabelle's shower. "Yes, you are. This is happening!" she called as she slipped into the bathroom, not giving Isabelle a choice.

Isabelle sat in silence. From where she was sitting, it felt like Freya had slapped her in the face and told her to just get on with it. Being surrounded by people sounded like the last thing she wanted right then, though.

She could hear Freya singing in the shower. *She wouldn't force me to do something like this unless she thought it would help, though. Right?* Freya was looking out for her; she always had.

When Isabelle heard the shower stop, she got up from her bed. If Freya was really trying, she wasn't going to throw that back in her face.

Let's do this.

She walked over to the bathroom door and lightly rapped on the wood. "Come on now, princess, it's my turn!" she called sarcastically.

Freya poked her head out of the door, a towel covering her. "Princess?" she asked with a frown.

"You were singing away like a Disney princess," Isabelle said with a smug grin.

Freya's face turned bright red.

"Now, get a move on if you wanna hit the shops."

***

They caught the train, headed to the nearest city and shopped their hearts out, bouncing between looking at clothing, makeup and beauty supplies. Freya convinced Isabelle to buy dresses and tops she wouldn't have chosen for herself but secretly wanted to wear and Freya even bought Isabelle one little, dark red dress she had refused to buy. Isabelle thought it was too revealing but Freya reminded her that was the whole point.

By the time they got back to Isabelle's flat, it was late in the afternoon. "Babes, I'm exhausted. I'm not sure about tonight." Freya slumped on Isabelle's bed, dramatically throwing the shopping bags to the ground.

"No! No, you were the one who suggested it!" Isabelle couldn't believe what Freya was saying. She put her bags down and threw her hands on her hips.

"I dunno… I'm just so tired and I'm not sure I wanna anymore." Freya defiantly rolled on her side, ready to take a nap.

"I can't believe this!" Isabelle was getting annoyed, and Freya let out an obviously fake snore. "Okay, what's going on?" Isabelle laughed.

"Well, I think the only thing that will wake me up and get me ready for tonight is seeing the little red dress I brought you today…" Freya said, hiding her smirk.

"What? No way—I can't wear that out!" Isabelle was embarrassed by the thought of wearing it at all.

"Well, then, I guess I'm off to sleep! Night, night." Freya knew precisely what she was doing.

"Fine," she reluctantly agreed, throwing up her hands. "I'll wear the stupid dress."

Freya bounced from the bed as though she had been electrocuted. "Perfect! I can't wait to see you in it again. You're gonna be turning heads tonight!"

Isabelle rolled her eyes but started getting ready for the night. Makeup, hair and—when it came to the outfits—though Isabelle tried to fight against it, she eventually caved to Freya's insistent badgering to wear the red dress. It was a relatively simple design, tight to the body with small straps for her shoulders, but it showed off all of Isabelle's curves in a way she usually shied away from. Once it was on, she looked in the mirror.

"Oh…my…*God*!" Freya gasped.

Isabelle, however, tried to cover herself. "Shut up," she whined to Freya. "Why do you always have to do that?" She moved her hands to cover her cleavage.

Freya started laughing. "I mean, look at you! How do you expect me to be to *not* say something?"

Isabelle turned and left the bedroom. "For God's sake," she said over her shoulder. "Just get ready, woman."

In the kitchen, she picked up her phone, no messages. For a moment, she thought about what it would be like to message Patrick.

Normally, I would send him a picture of an outfit like this…

She breathed through her nose and softly put her phone back on the table, leaning back in her chair. She felt deflated and the last thing she wanted to do was go out. She occupied herself with daydreams of curling up in bed and hibernating to escape everything.

After ten minutes, Freya left the bedroom and Isabelle rolled her eyes. "Took you long enough!" she snarked.

Freya headed over, looking like a model in a royal blue, backless dress. If Isabelle couldn't take her eyes off her then no man in the club would be able to—that was for sure.

"You're so hot," Isabelle blurted, a light blush rising to her cheeks.

Freya, however, ate the compliment up and started pulling off all sorts of poses. Isabelle couldn't hold in the laughter.

"Right, Miss Runway, let's head out."

As they left the building, the heavens opened and both the girls ran to the nearest taxi, using their bags to protect the hair they had spent so much time perfecting. Driving to the club, Isabelle looked out the window and watched the rainy town fly past; she couldn't remember the last time she had done something like this. It had just been her and Patrick for so long but for years beforehand, she had loved nights out at a club with her girls. When had that changed?

Outside the club, once Freya had left the taxi, Isabelle forced herself to pull out a small hand mirror from her bag and look at herself. She breathed in a sharp huff of air. "You can do this!" she whispered to herself.

When she left the taxi, she spotted Freya talking to the doorman by the club's entrance. The doorman looked like a goliath to Isabelle, but Freya laughed and joked with him as though they were old friends.

"Ah 'ere she is. Come on through, ladies. Have a cracking night." The doorman unclasped the rope, stopping the waiting line heading into the club, and ushered them through.

"Is this, okay?" Isabelle nervously asked Freya. It was the first time she had ever cut the line at a club.

"Of course, babes—I know the owner. Follow me, I've got us a booth."

The club was much bigger than Isabelle had expected, and hundreds of people were dancing. The music pulsated through her body, each *thump* of the bass adding to her anxiety. She focused on Freya and followed her up a flight of stairs, to a mezzanine of booths.

Isabelle looked around; everyone looked like they had money. She even noticed some famous people from a TV show she'd watched years back.

"Oh my God, Freya, do you know who that *is*?" Isabelle was a little star-struck but followed Freya.

"Oh, him? Slimeball, he is. All the girls stay away from him."

Isabelle's mouth hung open; how did Freya know these people?

They finally reached their reserved table where a bottle of chilled prosecco waited, two glasses close by.

"Babes, welcome to one of the best nights of your life." Freya immediately started pouring the prosecco. "Drink up!" she cheered.

Isabelle thankfully took one of the glasses and all her worries left her body for a moment.

"With friends like this, who needs a man?" Freya shouted over the music and Isabelle giggled.

That was the start of a night filled with dancing, free drinks, men hitting on them both—and even more drinks. They danced until the early hours of the morning.

Freya had wanted Isabelle to have a night where she let her hair down and be wild—and she couldn't have been more right. This was what she had needed.

Isabelle was smiling, laughing and just acting like her usual self—the one no one had seen in a long time.

The night was winding down and they were both very drunk. Isabelle begged Freya for one last dance but, exhausted and drunk, Freya told her she wanted her bed. "Go on, go down for one last song. I'll watch you from here."

Isabelle was annoyed but shrugged it off. "*God*, fine," she whined with a small smile on her face. "One more song." She bent down, hugged Freya, kissed her on the cheek and shouted, "You're the best!" With that, she bounced down the stairs.

That was the last thing Isabelle would remember about her night with Freya.

Chapter 45

ISABELLE

Isabelle's head was banging, her mouth was dry, and she desperately needed water. She slowly opened her eyes and the sunlight from the window hurt her eyes, so she covered them with her forearm. But as her eyes adjusted, she slowly realised she was naked.

Clutching the bed sheets to her chest, she looked around the room. She had no idea where she was. Her heart was beating out of her chest but, before she even had time to react, the door slowly creaked open.

She shot out of the bed, covering herself with the sheets.

"Morning—oh, everything okay? I've brought breakfast."

A man was standing in the doorway, wearing a white dressing gown. In his hands was a metal tray, loaded plates and mugs on top. Isabelle stood, mind still running wild as she wondered what had happened the night before. Her head was banging from the hangover. She looked around for her clothes.

"Oh, are you looking for your dress? It's hanging in the living room. Do you want me to go get it for you?"

Isabelle sheepishly responded, "…Please."

She couldn't bring herself to look the man in the eye. He put the tray on the bed and disappeared from the room and Isabelle immediately sprung to action and looked around for her underwear, finding them at the base of the far wall. When the man returned, she was back beneath the sheets, waiting.

He walked in holding a hanger with her dress on it. "Here you go, sorry for the wait. Is everything okay, Isabelle?" He held out the hanger and passed the dress to her.

"Um, yeah, I'm okay. Can you turn around, please?"

The man chuckled but did as she'd asked. "So, I'm guessing you don't remember my name?" he joked.

Isabelle felt awkward and got dressed as quickly as possible before responding. "I'm sorry, I don't remember," she said, composing herself as she scanned the room for her phone.

"Well, can I turn around now to introduce myself?" he asked only a little sarcastically.

"Uh, yes—yeah, of course, sorry."

He laughed as he turned back around. "No need to be sorry. I'm Eric. Nice to meet you—again."

Isabelle finally looked at him properly. He was tall, his dressing gown was open showing his lean, muscular naked body. His face was like it was chiselled to the point of ridiculousness and all Isabelle could think was that the guy in front of her was formed in the image of some ancient Greek sculpture. She was in awe—she had never seen someone like him before.

"Hey, my eyes are up here," Eric joked, gesturing with his finger for her to look up.

Embarrassed to have been caught staring, she looked away.

Eric walked over to the bed and sat next to the tray he had placed down on the bed and Isabelle noticed he'd made omelettes and fresh coffee with orange juice.

Isabelle eyed the coffee longingly. She was starving.

"Why don't you sit with me and have some breakfast?" Eric tapped the bed next to him.

Isabelle did precisely as he suggested, and he picked a cup of coffee up and handed it to her. Isabelle took it thankfully and took a sip,

"Wow," she was surprised. "This is really good."

"Thanks, I roasted the beans myself." He said proudly before taking a sip of his own.

Isabelle sat and eventually ate some of the omelettes with Eric's encouragement. She was quiet, though, and could only wonder who this guy was. Why was she there and did she sleep with him?

After Isabelle finished her breakfast, she finally broke the tentative silence by asking, "Where is my phone?"

He grinned, tapping his dressing gown pocket. "I have it here."

Isabelle was perplexed. "Okay… well, can I have it back?" she asked sarcastically her hand held out.

Eric let another chuckle as he passed the phone to her. "God, you're a funny one in the morning, aren't you?" he said and shuffled back on the bed to lay down with his hands behind his head.

Isabelle grabbed her phone and saw she'd missed dozens of calls and a lot of messages from Freya. The ball dropped and she finally realised what had happened.

She just left with Eric. She didn't call, message or even *tell* Freya where she was going. She felt like a monster; her friend had taken her out to cheer her up and Isabelle had left her—*worried* her—instead.

"Sorry, I need to make a call." Isabelle didn't wait for a response and rushed out of the room.

She immediately started to call Freya, and the line rang for a while before a groggy Freya answered it.

"H—hello…"

Isabelle spotted a clock on the wall and winced. It was 6 am—it was no surprise she'd woken Freya up.

"Hey… it's me."

There was a small pause. Then, "What the actual *fuck* happened last night?" Freya yelled. Her dozy tone was replaced by something which could cut glass. "You just vanished! I was terrified that something had happened to you! What happened? Are you okay?"

Isabelle had known she was due a tongue lashing but she had never heard Freya quite this angry. "I met this guy, and… well, I ended up going home with him—"

Freya snapped. "Seriously, Isabelle? You just left with some random guy? What if something had happened? No one knew where you were. I couldn't get hold of your phone all night—I was scared out of my mind!"

Isabelle's guilt made her feel incredibly small. "I'm so sorry, Freya. I really am." Isabelle started to get a bit emotional. She could hear from Freya's voice that she was as well.

"Message me where you are and I'll come get you with Albie, okay?"

Isabelle nodded. "Okay, yeah. I'll do that now, thank you."

Freya took a deep breath on the phone. "I'll see you shortly."

She hung up.

Isabelle crashed down on a sofa, the full realisation of what she had done bowling her over. She sent Freya her location as promised and threw her head into her hands; she wanted to scream. Suddenly, she heard a knock.

"Hey in there, how are you doing?"

Eric was standing at the door.

She didn't mean to be, but Isabelle was again stunned by how good-looking he was. It distracted her briefly before she realised, she hadn't responded.

"Yeah, I'm—*uh*—I'm gonna go. My lift is on my way."

Eric walked towards her. "Oh, what a shame." He gently sat beside her, brushed her hair back from her face and placed the strand behind her ear. "Would have been nice to have you all to myself today."

Isabelle's heart clanged against her chest as butterflies erupted in her stomach. She forced herself to jump up from the sofa; her heart was pounding, and her breaths were heavy.

"I'm sorry," she said, flustered, "I have to go. I have something to do today."

She adjusted her dress awkwardly as Eric leaned back into the sofa and threw his arm across the back of it, laughing. "You want to stay, don't you?" he asked.

Isabelle blushed. "No! I—what you mean?"

Eric got up and stood next to her, placing a hand on her chest. Isabelle couldn't move as his eyes locked on hers, her legs turning to jelly beneath her.

"Oh, yeah," he gave her a small smirk. "You definitely want to stay; your heart is giving you away." Slowly, he leaned in closer to Isabelle's face and whispered, "I want you again."

His words caused something primal to wake inside Isabelle and she launched herself at him without another thought, kissing him fiercely as he pulled her in close. His desire—it ignited something inside of her and made her bolder, reckless.

At that very moment, her phone started to ring. It was Freya.

"I—" she shook her head to clear it. "I have to go."

Eric kissed her neck. "No, you don't," he said easily. "You're going to stay here with me."

Isabelle couldn't resist kissing him again. Her hands slid up of their own volition and attempted to remove his dressing gown. As slid it from his shoulders, it fell back from his body and hit the floor with a soft *thud.*

A loud, heavy knock sounded at the door and Isabelle jolted and ran to put her shoes on.

"I think you're going to have to come back here later, aren't you?" He was still naked and seemed completely unashamed about it; this, for some reason, was very attractive to Isabelle and she could hardly keep her eyes off his body.

"I dunno… maybe?" she started to head towards the door and Eric walked over to his desk, picked up his business card, then walked over to Isabelle and slid it into her hand.

"I'll be waiting for your phone call."

Something about Eric made Isabelle lose all logical thinking. She was tongue-tied around him and nodded, taking the card. He turned away and slid his dressing gown back over his shoulders.

Another heavy knock sounded at the door and Eric walked over and it was for Isabelle. Albie filled the door frame, filling it. He looked Eric up and down and scoffed.

"Come on, you," he turned to Isabelle. "Let's get you home."

Eric grinned at Albie. "How you are doing there? You're a big fella, aren't you?"

Albie glared into Eric's eyes and rolled his boulder-like shoulders. Isabelle couldn't believe how terrifying Albie looked when he tried; his face was monstrous and his fists were clenched, so at odds with his usual, easy-going nature. She could tell he wanted to knock Eric's head off.

Eric, however, laughed once more, like everything was fine and Isabelle took that as her cue and squeezed past Albie, who was still standing in the doorframe.

"Call me, baby," Eric said. He continued to look Albie directly in the eye before slamming the door in Albie's face.

Isabelle pulled Albie away, his limbs stiff and jaw set. "Woah, Albie, are you okay? I've never seen you like this."

Albie instantly relaxed, body loosening to his usual friendly, happy state. "I bloody hate guys like that. I've met a load of blokes with that kinda pompous, 'I'm-better-than-you' attitude; I don't like him one bit. Isabelle—stay away from him, yeah?" he told her as he led her to the car.

Isabelle frowned. She didn't really understand what Albie meant; Eric had been fine.

As they got to the car, Isabelle saw Freya sitting in the front seat, looking directly out of the front window. "I'm glad you're okay," was all she said when Isabelle slid into the back seat. Freya didn't turn to look at her.

Isabelle knew she would be upset but, seeing her made her shame at her mistake hit harder.

Albie finally got into the car. "Yep, exactly what you thought," was the first thing he said. Freya just tutted.

Isabelle was confused. "Sorry, but what does that mean?"

Freya, clearly not enjoying her tone, turned and shot her head around to glare at Isabelle. "It means you abandoned me and went home with an absolute cretin—*that's* what it means."

Isabelle attempted to respond but Albie pulled Freya back. "Come on, let's just get her home and cool off. We can talk about it later, yeah?"

Freya forcedly sighed and threw her hand in the air. "Fine. Let's go."

The car ride to Freya's flat was short but it felt like it took eons. The air was cold. No one spoke a word.

Isabelle couldn't stop thinking about everything that had happened over the last few days, thoughts of Patrick only broken up by those of Eric as he stood in front of her that morning. It was maddening—so much so that, every time she had that thought, she forced herself to snap out of it.

They rounded the corner to Freya's place.

"Do you need a shower?" Freya asked. "I've put some towels and clothes out for you."

Isabelle nodded. "Yeah, that would be great. Thank you." She knew that, even though Freya was furious, she was only angry because she cared.

They parked up and headed in; Isabelle went straight for the shower where she contemplated what she would say. Afterwards, she wrapped one of the towels Freya had left for her around herself and walked out of the shower. She overheard Freya and Albie talking as she got to the hallway.

"Babe, you need to calm down a bit; she knows she messed up. You can't hold that over her head—she needs us right now." Albie was the voice of reason, as usual, Isabelle thought to herself.

"I know," Freya sighed. "I know, I just can't believe her! After what happened with Patrick, I thought a night with just me and her would be exactly what she needed but, no, she had to sneak off with some scumbag."

Isabelle turned. She didn't want to hear any more and headed to the spare room where Freya had left her some clothes.

She didn't understand why they keep saying Eric was a creep or a scumbag. She sat on the bed drying her hair, muttering to herself but her thoughts sporadically drifted back to Eric. She glanced at the bedside table where she'd put his business card.

She got changed and flopped on the bed. She was exhausted, all she wanted to do was sleep. But she turned and looked at the card one more time.

"What would it hurt…"

She picked up the card and tapped the number into her phone. She couldn't call him straight away in case Freya and Albie heard her talking to him, so she settled on a text.

Hi, it's Isabelle. I can't come around today but what are you doing tomorrow around 6?

Her courage surprised her. She had never done something like this before!

There was something so alluring about Eric—she just had to see him again. She laid back on her bed and, without realising, fell asleep.

Chapter 46

ISABELLE

Isabelle woke and groggily rolled over to look at the time. It was 3 pm. She had slept almost the entire day, which wasn't that surprising to her considering everything that had happened recently.

She slowly got off the bed and looked at her phone; two texts from Eric. She thought about opening them but ultimately decided against it. "I'll look later," she pacified herself. Right then, she needed to get home and set about collecting her things.

A few minutes later, Freya knocked on the door. Isabelle had forgotten she still had to talk to her about last night. "Hey babes, I heard you shuffling. Can I come in?" Freya asked, no longer as angry as she had been before.

"Yeah, come on in."

Freya pushed the door open, and they sat on the bed facing each other. Isabelle felt nervous, she didn't know what Freya was going to say.

"So, I had some time to cool off… you know you messed up—you don't need me to tell you that. I'm not your mother so I won't scold you like a child but, babes, you can't be doing that shit to me; it's not what you do to your friends." Freya reached out and held Isabelle's hand as she was talking to her.

Isabelle sighed, her chest straining. "Yeah, I know. I'm so sorry, Freya. I—"

Freya held her finger in the air. "Were gonna leave it there, yeah? You've apologised. Let's move on. Just promise me one thing—don't do that shit again… or ill kick your ass." She grinned.

Isabelle laughed. "I promise."

Freya grabbed and hugged her. "Oh, God—and please leave that guy as a mistake and don't go back," Freya laughed.

Isabelle bit her lip. She didn't want to tell Freya that she had already organised to meet him again. She *mhmm*'d and hugged her back tighter.

Isabelle ended up staying at Freya's for dinner. Albie cooked and they had the chance to talk. Then, she headed home. Within minutes of walking through her door, she'd thrown her bag to one side and headed to her bed.

"How am I still so tired?" she wondered aloud, covering her eyes with her forearm.

She laid in silence for a moment, but it was painful—intrusive thoughts spiralled around her mind and remained no matter how much she tried to push them away. Patrick. He was at the centre of it all.

Tears began to roll down her cheeks as she went over everything in her head once more. She hardly heard it when her phone began to ring and reluctantly leaned across the bed to grab it.

Eric was calling her.

She contemplated picking up for a moment before her curiosity won out and she hit 'answer'. "Hello?"

"Ah, so she is alive! Thought you might be avoiding me," he quipped.

"Yeah, sorry I didn't get round to texting you back… I fell asleep. Everything okay?" she asked.

"Fell asleep, did you? Well, texting me about meeting me tomorrow and then ghosting me surprised me."

Isabelle became defensive. "It wasn't intentional, you know?"

Eric sniggered, "Woah, woah, sassy pants. I'm pulling your leg! I guessed that hulk of a man talked you out of speaking to me."

Isabelle grimaced in embarrassment. "Yeah, he's a bit protective. He wasn't a fan of you…" She bit her lip. Why had she told him that?

She thought about her conversation with Freya. Freya had also told her to stay away from him. Where are they both right?

"Well, it's a good job I couldn't care less about what he thinks of me, eh? I'm more interested in you—he's not my type."

Isabelle couldn't help but giggle and they spent the rest of the evening talking on the phone. She couldn't remember the last time she'd done this with someone. Eric was the opposite of Patrick—and she liked it.

"Right then, you. I'll see you tomorrow at 6 pm. You remember where I live?"

Isabelle quickly replied. "Yeah—"

"I still think you should come round right now." She could hear the grin in his voice.

Isabelle sat up and there was a short pause before she said, "Okay, then. Pay for a taxi and I'll come."

Even Eric seemed surprised. "I'll send one now. I'll see you shortly."

As he hung up, Isabelle started to freak out.

What am I doing?

It was 1 am. She had never done anything like this.

She grabbed her pillow and yelled into it. Yelling was better than all the stewing she had been doing recently. She made herself get up, stripped off, found her most seductive lingerie and slipped on a dress. As she put some perfume on, pulling her hair into a ponytail, she saw a car pull up outside. She grabbed a jacket and left.

On the way, she couldn't stop looking at her phone and fiddling with her handbag; she was nervous but excited. The taxi pulled up outside Eric's house. She reached for her purse.

"Nah, it's all good, darlin'. All paid for. Have a good night." The taxi driver said.

She slowly got up and over to Eric's door, taking a moment outside to compose herself. She took a deep breath before knocking once.

"It's open."

She turned the knob and stepped inside, finding Eric in an armchair. She walked over to him.

"Stand there," Eric commanded.

Isabelle was startled but stood in place as instructed.

"Take the jacket off."

She smiled as she threw her jacket to the ground, a thrill shooting through her which made her feel sexy and confident. "Good girl," he smiled. "Now do a twirl for me."

Isabelle turned on a dime and giggled.

"Do it again but, this time, be quiet."

His tone was stern, and she didn't know why, but did exactly as he said.

"Better," he praised, and she smiled coyly. "You look good. Now take it off."

"What, now? Right here?"

Eric just sat back in his chair and nodded, so Isabelle slowly unzipped the side of her dress and let it fall to the ground. She tried to cover herself with her arms and he finally got out of his chair and slowly walked towards her. She watched him approaching her like a lion stalking his prey.

He wore a tight black shirt with smart trousers. As he got closer, Isabelle could smell his cologne. She couldn't help but love the way it smelt. He slowly walked around her, looking her body up and down. He then gently reached out and moved her arms to stop her from covering herself. He then started to walk towards the bedroom.

"Follow me," he said, leaving her standing behind him.

His behaviour was new to Isabelle, but it excited her, and the newness turned her on even more. She quickly followed him, excited to see what he would demand next and, as soon as she reached the bedroom, he launched her onto the bed.

She bounced off the cushions and looked up at him, legs open wide on the bed. He slowly undid the buttons of his shirt, showing more and more of his well-toned chest with each one. Finally, he threw it to the floor and unbuckled his belt. Isabelle couldn't take her eyes off him.

She wanted him so badly it shocked her, but she didn't make a sound.

When he stood before her, naked, he asked, "Do you want me?"

Isabelle nodded and bit her lip.

"Tell me," He demanded.

"I want you," she begged.

At that, Eric grabbed both her ankles and yanked her towards him, causing the briefest spark of pain. It didn't bother Isabelle; she liked his dominance.

He held her legs and thrust deep inside her, making Isabelle cry out in pleasure. He was slow and powerful, but she wanted to beg him to go faster. He threw her legs onto his shoulders to thrust deeper, slower and harder. He looked directly into her eyes as he grabbed a handful of her hair, a wild glint to his eyes that both scared and thrilled Isabelle. She wanted more.

He pulled her in, kissing her savagely and ginned when he noticed how she enjoyed it when he was a bit rougher with her. He grabbed her hips, spinning her around so he could push her head into the mattress and Isabelle let out a surprised gasp before a groan of pleasure as he slid back inside her. His strong hands gripped her hips tightly as he put a leg up on the bed to penetrate her deeper.

Isabelle was close, she never had a man like this before. Eric played off the moans and noises she made, his thrusts getting faster and faster as Isabelle's body started to spasm. Her back arched and her heart was beating out of her chest, her breaths laboured.

She felt euphoric as her knees gave way and she collapsed onto the bed, rolling over with a big grin on her face as she pushed the hair from her eyes. Eric stood, muscles dripping in sweat as he watched her.

“I'm not finished yet,” he told her.

His eyes still had that dangerous glint, which excited Isabelle. She crawled over to him and kissed down his chest before saying, “I want more.”

He groaned and wrapped his hand around her throat, pulling her up to his eyeline while he kissed her. He then guided her back to the living room and his armchair.

Isabelle’s legs felt weak, but she didn’t resist. He sat down and let go.

“You’re gonna ride me like a good girl until I finish,” he told her.

Without a word, Isabelle turned around and slowly lowered herself onto him. He quickly spanked her ass, and the sudden action momentarily caught her off guard, but she didn’t hate it one bit and turned her head to smile at him.

They kept at it all night before finally collapsing into bed. Eric fell asleep almost immediately, but Isabelle laid next to him, a sweaty mess and breathing heavily. The usual tirade of thoughts had subsided, leaving only exhaustion in their wake, and she stared at the ceiling in pure ecstasy before slowly drifting off to sleep.

Chapter 47

ISABELLE

It was late when Isabelle dazedly woke the next day, calling out, "Patrick?" before rolling over and realising which bedroom she was in.

She sat up straighter and pulled the sheet around herself. "Oh," she said, deciding to get up. She walked out of the bedroom. "Eric? Are you here?"

She looked around but saw no sign of him. She was sore—they didn't stop all night. She walked to the kitchen and poured herself a glass of water, then took another look around at his house. She hadn't noticed it last night or the last time she was there, but it was clear Eric had money. She couldn't help but snoop around for a while before finally locating a note meant for her attached to the fridge.

Gone to pick up my car from the garage; here's some money, order us some food. Will be back by 10.

Isabelle sighed but then shrugged. "Hey, at least he drives."

She took a shower, threw on one of his t-shirts and ordered the groceries to cook something nice for him. By the time he'd arrived, she had prepared a lavish, full English breakfast.

He walked in, confused and surprised,

"You deserved a reward after last night," she teased.

They enjoyed breakfast together, finally getting to know each other a bit more. After eating, Isabelle got herself comfortable on his sofa and listened to him tell her about going travelling in his early twenties.

They spent the rest of the day together. Isabelle didn't even think about work.

***

At the office, Julia was furious that Isabelle didn't call to let her know she wasn't coming in the previous day. She approached Freya, asking her where she was, and Freya was equally annoyed. "Yet again, she has disappeared without telling anyone what is wrong with her!"

Isabelle was almost late for work but wandered into the office just about on time.

Julia caught her immediately. "Hey, where were you yesterday?"

It finally dawned on Isabelle that she had forgotten to call or text when she stayed at Eric's the day before. She was supposed to have been at work.

She thought on her feet and quickly made up an excuse. "I went back to my parents' house for the day after what happened with Patrick. I knew they wouldn't be there, but I just wanted to get away—"

Julia held up her hand to stop her. "I don't care, Isabelle. Just make sure you let someone know when you're going to be off next time."

Isabelle quickly agreed and apologised some more. Julia accepted her apology and sent her to work, and Isabelle finally let out the breath she'd been holding, relieved to get away with it.

She threw her bag on her chair and set about making a coffee.

Lunchtime came quickly and Freya charged over to Isabelle's desk and slammed her hands down on the desk.

"Come with me."

Isabelle jolted upright. Freya looked furious.

And, for the second time in less than 48 hours, that anger was aimed at her. She sighed and followed Freya into the ladies restroom.

"Where the hell were you yesterday?" Freya demanded. "You talked so much bullshit to Julia earlier—and I know you did. I could see it in your face! If you gonna lie, you gonna need to work on your poker face." Freya hissed the words to Isabelle, so as not to alert anyone in the office.

"I'm sorry," Isabelle sighed and scrubbed a hand over her face. "Look, I know I should have messaged. I just forgot."

Freya's anger was reaching new limits Isabelle hadn't seen before and she practically exploded then. "What the fuck, Isabelle? Twice—in *two days*—I've been worried about you. I didn't have a clue where you were!"

Isabelle's face twisted stubbornly as she fought back. "Look, I didn't *ask* you to worry." Freya took a step back to compose herself, taking a deep breath in. "Why are you being like this?" she questioned.

Isabelle had had enough and rolled her eyes. "I'm sorry, *mum*. I'll let you know next time I'm out past sunset, shall I?" Isabelle's sarcasm was cutting.

Freya levelled her with a steely look and a chill ran down Isabelle's spine. "I'm done," she said. "I won't waste my energy worrying about you. I've tried to be there for you, and you threw it back in my face. *Twice.* I'm done."

She charged past, knocking Isabelle's shoulder on the way. This infuriated Isabelle.

"I spent the day fucking Eric," she yelled but Freya had already left the bathroom by that point. She went to follow Freya but, as soon as she opened the door, she was met by Julia.

"My office, now!" Julia snarled.

After a dressing down from Julia, Isabelle was informed that she would be suspended for the rest of the week.

As she left the office, she immediately called Eric.

Chapter 48

ISABELLE

The week Isabelle was suspended marked the start of her new relationship with Eric. That initial week was filled with sex, being taken out to lavish dinners and grand events for their dates. Isabelle had never experienced anything like the things Eric showed her before—not with Patrick nor anyone else.

Over the weeks, it became apparent that his world was so different from her everyday life that she felt like an alien at some of the more grandiose charity events and fancy restaurants that he took her to. She always felt like she stood apart—so obviously other—but knew she did as Eric always brought her the most elegant dresses and accessories to help her fit in and make her feel like the most beautiful woman in the room.

He treated her very differently from how Patrick had treated her and often went days without talking to her. He'd then message her at random times and demand to see her, which riled Isabelle up. She was always soothed, however, by Eric's smooth apologies and she'd feel guilty for having ever been annoyed at all.

They did occasionally have arguments. Every time they had a spat, Eric would buy Isabelle something to cheer her up—clothes, handbags, a new phone or something she definitely wouldn't have been able to afford.

She grew used to not taking her purse with her when they went out together; she knew Eric would pay for anything. It felt like the perfect relationship for Isabelle, who enjoyed having someone dote on her every need. It came with some drawbacks, sure—but after what had happened to Isabelle with Patrick, she felt like she deserved to be treated like a princess for once.

Eric could be controlling sometimes, but Isabelle did her best to stamp that sort of behaviour out. All she wanted was for someone to treat her well and, despite his flaws, Eric did that.

Her relationship with her co-workers had dwindled until it was virtually non-existent. She and Freya didn't talk at all, and, because of that, Albie had started to give her a wide birth, too. It got so bad that she had to remind herself that she wanted to keep her job because Eric seemed to like hearing about it. She loved pleasing him so, even though work had become a cold and lonely place for her, just knowing she would be going to Eric's after got her through each day.

Isabelle sighed and pushed away from her desk. *Another day down.* She needed to pick up fresh clothes from her flat before heading to Eric's. She made sure to collect fresh ones once a week.

By the time she got back to her place, she missed Eric's more than ever. She hated being in her flat; it reminded her of everything she wanted to forget. Her new life of luxury with Eric was all she wanted to focus on.

She picked up her mail for the week and headed to the table to check if there was anything she needed to open now; if not, she would just leave it for another time. By this point, bills plastered with 'final notice' and 'overdue' covered her kitchen table, but she couldn't bring herself to care about them and ignored them, instead.

As she placed down yet another envelope, a loud bang at her front door made her jump. She dropped the rest of the pile and quickly opened her door, smiling sheepishly when her landlady walked past her.

Isabelle had never had a problem with her before, but she was obviously pissed off at something now.

"Finally," the woman exclaimed. "I caught you!"

The landlady was an older woman, and it was painfully obvious to Isabelle that her properties were the only thing she cared about. "Caught me?" Isabelle asked.

"You haven't paid your rent for 2 months!" the old lady yelled.

Isabelle hadn't even realised her rent had been due. She wasn't sure what she could say to make the situation and found herself opening and closing her mouth like a fish.

"I want you out!" the old lady handed Isabelle a folded piece of paper.

Isabelle inhaled sharply. "You're evicting me?" she yelled back.

The old woman bumped past Isabelle, headed for the front door and slammed the door shut behind her. Isabelle was furious. She pulled two suitcases from under her bed and started to hastily pack her clothes and most-prized possessions. "I'll come back for the rest," she yelled as she opened the flat door.

She took another glance at her flat and emotion welled inside her but, she forced her feelings back down and ordered a taxi.

Not long after, she stood on Eric's doorstep, suitcases in tow.

"You off on holiday or something?" Eric laughed.

Isabelle wasn't in the mood and attempted to push past him and into the house, but Eric wasn't moving. His face dropped. "I'm gonna shut the door and open it again. We'll try this again, yes?" He shut the door in her face and swiftly opened it again. "Why hello, Isabelle. You off on holiday or something?" His tone was colder than before.

"I was evicted…" she said, unnerved by his actions.

"Well, don't stand out Come on in and tell me all about it." He opened the door wide and gestured for her to come inside.

Isabelle spent the next ten minutes telling Eric everything that had happened and he sat silently, sipping a whisky he had made before she arrived. When she finished, she carefully looked at his face and waited for him to say something.

"Oh, you're finished? Thank God." Isabelle was stunned but he continued before she had the chance to say anything. "I have a proposition for you," he said, sitting back in his armchair and swirling his whiskey.

"What do you mean?" Isabelle was thoroughly vexed.

"You move in here; you give me your wages every month and you will have to pay zero bills. You will live a comfortable life, and I'll make sure you don't have to worry about money at all."

Isabelle was taken aback. "What do you mean 'give you, my wages'?" She couldn't believe the words coming from his mouth.

He leaned forward and put his glass down on his coffee table. "You obviously can't handle your finances, so why don't I do that for you and give you spending money, instead?" His words were nonchalant. "I was thinking maybe five thousand a month?" He sat back in his chair, the corners of his mouth slightly inclined.

"I don't earn anywhere near that—what are you talking about?" Isabelle's head was spinning, Eric ignored her question. "I'll offer this to you one last time; I will give you five grand a month, a place to live and a life of luxury. All you must do is make sure your wages are wired to me every month. Deal?"

Isabelle took a moment to process this, the words *this is too good to be true*, taunting her mind.

Seeing the perplexed look on her face, Eric smirked. “You have till I finish my drink.” He leaned down, picked up his near-empty glass and placed the rim to his lips.

Isabelle saw the dribble of whisky he had left and quickly jumped to her feet. “Yes!” she instinctively yelled.

Eric smirked before throwing the last of his whisky down his throat. “Good girl.”

The next few days were like a whirlwind. Eric handled everything and sold everything that she had left in her flat. He then got her to throw out the clothes she brought with her and brought her a new wardrobe, claiming that it was about time she wore some proper clothes. Most upsettingly, he threw away the stuffed toy she and Freya had won at the funfair all that time ago.

Her protests fell on deaf ears, which hurt Isabelle, but Eric didn’t seem to care.

He paid off her outstanding debts, closed all her bank accounts and opened a new one for her in which he would deposit her spending money each month.

Isabelle's life was changing forever, and she knew it. She felt a little bit like she had surrendered everything to this man who now had complete control over her life. If she was being entirely honest with herself, the thought terrified her. She was confused about why she had to keep her job, but Eric warned her to keep working.

Part of her enjoyed having more money than she could imagine. She liked to buy anything and everything she wanted when the whim struck her and went shopping often. On one such day as this, after shopping for groceries, she stumbled upon a beautiful tabby cat laying on top of a low wall, soaking up the sun. Isabelle immediately melted and crept over, slowly pulling her phone out of her purse as she did so.

She opened the camera app on her phone and… paused. She had the camera pointed at the cat, ready to go, but she didn’t take the picture. The cat stretched out further as she stood there for a long moment—longer than she realised—and she found herself putting the phone away and walking off. She wasn’t sure why she didn’t take the picture—she wouldn’t normally think twice about doing so. Why didn’t she take the picture?

When Eric got home that night, he wasted no time in announcing that they would be going out for a nice dinner with a client of his. Isabelle was mid-way through cooking dinner at that point.

It wasn't unusual for Eric to want to show Isabelle off to his clients. She was never sure why he did it and never enjoyed the dinners but went anyway.

She agreed and turned the stove off without another word. She was hungry and at least she wouldn't be the one cooking their food.

The client dinner wore on that night, however, and Isabelle found herself gazing into space. Her lack of attention never affected conversations between Eric and his clients and, sometimes it would be minutes before something pulled her attention back. She was insanely bored; she could handle only so much business talk.

Her phone started to ring. *Thank God,* she quietly thought to herself.

Then, her heart stopped.

She quickly excused herself from the table—much to Eric's disapproval—and quickly rushed outside of the restaurant and Eric's view.

She stared at her phone in shock. *Why are you calling me right now*?

She took a deep breath before answering. "Hello, Patrick?"

Chapter 49

"Help me, please. Isabelle… it's Doc."

Patrick went on to explain what was going on and the pain in his voice was palpable. Isabelle couldn't stop the choked sound from repeating over and over in her mind. She didn't care how annoyed Eric would be by them leaving early to help a cat while he was in a meal with a client; she went and got him, anyway. Soon, they were in the car.

As expected, Eric voiced his annoyance the entire drive to Patrick's flat, but Isabelle blocked out the sound of his complaints. As soon as the car was parked, Isabelle tried to jump out of the car—but was stopped by the locks on the doors.

"Eric, let me out," she demanded.

"Well now; hold up. Exactly who is this person that you're ruining my night for?" he prodded.

Isabelle was flustered. "It's just a guy I work with who's disabled. He can't exactly rush his cat to the vet, can he?" She tried to open the door again. "Just let me out, Doc could be dying."

Eric reluctantly unlocked the doors and let her out. She ran as fast as she could to Patrick's door and pulled out her keys as soon as she reached it. She'd forgotten she even had a key to Patrick's place but was glad of it now.

"Patrick?" she called. "Where are you?" She looked around, not seeing him anywhere in the living room.

"In here!"

Isabelle ran, following the voice to the bathroom, and found Patrick's wheelchair blocking the door while he was on the floor, cradling Doc who was limp in his hands.

Patrick's expression was haunted—traumatised, even—as he asked, "What do I do, Isabelle? Please tell me what to do."

His pleading eyes pierced Isabelle. She quickly moved the wheelchair, dropped to her knees and threw her ear onto Doc's chest. "Tell me," she said quietly, still searching for a heartbeat. "What happened?"

Her tone was very stern and to the point; she needed Patrick to focus on her.

"I—I dunno," he spluttered, tears falling from his eyes.

She scanned the room and saw cat vomit on the floor. "Right, Patrick—you need to give him to me, okay?"

She could tell by Patrick's face that he wasn't completely okay with that plan.

She continued, making her voice as gentle as possible. "I'm gonna take him to the 24-hour vet right now, okay?"

Patrick gave Doc one last, soft hug before carefully passing him to Isabelle.

"You can trust me, Patrick. I'll look after him," she promised.

With Doc safely tucked against her chest, Isabelle stood and ran from Patrick's flat as fast as she could, leaving a weeping Patrick on the floor. She sprinted to the car, flung open the door, and threw herself in the passenger seat. "Quick, take us to the 24-hour vet in the town," Isabelle instructed.

Eric sighed. He wasn't happy. "If that thing is sick in my car, I'm leaving it on the side of the road."

Still, he sped off to the vet's and, thanks to how late it was and the speed of Eric's car, getting there didn't take long. When they arrived, Isabelle sprinted in with Doc carefully cradled close to her heart; some drool was already staining the dress Eric had brought her for this evening, but she didn't care.

The vet immediately took Doc away from her to start treating him and Isabelle sat down in the waiting room; it was the first time she had a chance to breathe in over an hour.

What just happened?

She took a second to process the bizarre events. The last time she saw Patrick, he was in a coma, but he had a wheelchair and looked so different to what she remembered.

"Why did he call me?" she accidentally blurted out.

The receptionist jumped—the room was dead silent before she spoke. Embarrassed, she rubbed her forehead and waited. Her embarrassment was short-lived, however, as the vet waved and came out to see her. Isabelle immediately pulled out her phone to relay any information to Patrick. "Is he okay?"

Patrick's bellow was so loud that Isabelle had to pull the phone from her ear so she could hear the vet.

"He's stable. We did some tests and think it might have been an epileptic fit." Patrick gasped on the other end of the phone but didn't interrupt. "He's going to stay the night, and we'll do some more tests but, depending on how he is tomorrow, he could be released with medication."

All Isabelle could hear down the phone was Patrick wailing with a spluttered, occasional, *thank you.* With that, the vet walked away.

"I'll bring him around tomorrow if they release him, okay?" Isabelle said to Patrick down the phone, but he didn't stop crying. "I'm going to go now. I'll message you tomorrow."

She hung up the phone and took some breaths before heading to the car park but, when she got there, she couldn't see Eric's car anywhere. Looking at her phone, she saw that she had multiple missed texts from Eric. The last read,

Get a taxi home; I've got work in the morning.

Eric was pissed off and the realisation had her chest tightening. What kind of mood would he be in when she got back? She paced for a while before ordering a taxi back to Eric's. He was asleep when she got back.

The next day, Isabelle woke feeling mentally exhausted. Eric had left before she had the chance to open her eyes, which she was thankful for. She went to work as usual and the atmosphere in the office felt a little less frosty than it usually was. Sure, no one spoke to her, but it was a little more comfortable.

At the end of the day, Julia intercepted her in the car park.

"Thank you for last night," she said. "My car is in the shop at the moment."

Her words surprised Isabelle, even though Julia was one of the few in the office who still spoke to her regularly.

"Erm, that's okay. I was just surprised, that's all..."

She hadn't asked Julia how Patrick was since that phone call and Julia seemed to understand her curiosity without her saying anything. "He's different now, she said, "different, yet the same. You should talk to him when you take Doc back." Her voice was normal, but her eyes were pleading.

She gave Isabelle a quick, tight hug and walked away.

Isabelle's mind was a mess, she could hardly string two and two together. She made her way to Eric's as per usual and, when she entered, Eric was on his laptop. He tapped away at the table and, without looking up from his laptop, he asked, "So, you gonna tell me who this Patrick guy really is?" It sounded like he was barely concealing his anger.

"It's just someone I work with; he doesn't even come to the office anymore."

She didn't want to tell him everything, but he was like a bloodhound that had caught its scent.

"Yet you know exactly where he lives? And, apparently have a key to his place?"

Isabelle froze. She couldn't think of an excuse.

She felt like a thief caught red-handed and took the seat opposite Eric. He closed the lid of his laptop and looked directly at her, his piercing eyes—which she was usually so mesmerised by—now seemed emotionless.

"We dated before," she told Eric about their time together, keeping most of their relationship to the CliffsNotes version.

Eric maintained the same expression on his face throughout and Isabelle finished by telling him about the accident.

"Right," Eric started, his voice impossibly low. "You can give him his cat back but, after that, I don't want to hear about you seeing him again, do you hear me?"

He stood up and walked over to Isabelle, placing his hand on her shoulder. He squeezed her shoulder tighter and tighter while he waited for an answer. "Are we in agreement?" he repeated.

Isabelle winced and nodded.

"Well, then," Eric's tone had flipped entirely. "Let's go get this flee bag. The vet has already called."

Isabelle nodded, glad of his friendly tone, and they headed off.

At the vet's, Isabelle got the rundown on how Doc needed to be looked after and collected the medication he would have to take going forward. She took as many leaflets as possible, signed the insurance company paperwork and collected Doc, who was waiting for her in a travel crate.

Doc was sleeping, and she didn't want to disturb him by stroking him, so gently took him to the car where she put him in the back seat.

Eric was acting very friendly, which confused Isabelle who had thought he might be upset—but she was thankful he wasn't acting as he had been when they had been sitting at the table.

They reached Patrick's flat, and Eric parked the car before turning to Isabelle. "I think I'll come in as well," he said, leaving no room for argument.

Isabelle tried anyway. "No, no, there's no need. I'll be ten minutes, tops."

She wanted to get this out of the way as soon as possible so Eric stayed as calm as possible.

Reluctantly, he nodded. "Okay. Ten minutes, then I'm coming in." His hands gripped the steering wheel tighter.

Isabelle quickly agreed and took Doc from the car before heading to Patrick's.

She let herself as she had the night before. "Hello?"

Within seconds, Patrick wheeled himself from the living room and to the hallway. He looked like he hadn't slept.

"I have someone here for you," she said with a smile. She felt sorry for him; he seemed so small to her now and his face was so sullen. She carried Doc into the living room without another word.

Patrick still hadn't said anything, and Julia's words rang in her mind. *He's different now...*

She placed Doc's carry case on the floor and opened the gate. Doc slowly emerged from the case, looking groggy from the medication. Patrick was clutching the armrests of his wheelchair as though in pain.

Doc stretched himself out and yawned before sniffing the air and managing to jump onto Patrick's lap where he nuzzled into his chest. Patrick finally let go of his armrests and picked Doc up.

"You scared me for a second there, buddy." Tears were slowly rolling down his face, but he was smiling even as the tears rolled into his mouth.

Doc let out a loud meow and rubbed his head against Patrick's before jumping away and heading to his water bowl.

Patrick wiped his eyes and looked to Isabelle who still knelt by the carry case, smiling. "Thank you so much, Isabelle; I can't ever thank you enough." Isabelle stood up, looking wooden. "Can I hug you?" he asked in earnest.

"Yes, of course... erm."

Isabelle walked towards Patrick but wasn't sure how to initiate the hug. Patrick held his arms out and Isabelle bent down, hugging him cautiously. He clutched Isabelle tighter and softly whispered into her ear three words; "I've missed you..."

Isabelle instantly pulled away with force. "How can you say that to me?" she demanded, her voice loud. "After all you did to me?"

Everything she went through while he was in his coma ran through her mind, topped off by his rejection when he woke. Her eyes filled with tears as she shook her head. "Fuck you, Patrick. Fuck you."

She grabbed the carry case from the floor, continuing. "You have no right to say that to me! No right at all!"

She started to storm out of the room but before she could, she turned. "And, for your information, I've found someone else—so don't you dare say that to me ever again."

She ran out of the room, slamming his front door shut behind her and crying as she ran. She tried to compose herself outside Patrick's flat but struggled to stop her tears. Makeup smudged on her face.

"Isabelle?" Eric was walking towards her; it had been ten minutes.

She once again tried to rub away the tears, but it was no use. As he reached her, she threw her arms around him and sobbed into his shoulder.

"Go back to the car and wait for me," was all he said, pointing her to the car.

She nodded and walked away without a fight.

Chapter 50

PATRICK

There was a loud knock at the door, Patrick wheeled over thinking Isabelle might have forgotten something. Without care, a man stepped inside with force and Patrick wheeled away in shock.

The man stood and looked Patrick up and down. "So, Patrick, is it?" He walked past Patrick and around his home, not saying a word.

Patrick wheeled himself into the living room and grabbed his phone and the man entered a moment later. Doc arched his back and hissed at him.

"Oh, shut up, you fleabag."

He walked over to Patrick, grabbed both armrests and pulled him close to his face.

"She's mine now," he said. "If I ever hear about you again—" The man's eyes locked to Patrick's and Patrick found he couldn't look away, gulping once.

Satisfied, the man pushed on the armrests and sent Patrick careening into the wall.

Eric laughed. "I'm Eric by the way. Pleasure to meet you." Nothing was said, Eric just kept pacing around.

"God, this is pathetic, isn't it? What—you have nothing to say?" He wandered over to the window. "See, look—you've made her cry. What do you have to say about that?"

Patrick looked down at his lap where the phone was still clutched. What was happening? His heart felt like it was about to beat its way out of his chest.

"Whoops!" Eric pulled Patrick's TV onto the floor with such force that the screen smashed, sending a jolt through Patrick. "Well?" Eric goaded. "What do you have to say?"

Under his breath, Patrick finally spoke. "I'm sorry," he said.

Eric walked towards him, cupping his ears. "He speaks! Repeat that—but louder. So, I can hear it."

Patrick apologised louder and Eric let out another menacing laugh.

He then walked past Patrick, rustled his hair and said, "Good boy. Now, remember what I said." As he strode away, he loudly called back to Patrick. "Oh, and if you get any ideas about telling anyone about our chat… just remember, I know where you live."

His tone was jolly and so out of place with his words. He laughed again before slamming the door and Patrick finally breathed.

It wasn't long, however, until these breaths transformed into hyperventilation and his body was shaking. Doc jumped onto his lap to try to comfort him. He was in a state of complete shock.

He had no idea how to react.

He tried his best to calm down but, ultimately found himself reaching again for his phone and calling Julia. But, when she picked up the phone, he couldn't say a word.

Julia could hear the panic in his breathing. "I'll be right there."

Within half an hour, Julia was there—comforting him. The TV was on the floor and Patrick was in such a state that Julia had no idea what had happened. When Patrick still couldn't tell her, she decided to help him into his bed so he could try to relax. She then went to clean up the mess in the living room.

A while later, after Patrick had calmed down, he called out for Julia, unsure if she was still there.

She was at his side in an instant, "Are you okay?" she asked, hands fluttering to help in some way.

He nodded. "Is Doc, okay?"

Julia reassured him. "He's okay. I've given him his medicine for the evening and he's sleeping."

Patrick let out a sigh of relief.

"I've got to ask you, Patrick—what happened?"

Patrick shook his head. Eric had been so menacing, and he didn't want to alarm or involve Julia, so decided to make up a story to appease her.

"The TV wasn't working. I tried to check the wires in the back, and it fell."

He was a terrible liar. Julia sat, momentarily thinking about what he had said before seeming to accept the story.

"I see. Well… well it's a good job you needed a new TV, anyway. That TV was as old as me," she laughed.

Patrick put on a half-limp smile to acknowledge her joke, but he was still horrified about what had happened. He asked Julia to stay the night on his sofa and she reluctantly agreed. He said he wanted someone there to look out for Doc. In all truth, he wanted someone else with him in case Eric came back.

Chapter 51

ISABELLE

Over the next few months, Isabelle's life changed again. Work was the same cold and lonely place, but her home life was what had really altered.

Eric sold all the clothes he had brought for her when she'd first moved into his place and replaced them with modest, plain garments to 'seem more professional', as he'd told her. He was right, she supposed, she needed to grow up and start acting her age. Slowly, she lost all validity of her own thoughts. She became a mould that Eric poured his wants and ideas into until she was less Isabelle and more Eric's project. Like clay in his hands, he moulded her to his every whim day to day.

Ever since the incident with Patrick, there had been a change in Eric. He had stopped treating her as a trophy—something precious to show off to the world—and instead was more callus, more demanding… in every way. He synced up their phones and told her it was in case she ever needed help—which she believed.

Isabelle never felt unsafe when she was with Eric. He was looking out for her. Yes, he would blow up at her at times but, in his defence, she often messed up and couldn't blame him for his reaction. She wanted to make him happy and kept telling herself how much she was looking after him and making her life better.

The money he had been giving her every month stopped. If she needed anything, she asked him for the money, and he would give her roughly what he thought it would cost and liked to have the receipts and change for all purchases when she got home. It was to help her learn better personal finance skills.

As the months went on, Isabelle started to lose significant amounts of weight. She became sheepish, jumping at the smallest sudden sounds around the office, whether it was Julia yelling at Albie or even a stapler being dropped. She was a shell of her old self and had lost all the confidence and light from her eyes. She wasn't sure how she felt anymore.

Her routines changed. Normal days in Isabelle's new life would pan out just so. She woke at 4 am to make Eric's breakfast and pack his lunch. Even if he decided he didn't need a packed lunch, she made sure to make it. At 6 am, she would wake Eric and, depending on his mood, she would either be greeted with a smile and a kiss or he would tell her he needed sex to wake him up properly. She obliged him either way.

The highly stimulating, erotic sex they'd initially had had fizzled into something more clinical. There was no passion anymore, just him using her for whatever he needed or wanted.

Then she would dress and get ready, before leaving for work after showing Eric what she would be wearing that day. If he was in a good mood, he would kiss her goodbye. These kisses kept that small flame alight within Isabelle. If he was in a bad mood, he would ignore her.

Lunch at work was always eaten alone at her desk and she'd taken to sometimes working through lunch to ensure she wouldn't be home late—Eric had started to get more and more annoyed if she was.

At 5 pm, she would head home. However, she did sometimes stop at the local convenience store to ensure she had everything for Eric's dinner. He always told her what he wanted the night before. While the dinner was cooking, she would clean, hoover the floors and dust or scrub the bathroom. Then she would wait for him to get home and usually read while keeping dinner warm enough in case he was late.

Sometimes, it had gone 7 pm before she received word from him, telling her that he was going to a work meal or that he had already eaten and not to wait up. She hadn't been invited to one work meal since the night when they took Doc to the vet.

When he eventually got home, he would eat dinner with her—often regaling her with some fantastic deal he'd made or meeting he'd had. He never asked her about her day or who she'd talked to. He would congratulate her on being so professional if she didn't have much to tell him. Once, she'd told him that Iris had come over to her desk to natter and he'd said that she needed to cut that out and act more professional.

After dinner, she usually went to bed and left him to his own devices. When he eventually joined her, he would either kiss her on the forehead before heading to sleep—or he would wake her, expecting sex.

This was her life now.

Every day was a new march to fit Eric's drum. She didn't fight back or resist in any way. She told herself everything he did was to help her improve her life. He was doing it because he cared.

Isabelle's work was starting to become affected; she would often rush projects or tasks to get them done as quickly as possible rather than taking her time. One day, as lunch ended, Julia asked Isabelle to come and see her in her office.

Isabelle crept towards Julia's office, unsure of what she had done. Would Julia yell at her? She really didn't want that, especially from Julia.

When she got to the office, Julia was waiting for her. "Have a seat, Isabelle." She pointed to the seat in front of her desk.

Isabelle perched on the edge of the seat.

"Isabelle, do you realise that, over the last month, people have been having to fix your work for you?"

Isabelle was startled. "What? What do you mean 'fix my work'?"

Julia explained how Freya and Albie were taking turns to go over her work on top of their own over the last month without Julia asking them to. Isabelle didn't understand why they would want to help her. They hadn't spoken for months now.

Noticing the puzzled look on her face, Julia continued, "We have all been worried about you, Isabelle. I don't know what happened between you all, but they obviously still care about you. Iris brought this to my attention this morning after she found out."

Isabelle broke down. She'd thought everyone hated her. She was overwhelmed by the emotion she had pushed down for so long and hit a breaking point.

She sat, head in her hands, and sobbed. Julia passed her over some tissues, which Isabelle happily took.

"Is there anything you need to talk about? If there is, I'm here for you," Julia asked compassionately.

Thoughts of Eric flooded Isabelle's mind. *What would he think if he knew about this?*

She quickly cleaned her face with the tissues and composed herself. "No, I'm fine Julia. Don't worry, I'll do better. I'm sorry for letting you down."

Julia was bewildered by the sudden, emotional change in Isabelle. She took a moment before asking, “Do you still want to be a journalist, Isabelle? I might have someone—”

Isabelle cut her off. “I should get back to work. I won’t let this happen again, Julia; I’ll work harder to make sure I'm not a burden on everyone.” She got up and started to head towards the door but paused as Julia spoke.

“Well, one; you’re not a burden. Two… you know where I am.” It was clear that Julia was annoyed by having been cut off but let she let Isabelle leave.

On the way back to her desk, Isabelle could feel eyes on her. When she glanced around, she saw Albie leaning against Freya’s desk as usual but, this time, they were looking over at her. She flushed and looked at the ground until she reached her desk.

The rest of the day, she couldn’t stop overthinking all Julia had said. Why was Julia so worried about her? Was it about her work?

Was… *she* different?

If she was, then she was a better version of herself. Eric was helping her; she told herself this over and over.

At the end of the day, Freya smiled at Isabelle as she passed her.

Unsure of what to do, Isabelle lowered her head.

Chapter 52

PATRICK

Patrick woke to a knock at his door. It took him some time to get out of his bed and into his wheelchair, but his jaw dropped as he answered it.

"Iris?" he asked, as though in disbelief. "What are you doing here?"

She was dressed for work and held multiple bags. "Well," she gestured for him to move. "Are you going to leave me standing out here all day?"

He wheeled backwards and let her in, and she blew past him in an instant.

"Have you got a table or something?"

Patrick was still bewildered about why she was in his flat but directed her into the kitchen. She threw her bags onto the counter and started to rustle through them, looking for something. Doc wandered in, looked around, and nibbled at his food like nothing was amiss.

"Oh," Iris said, giving Doc a sideways glance. You have a cat… fair. I'm more of a dog person, myself—oh, here it is." She pulled out a badge from her bag with Patrick's face on. "Julia asked me to come round and give this to you; I hear you're coming back to the office next week?" She passed him the badge.

"What? No, I'm not—I'm not coming back… Iris, I don't know why you thought I was." He looks down at the badge.

"Why not? Julia seemed pretty sure you were, or I wouldn't be here." Iris said, tone emotionless.

Patrick thought, trying to think of a justification for why he couldn't go back to Iris. "It would be too hard with Isabelle there—and I fell out with Albie. Freya probably hates me, too."

Iris scoffed at him. "Seriously, Patrick. Grow the fuck up. It's work, not a social club. Do you think I go there five days a week because I'm friends with everyone? No—and if I'm frank, Patrick, I couldn't care less if they didn't like me."

Patrick was shocked by her brutal honesty. "But—" he spluttered. "It's not that simple, Iris. Things happened with me, Isabelle and Albie—plus, everyone's lives have moved on. They wouldn't want me there."

Iris put her hands on her temple, rubbing her head as though in pain. "Right, I'm gonna lay it out plain and simple for you. You're being self-absorbed. Not everything is about you, Patrick. Yeah, from what I hear, you screwed it up with Isabelle. So what? Deal with the consequences of your actions!" She picked up her bags, ready to leave. "And Albie?" she continued. "Seriously? You're worried about *him* holding a grudge? I doubt he has the brain capacity for that."

She walked past him and started to walk down the hallway. He watched, gobsmacked.

"Just grow a pair of balls and come back to work. I'll see you next week."

Patrick felt like she had walked in and dropkicked him. "Iris—" Patrick stopped her as she was about to shut the door. She turned, giving him a bland look. "Thank you."

She smiled and closed the door without response.

Patrick needed coffee. A tornado had just blown through his house—he needed a pick-me-up. Doc jumped onto the counter. "She was telling me the truth, wasn't she Doc?"

Doc sat, licked his paw, and meowed.

"I think... I think I needed that. Do you think Julia sent her on purpose?"

He messaged Julia, thanking her for sending Iris around with the badge and asked her to take him with her to the office when she went on Monday. He spent the rest of the weekend trying to build up the courage to make amends with the people he hurt. After what Iris said, he knew it would be easy to start with Albie.

Isabelle? Now, that was a different story. He had no idea how to approach her.

On Monday, his first day back, he put on his old work clothes. They didn't fit him anymore, but he had nothing else. He had woken up 3 hours before Julia was due. He needed some time to prepare himself. He had breakfast with Doc and took a moment to compose himself.

Julia knocked on his door precisely on time and he opened it, expecting her to come in, but she waited outside.

"I'll lock up for you, don't worry. Now, come on or we'll be late."

It took Patrick a while to breach the door of his flat. It had been months since he had been outside, and he couldn't hide the anxiety it gave him to do so.

To him, it felt the same as if he were preparing to do a bungee jump for the first time with a grave fear of heights. Julia didn't rush him after seeing the look on his face and allowed him to take his time. Eventually, he slowly rolled out of his door. Julia quickly got around behind him and locked it before grabbing hold of the chair's handles.

"Right, we best be off." She started to push Patrick onto the public path, heading to the office. Patrick was clutching at his armrests. Everything seemed enormous to him; he had never felt so small. The cars, which seemed to fly by, made him jump every time. Julia tried to talk to him, but he found it hard to hear and talk to her while she was behind him.

The walk wasn't long but to Patrick, it had felt like a marathon. His heart was racing. Every minute thing he had taken for granted before was now a challenge or something to fear. Simply crossing the road had turned into an ordeal, with Julia looking for a drop curb to take his chair down and back up again when crossing the street.

By the time they reached the office, he was exhausted. "I don't think I'll ever get used to that," he muttered as Julia walked past him to open the door.

She helped him inside before walking off. "You've got this from here."

She left him in the doorway and walked to her office.

Patrick sat, unsure of what to do. The office seemed so much bigger than he remembered.

Inside, he looked around and saw Albie and Freya in the kitchen and immediately cast his gaze down; he felt guilty even looking at them.

His guilt was interrupted as Iris bumped into his back. "Oh, sorry. I didn't see you there. What are you doing sitting in the doorway?"

Patrick was oddly glad to see her. "Hi, Iris. Erm, where do I go?" he quietly asked.

Iris walked past him, tutting. "You're not a kid, Patrick. Figure it out." She headed to her desk, and he felt stupid for asking.

"I go to my desk… God, I'm so stupid," he muttered under his breath and slowly rolled to his desk where he immediately encountered a problem: his desk chair was in the way.

He didn't know what to do and sat, thinking of ways around it, before a large hand landed on his shoulder.

"'Ello, 'Ello. What do we have here, then?" The bellowing laugh came from behind him.

Patrick slowly turned to find Albie's hulking figure in front of him. *How is he bigger?*

"'Bout time you came back; I was outnumbered over here!" Albie's cheerfulness was infectious, and Patrick smiled slightly. He'd missed this.

"Good morning, Albie."

Albie smiled back. "Morning, mate. Is this chair in the way?" He quickly pivoted around Patrick and pulled the chair out of the way for him.

"Thank you. I wasn't sure what to do."

Albie jumped in the chair and wriggled around on it. "Nah, all good, big man—just ask. I've got you. I'm stealing this chair, though, if you don't need it?"

Patrick looked down at his chair and looked back up to Albie, quirking a brow. "Feel free, I guess?"

Albie grinned. "Sorted! Cheers, bud. Catch you later." He got up and put a knee on the chair, ready to sweep away like he was riding a scooter. Patrick couldn't help but smile—it was good to see him again. "Good to have you back big man," Albie said as he sped away to his desk.

Patrick hadn't known what to expect from Albie, but he had just been himself and it relaxed Patrick to know that, while so much was different, that hadn't changed.

He pulled himself behind his desk and it was strange, but it felt good to be back. After a moment, he got to work, zoning out the rest of the morning and violently tapping away at his keyboard—back with a vengeance. He didn't even notice when Isabelle came in. He was in his element.

No one approached him the entire morning and Patrick was glad. By lunch, people started to leave until it was just him, Isabelle and Iris left in the office. He hadn't thought about lunch. How could he forget about lunch?

He decided he would just work through the break, but Iris wandered over to him. "Don't tell me you didn't bring any food?"

Patrick nodded embarrassedly, and Iris held out her hand. "Oh, for God's sake. Give me some money, then. I'm only doing this once."

Patrick pulled out his wallet and gave her some money which she took before returning shortly with a convenience store bag of lunch for Patrick. "Here, take this. Just don't forget next time—I won't be doing this again."

Patrick smiled. "Thanks, Iris, you're a good friend."

Iris's eyebrows raised like she hadn't expected him to say that and nodded her head once before walking back to her packed lunch.

Patrick sat and ate the lunch Iris grabbed for him. As he ate, he looked around the office; everything was as he remembered, and it put him at ease. He felt safe here, he realised. It was like the old days, him eating lunch alone.

As he scanned the room, his eyes caught Isabelle's eye, and his gaze stumbled. "Erm—hi, Isabelle." Patrick held up a hand up to greet her.

Isabelle noticed him, nodded, and looked back down at her desk.

Patrick slowly lowered his hand, a sense of awkwardness creeping over him. Iris approached his desk with a note, placed it down, and left. The Post-it note just said, *Leave her alone.*

Patrick looked over to Iris who, in turn, gave him a death stare.

Patrick kept to himself for the rest of the day, not wanting to make any more waves. He did catch Freya glancing over at him a few times but, when he noticed her, she would quickly look away. It was more than Patrick had thought he would get from her today.

As the day was wrapping up, he knew he had to talk to Albie. He waited until Albie was in the kitchen alone before rolling over to him.

"Hey, Albie?"

Albie was facing away from him and jumped. "Cor! Trying to sneak up on me, were ya?" He gave his trademark laugh.

"Can I talk to you for a moment?" Patrick sheepishly asked.

"Yeah! Course, big man; what can I do you for?" Albie leaned back on the kitchen side and crossed his arms.

Patrick shuffled slightly in his chair and let out a breath. "I wanted to apologise for my outburst the last time I saw you. I wasn't—"

Albie held his hand up. "Hold your horses. I was a bit of a dickhead, myself. Water under the bridge?" He held his hand out as though waiting for a handshake.

Patrick, somewhat flabbergasted, met Albie's hand with his. Albie then crushed his hand, shaking it.

"Good man, you should come to lunch with me tomorrow like the old days!"

Patrick nodded in agreement and they both headed back to their desks. He felt elated—it was good to know that he and Albie were good again.

Juila took Patrick home that evening, and he struggled to keep his eyes open all the while. She then told him that it would perhaps be best to stagger his return to work, and that they should first start with just three times per week.

She then told him that she was proud of him, making his heart swell, and to get some rest.

The next day, Albie called Patrick at lunch to complain that Patrick had stood him up. Patrick apologised and explained how exhausted he was and that he needed some rest.

"Sounds like we need to build you up; you need some bloody stamina!"

They laughed and Patrick asked Albie to come around to help him exercise as he had offered before. He needed to get to the point where he could wheel himself around outside the house with ease.

The following month went by quickly, and Patrick enjoyed being back in the office. His friendship with Albie was stronger than before and they often went to lunch just the two of them. Freya often declined to come and was still cold towards Patrick.

Albie began going over to Patrick's place with weights and resistance bands and worked out with Patrick at home. When they first started, Patrick felt awkward and embarrassed at how little he could manage—but Albie surprised him once more. He told Patrick how he had been taking a course and wanted to become a personal trainer and told Patrick how he might get him walking with a walking stick in the future. Patrick was completely taken aback; he hadn't realised how great of a friend Albie had been to him all this time.

"Thanks so much, Albie. You're a real mate."

His words caught Albie off guard and, embarrassed, he punched Patrick softly on the arm.

"Come on," he said. "We have stretches for you to do, so none of that soppy shit, okay?" Albie scoffed but couldn't help but smile.

Chapter 53

ISABELLE

When Isabelle walked into work that first day and saw Patrick at his desk, she couldn't stop her mind from racing. She didn't know what to do or say. At lunch, when she realised, he was just going to sit at his desk, her heart had started to pound. She was glad that Iris had been there at least, so it wasn't the two of them, alone.

When he'd said 'hello', she'd wanted to say it back but had resisted. All she could think about was how Eric would react if he found out. She didn't have the brainpower for all this right now.

The next day, when he wasn't in, she was strangely disappointed, however. Seeing him toil away at work in the corner of her eye was nostalgic. It made her think of the past, which comforted her despite still being painful.

She started to notice that he was coming into the office every other day and working from home the other two. He would greet her every time he came into the office.

She never responded—but she didn't really know why.

Her days were the same as always, but the one difference was getting to see Patrick trying his best to get back to work. Knowing him, she knew he was trying his best.

Finally, one morning, she responded to his good morning with one of her own.

He looked so shocked when she said it that it made her laugh a little.

Over time, these 'good mornings' evolved into brief chats—mainly about Doc. These small conversations cheered up Isabelle in a way she hadn't felt for a long time. She didn't interact with anyone much outside of Eric.

Isabelle sat down and started to eat that evening after serving Eric his. He was telling her about his day; he had a lunch meeting which he'd enjoyed.

She tried to act like she cared while eating, nodding along and asking obvious questions. He turned the tables on her, asking her to tell him about her day. It was a rare, good day for her; he never asked her questions. She told him about being thanked for doing an excellent job by Julia, sitting in the sun eating her lunch and Patrick showing her a new picture of Doc—

"What the fuck did you just say?" Eric slammed his cutlery on the table.

Isabelle jumped; her heart stopped. She realised, too late, what she just said.

"Did you say 'Patrick'?"

Isabelle put her arms out in defence, opening her mouth without making a sound.

"You never told me he returned to work, did you?"

Isabelle's head dropped. "I'm sorry, I didn't think—"

Without warning, Eric launched his plate across the room, and it shattered as it hit the floor. "You're *sorry*? For keeping secrets—from *me*? What are you doing behind my back, huh?"

He shot to his feet, walked over and launched Isabelle's plate, too. Isabelle was terrified. "I'm sorry! Please stop—I'm sorry!" Her fear was making her cry, and Eric tutted.

"What are these, crocodile tears? Are you trying to manipulate me? You snivelling, little bitch?" He pulled her up by the arm, so she was standing, too. "Now, look me in the eye and tell me you're not sneaking behind my back with that fucking cripple."

Isabelle's eyes pleaded with him to stop. "I would never do that to you, please."

Eric threw her arm away from him with so much strength that it knocked her to her seat before walking to the bedroom. "Clean that shit up." He yelled, pointing at the broken plates and food which covered the floor.

Isabelle rushed to the kitchen, grabbed the bin and hurriedly started to put the fractured pieces into it. As she cleaned, Eric came back from the bedroom and started to lay down the law.

"You're gonna stop working there as of tomorrow, you hear me?"

Isabelle's heart sank; her job was the one thing left in her life that she had chosen.

"No," she said under her breath.

Eric turned back to her, his face contorting with anger. "What did you just say?"

It hit Isabelle, then. She knew she had to take a stand, or she would be left with nothing. "I said no! I'm not gonna quit."

Eric lunged towards her, grabbed both of her wrists tightly and pulled her close to him. "No?" He threw her towards the table and her back slammed into the edge of it. Her back stung but she recovered quickly and stood tall. She'd found her confidence and was determined to protect the one thing in her life that he didn't control.

"Eric, I said *no*!" she shouted at him.

It took a split-second for Eric to clench a fist and throw a punch at her face. The blow connected with her temple and Isabelle fell, her legs giving way beneath her as her head cracked against the side of the table.

Blood began to pour down her forehead. Her vision grew fuzzy, and her head pounded. When she opened her eyes, Eric was crouched over her, slapping her cheeks. "Wake up right now."

His slaps had force behind them, hurting Isabelle more.

"See what you did?" he yelled over and over before standing up and walking off.

Isabelle tried to stand but the strength had been sapped from her body. Blood dripped from her brow. It hurt so much that she wanted to scream in pain but the blood in her mouth was stopping her.

Eric walked back into her eyeline wearing his jacket. "I'm going out and tomorrow you're leaving that fucking job, you hear me? When I get back, this shit better be cleaned up." He slammed the door behind him.

No longer scared to cry, Isabelle began to wail. He was a monster.

Her eye was beginning to swell to the point that she couldn't see out of it. She shakenly got to her feet using the table to pull herself up, went to the kitchen and grabbed her phone. Instinctively, she wanted to call the police but was scared.

She went to her contacts and phoned Freya.

The phone rang twice before Freya picked up. "Hello?"

As soon as Isabelle heard her voice, she started to cry again.

"Babes, what's wrong? What happened?"

Despite their issues, the care in Freya's tone was genuine and Isabelle cried harder, wincing in pain and crying out in a different way.

"Are you hurt?" Freya was trying her best to get Isabelle to talk.

"He… he hit me." It hurt to speak, and she winced again.

"Isabelle, listen to me… is he still there?" Isabelle forced out a *No* before

Freya jumped into action. "Okay, I'm coming with Albie now. We will be there in five minutes." Isabelle began to sob again. "I'm going to stay on the phone with you the entire time, okay? You don't have to say anything; just stay on the phone with me."

Isabelle heard Freya attempt to cover the phone as she told Albie that Eric had hit her; Isabelle's hands started to shake. She heard Albie swearing in the background and telling Freya that he was getting his keys.

She listened as they got in the car and started to drive while Freya tried her best to calm her down. She couldn't believe this was real.

"We're almost there, okay, baby girl?"

Speaking hurt too much, so Isabelle started to hum an acknowledgement. Within minutes, they had arrived. When they were outside the door, Freya asked Isabelle to let them in and she slowly got to her feet and opened the door.

Freya pushed it open the rest of the way and, when she finally saw Isabelle—her shirt covered in blood, her eyes swollen shut, looking scared and broken—Freya threw her arms around her. The strength in Isabelle's legs failed and she collapsed in Freya's arms.

"Were here, were here now," Freya kept repeating. "You're safe, you're safe." She looked over to Albie, her eyes on fire. "Get a bag and get her things. She's never coming back here," Freya ordered Albie.

Freya was cleaning the blood from Isabelle's face while stroking her hair, trying her best to reassure her.

"I've got it. Let's get her out of here," Albie said, and Freya thanked him.

"She needs to go to the hospital; I think she has a concussion."

Albie's fists were clenched, his fingernails digging into the palms of his hands as he nodded. Freya gently helped Isabelle to her feet. "Come on, babes, let's get you to the hospital."

Isabelle couldn't stop repeating the phrase, "He did it, he did it."

Freya got her to her feet and, as she did, they heard the front door open. Three heads simultaneously turned.

Eric started to walk into the room, his face morphing from shock to anger as he took in the sight of Isabelle in the arms of Freya and Albie. He made to lunge towards them, but Albie quickly got in front of both girls and threw a combination of powerful punches. Eric flopped to the floor.

Albie was bloodthirsty. He wanted to beat Eric until he was a stain on the floor and walked towards him as he scrambled away from Albie's imposing figure, expression horrified.

"Enough!" Freya yelled.

Albie stopped in place, breathing heavily like a monster, his eyes locked onto Eric.

"Take Isabelle out to the car now," she barked.

"You stay right there; if you move an inch, I will kill you." Albie pointed down at Eric. He walked backwards, keeping his focus on Eric. When he got to them, he picked Isabelle up effortlessly. Isabelle could feel Albie's heart pounding in his chest. She was terrified by the anger which emanated from him but, when she looked up at him, he was looking down at her with that same warm smile. "Come on, you, let's get you to the car." With that, he began to walk her out of the apartment. "You gonna be alright?" he asked Freya as he passed Eric, who was still snivelling on the floor and wiping his dripping nose.

She nodded. "I'll be right behind you".

Albie slowly led Isabelle out of the door, but Isabelle stopped and turned, she didn't want to leave Freya alone with him. Albie understood without saying a word and stood just ahead of her. Arm still around her supporting her.

Looking down at Eric, Freya crossed her arms. As soon as he thought Albie was out of eyeshot, Eric tried to reach his feet, but Freya swiftly kicked him in between the legs like she was aiming for a football.

"You're a pathetic waste of space."

She kicked him again, this time in the stomach.

"You're never gonna see that girl again, you hear me?" She kicked him one more time. "You hear me?" she bellowed at him.

Eric let out a *Yes* between ragged breaths. As she turned and walked out of the flat, Eric started laughing, spluttering on the floor.

Freya turned, surprised to hear him laughing. He pulled himself to his knees, holding on to his ribs. She shook her head and decided she had to leave and call the police. There was nothing left to do. As she turned, she saw the two of them standing there in shock, "come on let's get her down to the car."

Walking away, she pulled her phone out and called them, explaining what had happened and that they were taking Isabelle to the hospital.

When they got to the car, Albie helped Isabelle into the back seat closed the door softly behind him and turned to check on Freya. Isabelle couldn't help but watch. It was clear Freya was shaken and he walked up to her, putting his hand softly on the side of her face. "You okay, darlin?"

She just stared, pleading with her eyes to for them to leave. Albie noticed immediately, opened the passenger-side door for her and drove off.

They rushed Isabelle to the hospital, where she was diagnosed with a concussion. Her wounds were stitched and treated. She hadn't realised, but Eric had knocked one of her molars out, which caused the amount of blood to seep from her mouth. They cleaned and patched her up and took her to a private room. Freya didn't leave her side and refused to let go of her hand unless directed by the doctors.

The police took all three of their statements and Eric was resultantly arrested. Isabelle was told she had to stay the night at the hospital to keep an eye on her. Freya stayed by her side but sent Albie to get his hand x-rayed; it had swollen like a balloon. He came back a few hours later wearing a cast. He got Isabelle to sign and draw on it, making jokes all the while.

Isabelle was numb, though; everything that had happened didn't feel real. The only reason she knew she wasn't having a nightmare was because Freya held and squeezed her hand. It calmed her, though. Even after all they'd been through, she was still her friend.

Isabelle didn't really talk the rest of the night, but she did cry sporadically. Eventually, she managed to drift off to sleep.

Chapter 54

PATRICK

Patrick was starting to enjoy having a routine again: getting up to feed Doc, rolling to work with Julia and then working. He spent more time talking to Iris and enjoyed her no-bullshit way of speaking; she constantly pulled him up on things, but he appreciated it. He was glad to have a good friend in her.

He enjoyed it now that he and Isabelle were exchanging a few words and becoming more comfortable around each other. It was a slow process, but their small chats about Doc meant a lot.

He arrived at work at the same time as any other day. After a small chat with Iris—she told him he needed to buy an ironing board short enough to use because she was sick of seeing his creased shirts, making Patrick laugh—he wheeled himself to his desk. He was surprised, however, to not see Albie and Freya; they usually arrived before him. When he noticed they were officially late, he got to work but sent him a text to check-in. Albie texted him back quickly, telling him he'd have to take a bus. Patrick laughed and got back to work. He presumed he'd had one too many beers watching football or something; he was looking forward to seeing how he smoothed this over with Julia.

About half an hour later, Albie turned up. Patrick's eyes shot to the cast on his hand. He quickly pulled out of his desk and rolled to meet Albie at the door. "What happened? Are you okay?"

Albie looked slightly ashamed. "Ah… yeah, I'm good, mate. Was a muppet and broke my hand last night is all."

Patrick sarcastically tilted his head. "Well, I'm pretty sure I could figure that one out."

Albie let out a classic laugh.

"Come on, what happened?" Patrick asked.

"I let this douchebag Eric have its last night," he said, his shame quickly making way for pride.

This piqued Patrick's interest. "The guy Isabelle is seeing?"

Albie slapped his forehead. "Bugger, I probably wasn't supposed to say anything."

Patrick intensely asked again what had happened and Albie quickly explained in a hushed tone. Patrick immediately swung his wheelchair around and headed straight for Julia's office.

"I'm really sorry, Julia," he said. "But I need to take a few hours off."

Julia was surprised. "Oh? What's wrong?"

Patrick was impatient. "Can I?"

Julia raised a brow; she hadn't seen Patrick this impatient for a while. "You can have the morning; I expect you back after lunch."

Patrick got his phone out and ordered a taxi; it turned up quickly. "Where you off to mate?" the driver asked.

Albie answered for Patrick. "Round trip to the hospital. We're gonna drop him off, then bring me back here." Patrick looked at Albie, puzzled. "Well, you're gonna need my help, ain't ya?"

For a moment, Patrick had forgotten his wheelchair. He thanked Albie and, with his help, got into the taxi. When they reached the hospital, Albie told him where he had to go and left him there.

It was Patrick's first time outside the house by himself, a fact which hadn't even registered until they arrived. He made his way around the hospital to the ward Isabelle was in. He politely asked the nurse where Isabelle was, but they were reluctant to let him see her. As he was turning away, however, Freya rounded the corner and spotted him.

"What are you doing here?" she asked.

Patrick was still amped up and full of drive to see Isabelle. "I heard what happened from Albie and took a taxi here. Is she okay?"

Freya sighed deeply. "That bloody idiot, what's he doing going around telling people?" She stood, hand on hip, thinking.

"You have five minutes... and if she doesn't want you there, you're out, got me?" she asked sternly, eyes fixed on Patrick's.

He was slightly scared and nodded quickly.

"Come with me." Freya headed to Isabelle's room. When they reached the door, Freya paused. "Don't fucking upset her, you hear? Or I'll beat your ass."

She opened the door. "Hey, babes, you have a visitor. Are you up to it?"

Isabelle was surprised but nodded out of curiosity. The gumption left Patrick's body, but he slowly rolled himself into the room, regardless. "Hey, Isabelle." He looked up and saw her.

Her face was swollen and bruised and there was a large cut across her forehead which had been stitched together. Patrick was taken aback; he hadn't known what to expect.

He wheeled around her bed and parked his wheelchair. Freya headed to the door to give them some time. "I'll be back in five. If you need me, Isabelle, just call for me."

Isabelle nodded towards Freya, and she left.

It was just Patrick and Isabelle in the room. They hadn't been alone like this for a long time, and even the air felt awkward. Patrick wasn't sure what to say but knew he had to break the silence. "Are you okay?" He knew that was the dumbest question he could ask. He grasped his forehead. "God, I'm sorry; what a stupid question!"

Isabelle let out a little laugh. "It's okay, I'm doing okay-ish. But Freya is looking after me."

Patrick was glad to have made her laugh. "Oh good, she is bloody terrifying, though." Patrick decided to act silly. He wanted to make her laugh again, so didn't mention what had happened. He just wanted to see her smile.

Isabelle barely said a word, but lay listening to Patrick as he told her stories. He pulled out his phone and started to show her cute videos of Doc and told her all about Iris' near-daily critics he had been getting.

Isabelle smiled all the while. "I've missed you."

They were the first words she had spoken since confirming she was alright, and when she did, her words knocked Patrick back. He hadn't expected her to say that, and it hit him right in the chest.

She smiled at him until their allotted five minutes had passed, Freya came back to check on Isabelle. When she opened the door and saw her laughing with Patrick, however, she decided to leave them be for a while longer and headed to her car to sleep.

By the time Freya returned, Isabelle was asleep. "Time for you to leave, Patrick," she said.

Patrick agreed, "Yeah, Julia wants me back after lunch." He headed to the door.

"Let me see you out." Freya came up behind Patrick, grabbed his handles and started to push him. The aura Freya was giving off felt off; Patrick could tell she wanted to say something. "Are you okay, Freya?"

Freya stopped in place and spun Patrick around, so he was facing her. There was a pause where she surveyed him from head to toe before finally opening her mouth. "You treated her like shit, you know? You broke her heart. You fucked up, Patrick." Freya was furious and her fury was targeted straight at Patrick.

He attempted to interject and apologise but Freya continued without pause. "You know she went through hell while you were in your coma; she was there every day watching over you, talking to you, looking after you. And what thanks does she get? You discard her like a broken toy."

Everything she said hit Patrick like a ton of bricks; he knew she was right, and she took a breath to calm herself. "But, somehow, even though you were a giant tool—you helped today. I didn't think I would see her smile like that for a long time." She exhaled heavily. "If you gonna be helping her like this, you better promise me right here, right now, that you will look after her." She leaned down to look at him directly in the eyes. "If you don't... Patrick, you don't want to know what I'll do to you."

Her eyes alone warned Patrick that he didn't want to find out. He carefully said, "I promise."

Freya backed off the wheelchair. "Good, I'm gonna be watching you! Now, let's call Albie so he can get you back to work."

Patrick texted Albie while Freya pushed him to a bench outside the hospital. She parked his chair so that it was facing the bench and sat down.

Albie eventually arrived in the taxi with a big smile on his face. "Ah, look here, two of my favourite people finally talking to each other." He stood beside them and put a hand on each of their shoulders. "How's our girl doing?"

Freya stood up, shrugging his hand from her shoulder. "I'm gonna get back to her now; I'll call you later." She kissed Albie on the cheek and looked at Patrick for a moment like he was different, but she couldn't pinpoint the change.

She nodded towards him and walked off.

On the ride back to the office, Patrick thanked Albie for protecting Isabelle.

"Mate, no problems at all. I wanted to kick his ass more, but Freya stopped me." He didn't realise it, but he was tearing at the plaster on his hand.

"It's all good, Albie, you've done enough. Thank you" Patrick wanted Albie to know how much he appreciated his being there when he couldn't be.

Once they got to the office, they received a long dressing down from Julia for not telling her what was going on. Albie took the brunt of her wrath, however, and it took everything within Patrick to not laugh. The sight of Albie trying to give Julia puppy dog eyes was hysterical.

Chapter 55

ISABELLE

Isabelle was in hospital for two days. During this time, they carried out every possible test they could to ensure that she was healthy. She also spent some time talking to a therapist and found that even their brief meetings left her feeling overwhelmed as their conversations gradually started to crack open a box she wasn't sure she wanted to open.

They released her on the weekend and planned for her to continue seeing a therapist once a week from then on. Freya didn't leave her side once except to quickly run home, shower and change her clothes once the entire time she was in the hospital. She was like a lioness protecting her cub.

Freya took Isabelle to her car. "You wanna come stay with me for a while?" she asked Isabelle and helped her into the car. Isabelle knew she had nowhere else to go and that staying with Freya would allow her to feel safe, so she nodded in agreement.

"Good," Freya nodded, and that was that. "Now let's get you home."

Living with Freya was comfortable, and, luckily, her friend had a spare room, which was now Isabelle's. Isabelle was also secretly glad to finally see Freya and Albie together with her own eyes. As it happened, he basically lived at Freya's, too, so there were three of them.

Isabelle tended to spend most of her time in her room, only leaving it when Freya dragged her out to watch the latest trashy reality show with her. She hadn't spoken much since the incident, so it seemed Freya was trying her best to get Isabelle to do everyday things with her to help bring her out of her shell. It wasn't working though, and Isabelle still felt as though she were trapped somehow, unable to speak even if she wanted to.

After a week of living at Freya's, however, Isabelle began to feel more comfortable and started voluntarily spending more time with Freya in the evenings, only retreating to her room when Freya was at work.

Freya came into her room one Saturday and exclaimed, "I think we need a bit of fresh air!" She was energetic. "Let's go shopping and get some more 'you' clothes! What you've been wearing isn't you and you can't keep wearing mine—so let's go shop till we drop! On me!"

Isabelle wasn't sure about going out and didn't want Freya to feel as though she needed to buy her clothes. Freya's beaming smile and energy convinced her to try, however. "Okay," she smiled tentatively. "But can it be a short trip?" She said, almost mouse-like.

Freya was ecstatic and shouted, "Yes!" She got her out of the door as quickly as she could and dragged Isabelle into as many shops as possible. She tried her best to get her opinions on anything that caught her eye, and slowly, Isabelle started to get into the swing of things and picked out clothes she liked. She was even beginning to have fun.

Freya grinned the entire time. After a few hours, Isabelle started to lag. "Right, one more shop, and then we'll head home," Freya said, and Isabelle nodded in agreement.

Freya pointed out a beautiful red sundress with white polka dots in the shop. "Oh my God, Isabelle, this is so you—you have to get this!"

Isabelle's eyes lit up when Freya showed her. "Can I?"

Freya couldn't believe she asked. "Erm yes! Imma go buy it now. Wait here. I'll be back in a moment." Freya snatched the dress from her hands and darted to the cashier to buy it.

It was the first time Isabelle had truly been alone outside the house in a long time. She had been sticking to Freya like glue, and with her gone, anxiety started to twist inside her. She backed up to the closest wall near the exit. Her head was turning at any slight noise or person walking past her; her breathing started to accelerate, her heart was beginning to beat like an engine warming up and the noise in the shop began to get louder and louder. A male shop assistant saw Isabelle standing against the wall and approached her.

"Afternoon, my name is Nathan; how can I help you today?" He smiled at her and seemed friendly, but all Isabelle could see was Eric.

She shook her head, pressing herself further away and dropped to the floor. Her hands were held up in a defensive position and without a thought, she began pleading with him. "Please don't, please."

She kept repeating the words louder and louder and the shop assistant backed away quickly, his hands also held up as he looked around for anyone to help.

Freya sprinted over to Isabelle and dropped to her knees. "What happened, babes?"

Isabelle began to cry, shaking her head and uncertain. Freya levelled the shop assistant with a scowl.

"Woah, I didn't do anything. I just came over to offer some help."

Freya turned back to Isabelle, speaking softly. "You're okay, lovely. You're okay." She stroked her hair and hugged her. "Let's get you home." She helped Isabelle off the ground and, though it took some time, they eventually got home.

Isabelle quickly beelined to her room, where she buried herself under her duvet. Freya gave her some time before coming in to speak to her. She entered her room and sat on the end of her bed. "Babes, what happened?"

Isabelle couldn't bring herself to look at Freya. "I saw him, Freya. I saw him." Tears started to roll down her cheeks. "When that guy came towards me like that, all I saw was him."

Freya lay down on the bed next to her. "You safe here with me, babes."

They lay in silence for a while and, eventually, Isabelle drifted off to sleep.

Freya carefully got out of bed and let Isabelle sleep. On her sofa, she tried to process everything that had happened, muttering to herself. "Everything seemed fine. I should have taken her to the cashier with me."

When Albie arrived and found Freya close to tears, he wrapped her into his arms on instinct. "Hey, hey. What's happened, beautiful? Come here."

Sobbing into his shoulder, she mumbled the words, "I tried to help; I really did."

Albie stroked her hair and sighed. "Let it out darlin', let it out."

After a while, Freya composed herself. They sat talking about what had happened, and Albie said what he had been thinking for the last few days. "Look, babes, you know I love you, but you can't do this by yourself. Isabelle needs professional help. She needs to lean on other people, not just you."

Freya knew he was right but didn't want to accept it. She sat in silence in Albie's arms for a while.

"Come on then, you. Let's get some grub going." While he walked to the kitchen, Freya grabbed her phone and sent a message.

You need to come round tomorrow. I'll come to get you.

Chapter 56

PATRICK

Patrick wheeled his chair through Freya's front door. When she'd texted him that he should come over today last night, he'd had no idea what to expect but, as she opened the door and beckoned him through, he found that her flat was incredible. He could hardly even believe someone lived there; it looked like a show home.

Freya walked to the sofa and beckoned Patrick to pull up next to her. "Isabelle is struggling," she said, breaking the easy silence they had maintained throughout the entire car ride. "She needs to speak to someone about what happened, and I'm not sure if I'm the right person to get her to do it." The confession shocked Patrick, and it seemed to take something out of Freya to admit it. She looked at him, eyes pleading. "I'm trusting *you* to try. Please don't let me down, Patrick."

Patrick didn't really know what she wanted him to do but nodded his head, regardless. "Okay, erm, I'll try…"

Freya thanked him and directed him to Isabelle's room.

Once outside, Patrick knocked on her door. "Hey Isabelle… it's me. Can I come in?"

He heard a faint *yes* and Freya opened the door for him. He rolled in and found Isabelle sitting in bed, her legs crossed, reading. He pulled his chair up beside her and they sat in silence for a while.

"How you doing? Not seen you for a bit." Patrick's words were so awkward that Isabelle couldn't help but laugh.

"Yeah, I'm doing good," she giggled, covering her mouth.

Patrick wasn't sure what small talk to start, seeing as he had been called in for one reason. Lost for words, he decided that throwing himself into the deep end was the best option.

"So, I heard what happened yesterday…"

Isabelle immediately tried to stop Patrick from continuing, but he carried on.

"I think you need to speak to someone, Isabelle. Like someone professional. You went through a really messed up situation, anyone would be struggling."

Isabelle sat, stone-faced, so Patrick continued. "Talking to someone is always better than keeping this kinda thing in."

Still nothing from Isabelle. Patrick sighed. He realised he wasn't going to break through to her like this and wheeled himself closer so he could take her hand; she flinched when he did.

"Sorry," Patrick pulled his hand away on instinct. "Isabelle, when my parents' died, I didn't properly speak to anyone about it for most of my life; it was all-consuming. My grief was my life. I always rejected the help of professionals, and I only got worse. I was at my lowest when we were together, but you put the effort in with me to help me get better, no matter how long it took. I never got to properly thank you for that."

Isabelle's eyes began to well up.

"I'm gonna help you the same way you helped me, no matter how long it takes." Tears started to fall down her face. Patrick continued, "I know we're not together now, but I can still do this for you as your friend if you'll trust me to?"

Isabelle threw her arms around Patrick's shoulders, hugging him. She cried into his shoulder for a while, and Patrick, not wanting her to feel on edge, air-hugged her back.

Freya heard the crying and rushed in. "What's happening?" She saw Patrick awkwardly air-hugging Isabelle as she cried into his shoulder.

Patrick looked over to her, which made Freya hide a laugh. She slowly closed the door to give them more time as she could tell he wasn't upsetting her if she was hugging him.

"Thank you, Patrick," Isabelle stopped crying after a while.

"Erm. I mean, that's okay; I don't think I've done anything yet…" Patrick was a little confused. "So, well, I'm thinking—if you want me to—I could come with you to your therapy. Obviously, I won't come in with you, but I'll wait outside for you and be there if you want me to be after… if you like, of course?"

Isabelle was hesitant; she wasn't sure if she was ready to talk about it, but she knew that if Freya had called Patrick, she must have been worried about her. Plus, Patrick genuinely seemed like he wanted to help her. "Okay… I'll try. But it has to be a female therapist."

Patrick was surprised. "Yeah! Yeah, of course. I'll get Freya to see if she can find something for you and then we can organise something, yeah?" Isabelle nodded in agreement and Patrick looked deep into her eyes. "I promise, I'm here for you—whatever you need."

They sat together for a short while longer and Isabelle requested daily pictures and videos of Doc which Patrick, of course, happily agreed to.

Freya eventually knocked on the door, "Want me to drop you off home, Patrick? I need to go pick up Albie."

Patrick nodded in thanks and said goodbye to Isabelle.

"Thank you for today, Patrick." Freya was driving, and didn't look at Patrick. "After everything you put her through, I'm glad you're actually trying to make amends. But if you're doing this, you have to make sure to see it through. This isn't something you can throw away. You have to step up and be the best friend you can to that girl—no hidden agendas or anything like that, you hear me?"

Patrick, for once, spoke up for himself. "I wouldn't have agreed to it otherwise, Freya. I just want to do for her what she did for me, nothing else."

Freya's face relaxed slightly as her shoulders lost some of their tension. "You're making it hard to hate you still, you know?"

***

Isabelle started therapy the following week and, for the next few after, Patrick's being with her was the only thing keeping her there. It was all too much for her at the start and she'd be exhausted by the time Freya arrived to pick them up.

Still, over time, she trusted Patrick to calm her and help put her mind in a different state after the therapy. A slight routine started to form. They'd walk around a local park and stop at a coffee shop near Freya's place. He thought it would be best to stay away from *Rachael's.*

Their friendship grew stronger with each day, and they started to joke around with each other like they used to. It was a chance for them to be friends—something they hadn't gotten to be before.

Patrick was incredibly attentive towards Isabelle, looking out for her in any way he possibly could. This led to him spending long periods of time around Freya's place. At first, Freya was as frosty as ever with him, but after a while, she slowly warmed up to this new Patrick; he was so different from she'd met all that time ago.

When Isabelle had been going to her therapy for a while now, she told Patrick that their autumn walks in the park were something she looked forward to every week. Her therapist was a woman and Isabelle felt comfortable opening up to her, even though having her listen brought Isabelle to tears.

As the sessions went on, and Isabelle told her therapist all about what happened with Eric, she began to understand it wasn't her fault that it happened. It was an abusive relationship, and he was at fault, not her. Thanks to her therapist, she was slowly getting better. She had re-joined everyone at work on a part-time basis and everyone in the office constantly checked up on her. This annoyed her, but she appreciated them more and more.

She still had a tough time trusting men, which caused her to have sporadic panic attacks when out in public. Albie and Patrick had become the only men she trusted in the world.

Chapter 57

PATRICK

A problem was bubbling beneath Patrick's skin—the more time he spent with Isabelle, the more his old feelings for her were triggered until it dawned on him that he'd never actually dealt with his feelings for Isabelle after his accident; he'd just locked them away. Slowly, those locks were rusting into nothing. He didn't know what to do. He was proud of his friendship with Isabelle, but deep in his heart, every time he saw her smile his way, that old love for her rose to the surface. He knew he had to keep things platonic, but he was struggling.

It was an overcast autumn day when Patrick suggested to Isabelle that they head down to the beach for a coastline walk and some lunch when it wouldn't be busy. Isabelle liked the idea and took him up on the suggestion.

They shared a taxi and started to walk down the coast. It was a windy day, so Isabelle had to help Patrick at times by helping him through the headwind which slowly pushed back the wheelchair, no matter how much effort he put into propelling himself forward. They laughed about it and stopped at a lovely seaside restaurant that served freshly caught fish and chips.

Yet, mid-bite, Patrick drifted off into space.

"Everything okay, Patrick?"

Isabelle broke his concentration, and his gaze snapped onto hers. "Oh yeah, of course… I was just thinking about the last time we were down at this beach."

It was as though a light had been switched on within Isabelle's mind. "Oh, with Freya and Albie!"

Patrick nodded. "Yeah, that was such a fun day; maybe we can do something like that in the summer… Not sure how it would work with me, though," he said, looking down at his chair.

"Oh, shh—that won't be a problem! It'll give Albie a chance to use the muscles he works so hard on all the time."

They laughed, paid up, and left the restaurant to continue their seaside walk.

Together, they walked up to the edge of the coastal wall and looked out at the sea. Patrick's emotions were practically choking him. He knew, at some point, he would have to confess his feelings to Isabelle. Coming to this beach was the final nail in the coffin.

"Hey, Isabelle?" Isabelle continued to look out at the waves as they crashed against the rocks. "I wanted to tell you something."

Isabelle turned and leaned against the railing, looking at Patrick. "Of course," she smiled, "you can tell me anything."

It was the same smile that had made Patrick melt the last time they were here. Patrick knew it was now or never. "I love you, Isabelle; I've loved you ever since you stopped me outside of work that day, begging to see pictures of Doc."

Isabelle's face dropped. She took a big step away from him.

Patrick continued, needing to get the words out. "Look, I'm sorry. With everything going on right now, this might not be the right time but spending this time with you recently has made me realise something I think I've known for a long time now… I'm in love with you, Isabelle. Absolutely, truly in love with you."

Isabelle stood frozen still.

"Isabelle?" Patrick started to slowly roll towards her.

This snapped Isabelle from her stunned state. "Why?" she cried out, her tears starting to flow.

Patrick hadn't known what sort of reaction he would get but this was the opposite of what he had hoped for.

"Why would you tell me this now?" she started to sob. Patrick attempted to comfort her, but she flinched away. "No! No, Patrick, stay away. I need time to think." She ran towards the car park.

Patrick sat on the coastal walk. "What have I done?"

Cold autumn rain started to fall on his head.

Chapter 58

ISABELLE

Freya picked up Isabelle from the beach, but she refused to tell her what had happened. She just wanted to go home.

Freya had attempted to ask, "What about Patrick?"

This set Isabelle off again, so Freya sped away. When they returned to Freya's, Isabelle shut herself away, alone in her room.

A large part of her didn't want to go to work, but she really didn't want to let Julia down after she had been so understanding of her needing some time off after the incident. Plus, she knew that she would have to face him eventually. So, leaning on Freya for strength, she went in the next day. She was anxious all the way to the office and her anxiety lifted when she realised this was one of the days Patrick had off to rest.

Julia poked around her office, "Isabelle, could I speak to you before lunch?"

Isabelle's heart sank; her head had been on a different plane all day and one sentence brought her crashing down to earth. She got up from her desk and took a slow walk to Julia's office. The walk was 10 meters, but it felt like a mile. When she opened the door, Julia was at her desk and waiting. She looked stern and somewhat ominous as she gestured for Isabelle to take a seat.

"Good morning, Isabelle. I wanted to do a sporadic evaluation with you today."

Isabelle's eyes widened, and she had to stop her jaw from dropping in shock. "An evaluation?" she repeated, anxiously rubbing her hands together.

"I want to talk about your progress while you have been with us."

I'm going to lose my job. Her heart was halfway to pounding out of her chest; things had just started to pick up slightly for her. Why now? Did the universe hate her?

Julia was staring at her like she was waiting for a response; Isabelle panicked and blurted out, "Thank you…"

Julia's eyebrows lowered. "Excuse me?"

Isabelle started to turn red. "Sorry, I don't know why I said that…" she looked down at her hands.

"Right, let's start this evaluation, shall we?" Julia picked up a pencil and paper and got ready to write.

"You've been with us for what—about 2 and a half years now?" Julia looked up, expecting a response.

"Erm, yeah, I guess so," Isabelle replied timidly.

Julia nodded. "Would you say working at this company has helped you reach the goals you outlined in your interview?"

Isabelle was confused. "Goals I told you about in my interview?"

Julia put the pencil down for a moment and stopped writing. She then pulled a piece of paper from a folder on her desk and read aloud. "I asked where you saw yourself in five years of working for this company… Do you remember what you told me?" Julia prodded.

Isabelle racked her mind. "I'm really sorry, but I don't…"

Julia sighed before reading from the page again. "You told me," Isabelle began to look down at her lap again. "You wanted to interview people for a news network or a show on TV. You planned on being with the company for a while you looked for an intern position somewhere so you could get started on the journey." Julia looked up, a small smile as she continued. "You then said you knew that's not what people should say at a job interview but that you thought honesty was more important than anything."

The silence in the air was palpable. Julia softly placed the paper on the table as emotions built inside Isabelle. Neither said a word; Isabelle's eyes started to fill up with tears and though she tried to fight it, she couldn't stop the one tear which fell down her face. As soon as one fell, the rest soon followed. Her emotions soon overwhelmed her, and she started to sob.

Julia was stoic throughout and let her get it out for a few moments before pulling a tissue box from her desk and handing it over to Isabelle.

Julia finally broke the tension. "Do you know why I've brought this up, Isabelle?" Julia asked softly.

Isabelle shook her head and wiped away her tears. "I brought this up because I know what you have been through recently. It's a lot for anyone to cope with. I'm proud of how you have kept going." This caused Isabelle to whimper. "But… even with everything that has gone on in your personal life, I think you have lost sight of the goals and dreams you had when I first met you."

Isabelle continued to sob but now with her head in her hands. It was all too much, and her head was swimming. How had she let go of so much in such a short span of time?

"I didn't call you in to make you feel bad about yourself; I wanted to make you remember the woman I interviewed and her goals and ambitions. If I'm being perfectly honest with you, I didn't expect you to still be with the company based on the woman I spoke to two and a half years ago." Julia got up from her desk, circled so she was just in front of Isabelle and perched; she stroked the top of Isabelle's head comfortingly. "I saw something inside of you that day that reminded me of a younger version of myself. Ambition, drive and a flame within that was hungry to move to the next step up in life."

Isabelle finally lowered her hands, and Julia could see her wet, swollen and red face; she wiped the sleeve of her blouse. "Isabelle, I want you to take the rest of the day, go home and think about what I've talked to you about today."

Isabelle nodded in agreement.

"Good, and I want you to come back tomorrow and, when you do, come straight to me and we'll have a talk, yeah?" Isabelle nodded again. "Right now, take a moment and then grab your stuff and head home."

Julia approached a coat rack behind her door and picked up her bag. "I'm gonna head to lunch; I'll see you tomorrow, my dear." She quickly left the room and shut the door behind her, leaving Isabelle silently sitting on her chair.

Her world had been shaken and, like she was experiencing the aftermath of an earthquake, the silence was deafening.

After using most of Julia's tissues to wipe the makeup from her face and taking multiple deep breaths, she built up the courage to peek out of the door. There was no one in the office and she let out a sigh of relief before quickly walking over to her desk and collecting her things. She stood in front of her desk for a moment, her bag on her shoulders, and thought of all the amazing times she'd had in this office with Freya, Albie and Patrick. All the laughter, longing stares and inappropriate jokes she overheard—the latter being from Albie. And only recently had she gotten to know Iris properly. She started to get emotional again and, before she could let her emotions take over, she ran out of the office.

Chapter 59

ISABELLE

On her cold walk home, she finally let herself think properly about everything Julia had said to her.

"I really didn't say a thing, did I?" she muttered to herself; she wasn't sure if Julia had overstepped the line, whether it was exactly what she needed to hear or both.

Does she have good intentions, or does she just not want me there anymore?

Lost in thought, she arrived at Freya's flat much quicker than she had realised. She entered, threw her bag on the floor and flopped onto the sofa. It was only halfway through the week and within that time, she'd had two people express how they felt about and saw her in a short span of time—and she hadn't been ready for either.

What does she expect me to tell her tomorrow morning? Why did she tell me all of that?

She laid down on the sofa, looked up at the ceiling and thought more about the day Julia had interviewed her at *Rachael's.* Just thinking about the cake, the owner had given her made her long for who she had been in the past.

When she thought of work, the first thing that came to her was bumping into Patrick that very first day. She smiled before that old heartbreak of hearing, *Patrick doesn't want to see you,* shattering her heart to pieces. A tear slowly rolled down her cheek.

Then Eric...

She jumped from the sofa, shaking her head. She wasn't even going to touch that one—not now she had so much going on. She decided to take a long shower and, beneath the water, started to think about the job.

When she got out of the shower, she changed into some comfy jogging bottoms and a t-shirt before flopping on her bed.

Her job was the only constant she had, considering everything that had happened in the last couple of years. Why would Julia say all of that to her? Was she not doing a good job anymore?

Just thinking about that made her laugh, what with all the times Freya had saved her from making more mistakes than anyone would even dream. She kept thinking about the faces Albie would pull when he could see her stressing out and asking for help.

Do I even like this job?

She sat up in bed, Julia's words ringing.

"…I didn't expect you to still be with the company…"

The realisation hit Isabelle like a truck, and she grabbed her pillow from behind her and clutched it to her chest. "She's right. This wasn't my plan at all. I just wanted to be here until I could pursue my dream." She was so confused. "Why have I stayed here for so long?"

She thought about her pivotal moments there and slowly realised that the one common factor was Patrick. He was always involved somehow, whether it was a good or bad moment. Was he the only reason she had stayed?"

Isabelle spent the rest of the night in her bed; she was hungry, but her mind was so scattered that she didn't even realise Freya had gotten home. All her mental energy was spent thinking about what Julia had said.

"I think I hate my job?" she said aloud. "I think the only reason I'm still here is the people; I don't want to work a boring office job for the rest of my life."

She started to think more about what she wanted to do with her life and the understanding that Julia had confronted her with my past self today was to help her realise this finally hit her.

"She wanted me to remember who I was… I was someone with a dream and a goal! And—what am I now?" She finally got under her duvet. She knew, then, what she needed to do.

She fell straight to sleep that night for the first time in a long time.

***

"It's starting to get chilly in the mornings again," Julia muttered. Autumn was Julia's favourite time of year, and she smiled as she got into her car. She got to the office early that morning as she wanted to be the first in when Isabelle arrived. She hoped she hadn't been too harsh to her yesterday.

She unlocked the office door, flicked on all the lights—filling the office with colour—and headed to her office. She then pulled out the thermos her wife made for her every morning in the colder seasons; pouring herself a morning coffee from home in the office never failed to make Julia smile.

As the minutes ticked by, the office started to fill. First was Iris, followed by Freya and Albie and last was Patrick, who rolled in just before the start of office hours. Julia was surprised, and she wondered where Isabelle was. Half an hour passed before Julia started to worry.

She got up from her desk, ready to ask Freya, but her office phone began to ring the second she did.

"Yes, hello? Julia speaking."

She had picked up the phone with some urgency but slumped in her chair as soon as she heard the caller.

"G—good morning, Julia. It's me, Isabelle." She sounded extremely nervous.

Julia acted how she typically would. "Good morning, where are you? You're late."

Isabelle was quick to respond. "I'm really sorry—I'm on my way; there is a good reason I'm running a bit late today, I promise!"

Julia crossed her legs and waited for her excuse.

Isabelle carried on. "So, after our chat yesterday, I was upset. I thought you were trying to upset me or something…"

Julia frowned. "Right, and your conclusion?"

Isabelle took an audible breath. "After some time, I realised you were completely right about everything you said. I've put everything I've ever wanted on the back burner… I think I've figured out I don't like this job, but I love the people like family—but I think the time has come. So, Julia, I would like to—"

"Due to the financial climate, we're going to have to let you go and this is your official notice. You're being made redundant in thirty days however, due to confidentiality, I would like this to be your last day," Julia cut in before Isabelle had the chance to finish her sentence.

"What? What do you mean?" Isabelle's voice went up an octave out of surprise.

Julia sat up, uncrossed her leg and started writing on a piece of paper before responding. "Isabelle, I couldn't be prouder of you; it takes a lot of heart and courage to say what you just tried to say."

Isabelle started to sob down the phone. "But why? Why now?"

Julia smiled. "Oh, Isabelle, I feel like I can say that I know you pretty well at this point, right?" Isabelle sniffled and agreed. "Well, I know that if you want to set your heart on something, you can achieve it. I've seen it here and in your personal life. You're strong-willed, and I know for a fact you will achieve everything you told me in your interview." She could hear Isabelle trying to catch her breath between tears; Julia was trying her best not to get too emotional and be that brick wall she knew she needed her to be.

"I could have hired five other people over you. You were—let's be honest here—completely inexperienced, and I could tell you were beyond uninterested in being here on the first day. But I hired you because I saw something in your personality that was like a dog chasing a bone; no matter how hard it was, you were going to get there no matter what anyone told you. From your first day on the job, you immediately impacted the office; you brought life and energy that I'd not seen here for a long time. So, I couldn't be happier with my decision to hire you and, as my gift to you, I'm going to give you the last push you need…" Julia had to stop herself from choking up.

"I was going to tell you about this once I found the right time, but I have a contact that I wanted to put you in touch with that works for the local news if you're interested?"

"Thank you… thank you so much, Julia." Isabelle was an emotional mess. She knew Julia was showing her a kindness that she had yet to experience and was overwhelmed.

"Now, Isabelle, it's time for you to stop crying and be that girl with fire in her eyes."

Isabelle wiped her eyes with her sleeve and composed herself. "Thank you for everything, Julia; I will make you proud."

"You may come to the office at lunch and pick up your things. After that, the next time I want to see you is on my TV, okay?"

Isabelle was full of energy. "Yes, boss lady."

Julia didn't respond and just put the phone down before turning her chair away from the office door and letting herself feel the emotions that had built within her.

Chapter 60

PATRICK

The morning had been stressful, and Patrick was exhausted, but when he looked up at the clock, he saw he still had twenty-five minutes until lunch. He leaned back in his wheelchair and surveyed the office; he had been so absorbed by his work that he hadn't noticed that Isabelle wasn't in. He looked around in case he'd somehow missed her but couldn't see any sign of her. Was she ill today or something?

He wheeled himself over to Albie's desk. "We doing lunch today, buddy?"

Albie jumped out of his seat. "Yeah, I mean, if you guys wanna?" He looked over to Freya, who was also getting ready to leave.

She picked up her bag and walked over to Albie's desk. "First off, Albie, please clean this desk. It's a tip!" She crossed her arms, glaring at Albies's—admittedly messy—desk. She looked at Patrick and the cadence of her voice became much softer. "And second, I think you should wait here for five minutes, babes, and then join us if you want to."

"Erm, okay. I guess I'll meet you there." Patrick contorted his face in confusion and wheeled himself back to his desk. "She called me 'babes'." What was going on? Had something happened? He grabbed his phone to see if he had missed anything but there was nothing. "What's going on?" he was starting to get anxious the more confused he got.

"Alright, mate, see you in a bit." Albie nodded towards Patrick as he left with Freya. Patrick sat in his chair. He didn't know why Freya wanted him to stay back. "What the hell is going on?"

Iris was the last to leave for lunch and she waved goodbye to Patrick before bumping into someone coming into the office. "Oh, I'm so sorry—I didn't see you there, Isabelle. I hope you're feeling okay. See you later."

The air escaped Patrick's lungs. He hadn't had a one-on-one

conversation with Isabelle since the day they had gone to the beach. His heart started to pound.

Why am I so scared right now?

When she caught Patrick's eye her face twisted in surprise.

Had she not known he was going to be here? Patrick's fear morphed into curiosity; he pulled his chair out from his desk and slowly wheeled his way over to hers, meeting her at her desk. "Hey, I was surprised to see you; I thought you weren't feeling good today or something?"

Isabelle sat at her desk and turned to face Patrick. "No need to worry, I'm fine," she said through a somewhat pained smile.

Patrick could see something was wrong but couldn't figure out what; it was so unlike her to come to work late—let alone dressed in a t-shirt and jeans. Even her face looked different; she wasn't wearing makeup, and he could see how tired she looked—like she hadn't slept in days.

Patrick was getting worried. "Has something happened?"

She dropped her head and started pulling things from her desk and putting them in her bag. "No… I mean yeah—do you want to go for a coffee?"

Patrick nodded as she grabbed a few more things from a drawer. "Right—let's head off, shall we?" she said as she stood up, offering him another pinched smile which he could tell was forced.

Patrick nodded and followed. "Where would you like to go?"

She paused at the door to the office for a moment without saying anything.

"Isabelle?" Patrick snapped her out of a trance.

"Let's go to *Rachael's*—we've not been there for a while." Isabelle turned away from Patrick as she spoke, and he thought he heard a crack in her voice.

"Yeah, that will be nice. Let's head there now." He tried to make his voice warm to make her feel better.

They walked to the café in silence, not saying a single word to each other. Isabelle opened the café door, and they were met by warm welcomes from the married couple who owned the small café. "Good afternoon, Miss. I haven't seen the both of you for a while. Feel free to take your seats and I'll be over shortly."

Isabelle shot him a smile before heading over to their usual table. She moved the chair away from Patrick's side of the table and sat down. Patrick rolled into the space and put his brakes on, softly prodding, "What's wrong, Isabelle? Something's not right."

Isabelle's eyes were starting to water but, before she could say anything, the old man arrived at the table, and she shot him a broad smile.

"Here you go, Miss—your usuals." he placed a tray on a table with the exact order they had the first time they ever came for lunch together. He took each coffee and plate off the tray and placed them elegantly onto the table and they both sat silently and watched him. Once he was finished, he took the tray from the table and held it under his arm. "Please enjoy," he said with a gentle smile.

The silence drew on a moment longer as the pair looked at the lunch on the table. Patrick finally broke it and lifted his hand, intending to place it on Isabelle's, but Isabelle pulled away as soon as he got close.

"Oh," he said softly. "I'm sorry, I shouldn't have done that. What's happening? Is this about the beach?"

After a deep breath, Isabelle put her hands under the table and replied. "Well, yeah, a bit—but that's not everything. A lot has happened these last few days."

Patrick picked up his coffee and took a sip. "Do you want to talk about it?" he asked, trying to sound as kind as he could. Inside, however, his heart was thumping. The air felt ominous.

"Patrick, I'm going to open up to you right now—but you have to promise you'll let me say everything I need to say, okay?" Isabelle's posture changed like she was building herself up to let everything out.

Patrick put his coffee back down on its saucer. "Yeah, okay. You've got me worried."

Isabelle took a deep breath. "Patrick, the other day at the beach, I told you I needed time to think about things, didn't I?" Patrick nodded slightly, listening intently. "Well, Julia also gave me a lot to think about this week; my head's been a mess." She let out a depressed chuckle and her eyes flitted away from Patrick's.

She continued, "Patrick, we have been through so much over the last few years. You've impacted my life like no one else—good and bad." Patrick's head dropped; guilt gnawed at him at just the thought of what he had done to her. "We have made so many special memories that I will cherish forever but I can't be with you right now."

Patrick's heart snapped. He had felt that this conversation was unlikely to be good but knowing that didn't stop her words from hurting. He looked up to find Isabelle looking at him with tears rolling down her face. It was clear she was hurting even more than he was. "Isabelle, I—"

Before he could continue, Isabelle interrupted him. “Patrick, please just wait. I need to finish.”

Defeated, Patrick nodded slightly again. “I'm leaving Patrick; I'm going back home to live with my parents for a while.” Patrick’s eyes widened; he wanted to shout out in opposition but knew how much Isabelle was hurting. He also didn’t want to interrupt her again. “I’ve loved it here; working with you, Freya, Albie, Julia and Iris has been one of the best experiences… but I hate it here just as much. After chatting to Julia, I realised some things about myself.” She wiped her tears with a napkin from the table and the brief pause left the room feeling empty. “I didn’t want to do this, Patrick. I’ve always wanted to be a journalist—you know that.” He nodded in acknowledgement, afraid to speak. “But, for various reasons, I’ve stayed here for far longer than I ever intended.”

Emotion was starting to build in Patrick and his eyes began to glaze over.

“I stayed for you, Patrick. I think I’ve been in love with you since we first had lunch here two years ago.”

A tear fell from Patrick’s eyes as he looked into Isabelle’s. He no longer wanted to interrupt her.

“Everything that you are is everything I want from someone, but Patrick—you broke my heart.” Isabelle’s voice cracked and she burst into tears. She tried her best to continue. “I hated you so much after you abandoned me after your accident, Patrick.”

Patrick could feel the anger coming from Isabelle’s teary voice and his hate for himself was building inside him again. He was ready to burst but did his best to control himself for her.

“I—I know I shouldn’t, but I can’t stop thinking that if you hadn’t stopped me from seeing you, our lives could be so different right now. I just know it.”

Patrick turned away from her. He couldn’t keep looking at her without breaking down.

“After everything happened with Eric, you were amazing, Patrick. Without you and what you did for me, I'm not sure what would have happened. But, if I'm being completely honest, Patrick, though my hatred was fading, it was always there.” Isabelle tried her best to compose herself but couldn’t stop the tears from falling and spoke through them. “When Julia called me into her office yesterday, she painted me a picture of who I used to be. I'm not that person anymore, but I’ve decided I want to be her again. I need to follow my dreams and start a new life for myself. A life away from you."

Patrick felt awful. He hadn't realised how badly he had impacted Isabelle's life. He was being selfish again. His selfishness had caused the accident—and it was causing her to feel this way. His head was on fire, his thoughts racing; how could he make amends? How could he make her stay? How could he take it all back?

"Patrick? Can you look at me?"

He had never been able to refuse her and looked up. "Patrick, I'm sorry. I shouldn't have held onto my hatred. When you told me you loved me, I realised that I could never truly hate you." They looked into each other's eyes intensely. "I'm leaving for my parents in a few hours, Patrick. I'm not sure if we'll ever see each other again after today."

She lifted her hand and placed it on his. He let their fingers lock, and she held on for a moment before pulling her hand away. Tears started to fill her eyes again before she looked at him one last time.

"I hope you understand, Patrick; I need to do this. And please, just remember how much you mean to me."

She picked up her bag from the floor and stood. Patrick's eyes never left hers as she did. She paused for a moment. "I'm going to miss you."

She turned away and ran from the café, leaving Patrick alone and broken in the café they'd first fallen for each other.

5 Years Later

Chapter 61

PATRICK

Patrick was woken by his overly loud alarm early Monday morning. The sun was beaming into his apartment, and he moaned grumpily as he sat up, grabbed his walking stick from the side of his bed and sauntered through to the kitchen. It was much bigger than the kitchen he'd had in his old place—much more modern, with everything in shades of white and grey and a large island in the centre of the room. The automatic coffee machine bleeped, letting Patrick know that a piping hot coffee was ready for him. He poured himself a large mug and sat on a bar stall next to the kitchen island. Within seconds of him sitting down, Doc jumped onto the island next to him.

Patrick looked over at him while taking a sip of coffee. "Big day today, buddy!"

Doc meowed back in agreement.

"I can't believe I have to do a TV interview today… I begged Freya to do it for me but she flat-out refused." Patrick groaned.

Doc jumped off the island, walked over to his bowl and sat—clearly expecting Patrick to give him his dinner. "I knew I shouldn't have gotten rid of that automatic feeder," Patrick laughed before emptying a can of Doc's favourite food into his bowl. "Last couple of years we've been here, you have definitely started to think of yourself as a little prince." Patrick ruffled Doc's head and left him to eat.

He slowly limped to his bedroom and looked through his clothes. "What the hell am I meant to wear for this? I've never been on TV before." He rifled through his many shirts, unable to make up his mind. Suddenly, his phone bed pinged three times in a row. Patrick looked—they were from Iris.

Let me guess, you don't know what to wear.

Patrick sighed before reading the following message.

In your living room, I've left out a suit, shirt and tie for you to wear. I'm sure you can handle the socks and shoes.

Patrick's fist pumped into the air. "Get in!" he exclaimed.

Thank God you have the best assistant in the business. You're useless sometimes, I swear.

Patrick could practically hear the smug, self-praising tone of Iris' last message. He threw his phone onto the bed. "I really need to talk to her about that," he muttered before heading into the living room to get dressed.

The living room was also bigger than the small, old apartment he'd lived in with Doc for a year—the large windows that wrapped around let in the morning sun. It was peaceful.

Patrick changed into his deep blue, fitted suit and white shirt and sat at a chair which overlooked the view from his window. Doc was already asleep on the stool beside him—it had become a routine for them both to take a moment of reflection before starting the day.

"We've come so far, buddy," he said softly, stroking Doc's fur as he soaked up the sun. Their moment of reflection was disturbed by a loud buzzer.

"Oh God, how am I late already?" Patrick put on his shoes, grabbed the same beaten-up old bag that he'd used years for years now and threw it over his shoulder. "Wish me luck, buddy!" he shouted as he slowly hobbled out of his apartment.

Outside was Albie, who leaned against the back of a nice car as he waited for Patrick. "Come on, lightning, we've got to get a move on." He laughed louder than anyone should at this time in the morning.

Patrick was confused. "What are you doing here? Shouldn't you be in the office today?"

Albie strutted over to Patrick and pulled the bag off his shoulder. "What you chatting 'bout, big man? This is a big day. I'm here for if you need your boy's backup." He grinned as he walked off. Before getting to the car, he turned back to Patrick, "Don't tell Freya, but I want to get a selfie with the interviewer—I'm a big fan." He laughed before getting into the car.

"You know Freya is gonna kill you one of these days, right?" Patrick couldn't help but laugh as he slowly walked over to the car and got in.

"It's gonna take about an hour to get there. You should be able to shake off the drowsiness from your pills by the time we get there."

Patrick was surprised Albie remembered such things but thanked him anyway and Albie let out one of his trademark loud laughs.

"Come on then, big man, let's get you to your five minutes of fame."

Albie didn't usually mention things like his pills and could imagine that he had received a call from Julia that morning to scold him and make sure he looked out for Patrick.

Before Patrick knew it, he sat in a makeup chair with a cape around him as if he were getting a haircut. He felt so uncomfortable as he sat there whilst Albie and the makeup artist chatted away behind him. Over the years, he had grown increasingly in awe of how Albie could seemingly make friends with anyone at any time.

"Right, you—sit and get pretty for once in your life; I'm gonna sneak myself a cheeky selfie with your interviewer." Albie slapped his thighs before getting up and leaving Patrick to himself.

"Behave yourself, please, Albie." Patrick tried to look stern but because of his nerves, it sounded like a mouse telling off a bear.

The makeup artist tried her best to get a conversation out of Patrick, but his nerves were getting the better of him and he couldn't seem to escape his head to talk back. Thankfully, she seemed used to it. "I'm done, sweetie," she said, whipping the cape from his neck. Patrick looked in the mirror and was shocked at how good he looked.

"Wow, you are amazing at your job. Thanks so much. I'm sorry for not talking much," he said with a smile, trying to hide his nerves.

"Ah, no problem, darlin'. Have a good one," she said and left the room.

Alone in the green room, sitting on the strangely comfortable sofa, Patrick tried his best to come up with any possible question that the interviewer could ask him—and an answer to match. Waiting and overthinking, he tried his best not to sweat too much so his makeup wouldn't start to run.

His phone rang and Patrick pulled his phone out of his pocket, saw who was calling, and picked it up instantly. "Freya… why am I here?" He sounded uncomfortable and nervous and almost rude, even to himself.

"Are you there? Hello?" The phone line cut.

Patrick immediately phoned her back.

"Good morning, this is Freya from We Care for You," she said in a positive, very professional manner.

"Erm, hi Freya, it's Patrick. Did you just call me?" He said, brows furrowed.

"Oh no," she said, tone pleasant. "I just called someone who must not have realised who they were on the phone to and was rude—that couldn't have been you, could it, babes?"

Patrick sighed. "I'm sorry, Freya." His cheeks reddened.

"Thank you, babes. Now, I wanted to speak to you before your interview and make sure you're ready and see if you need anything?"

In the following ten minutes, Patrick and Freya reviewed the PR answers that she would usually do if she was doing any interview for the company.

"Freya, you're so, so good at this! Why am I here right now and you're at the office?"

Freya laughed down the phone at him. "Babes, we're all partners in this, aren't we? It's about time you picked up some of the media slack, even if it's just this once, so I can do what I need to do today."

Patrick rubbed his brow. He knew she was right—he always asked her to do this sort of thing because of how anxious it made him but that wasn't necessarily fair. He held his breath, and Freya gave a comforting surge of encouragement. "You can do this, babes. Look at everything you have accomplished. Without you, this would never have happened. You've done the hard bit—a silly interview should be a breeze."

Patrick smiled. "What did I ever do to deserve you guys?"

Freya laughed down the phone. "You should be on soon, babes. Good luck, you've got this."

She sounded so confident that Patrick started to believe it and began to sound much more perky. "Thanks, Freya. I'll see you in the office later."

"We'll see about that," Freya said as she put the phone down.

Patrick paused. *What did she mean by that?*

A PA entered the room. "You're on in three. Please follow me."

Patrick picked up his walking stick and looked at himself in the mirror, he was growing fond of the walking stick. He actually thought he looked good for once. He smiled into the mirror before following the PA.

The PA led him to a brightly lit set where two modern-looking chairs facing each other were staged. Patrick made a point of trying to ignore the surrounding cameras. He was led to his seat and a microphone was fastened to his shirt.

Patrick didn't know what was happening; it felt like he had been picked up by a hurricane and thrown into an unknown land. He closed his eyes and took a deep breath, "I can do this," he muttered to himself. As he opened his eyes, however, his heart stopped.

Chapter 62

ISABELLE

30 MINUTES EARLIER

Isabelle was in her makeup chair reading the notes of her upcoming interview; the interview was with a new company that had won a lot of awards recently for their support of people who had experienced traumatic experiences. They provided affordable care and helped people going through these experiences back on their feet. They even had their own brand of walking sticks and wheelchairs available for purchase. As soon as her network had mentioned this interview was a possibility, Isabelle requested the job without knowing anything more. Her boss had given it to her immediately.

She spent the next few days researching the company and, to her, it sounded amazing. Thinking about her past and everything that had happened, she thought that Patrick could have done with help like this after he'd had his accident.

Had that been why she'd jumped at the chance to take this interview? She couldn't figure out why she was so drawn to it. As she read into the company more and more, she saw that all the interviews in the past had been completed by a woman called Freya and felt an immense amount of guilt. She hadn't contacted Freya for years after she'd up and left out of nowhere with no explanation.

She sighed. She'd message her tomorrow. She'd make sure of it.

Isabelle spent the rest of the week preparing for the interview. Since joining the network, she has become extraordinarily talented at making people feel comfortable and getting them to open up to her during her interviews. It was this skill that had helped her to shoot up the ranks at the TV network Julia had put her in touch with all those years ago.

When her makeup artist had finished, she wished her luck and, as she left, bumped into a large man standing at the door. "Oh, sorry love! You, okay?" she asked. "Need a hand with all that?"

Isabelle would have recognised the overly loud, bellowing voice that answered anywhere. "Albie?" Her head spun so quickly that she could have gotten whiplash.

Albie stood, filling the door frame, grinning like a Cheshire cat.

"Alright, darlin', long time no see." He held out his arm and, within a fraction of a second, Isabelle launched herself into them.

"I'm not your darling. Remember, you big dummy?" her lower lip trembled.

Albie let out a loud, bellowing chuckle and they hugged for a moment before Isabelle pulled away, checking that her makeup hadn't run.

"What are you doing here, Albie?"

He put his hand into his pocket and pulled out his phone. "Well, I mean—I just wanted to make Freya jealous by getting a selfie with our favourite TV presenter."

Isabelle got embarrassed. "Your favourite?"

Albie laughed again. "Of course, you muppet! Freya and I are your biggest fans. We've seen everything you've done so far!" He grinned, looking as proud as anyone could. "So come 'ere." He pulled Isabelle towards him and started to take as many selfies as possible.

Isabelle—though initially startled by Albie's presence—began posing as best she could. Albie took so many pictures that she was stuck for new poses. "As lovely as it is to see you, Albie," she laughed. "I have an interview to do in a moment." She walked over to pick up her cue cards.

"Oh, yeah," he said and shot a thumbs up her way as she turned to leave. "'Course, don't you worry. Imma love you and leave you. Break a leg, darlin'."

As he was, Isabelle shouted his way. "I'll give Freya a call—we should all get dinner soon." Albie didn't break stride. He put his arm in the air and shouted, "See you soon, darlin'!"

Isabelle flopped into a chair as he turned the corner. "What are the chances! I've not seen that big ox for way too long." She smiled just thinking back on the great times spent with Albie, Freya, and Patrick…

The last thought broke Isabelle's smile. She'd felt guilty ever since her last meeting with Patrick at *Rachael's* and had wondered what he was doing now.

Hold up, Freya and now Albie? That can't be a coincidence…

Before her mind could wander more, her PA burst into her room. "Come on, Isabelle, you're almost late. Get moving!"

Isabelle snapped out of her trance-like state, jumped into her shiny black high heels, and headed towards the set. "Maybe it's been long enough…" she murmured. "Maybe I can get in touch with him."

Before Isabelle could finish her thought, she froze.

"Isabelle?" Patrick asked, staring at her in shock.

Isabelle froze. It was the first time she'd been in front of Patrick in five years. Her heart was in her mouth, and she didn't know what to do or what to say.

She just stood there, her cue cards dangling in her drooped hands. Neither said a thing; there was just deathly silence as they looked at each other—both like they'd seen a ghost. Isabelle looked Patrick up and down; he wasn't in a wheelchair—he was sitting! He looked handsome in—what she could tell—was a costly suit, holding a walking stick.

She had a million questions and things she wanted to say. Still, nothing came from either of their mouths. Finally, a technician broke the tension. "Here's your microphone. We'll be ready to start as soon as you give us the nod." He put the microphone on her blazer and left.

Isabelle hooked her hair behind her ear and sat down opposite Patrick. Her heart was racing. She closed her eyes and took a deep breath. *I can do this.*

She opened her eyes, and Patrick was still staring at her. She got embarrassed but corrected her posture and finally spoke. "We need to be professional here. We can talk later in my office if you like?" she said in a hushed tone while covering her microphone.

Patrick didn't respond. He just nodded in her direction.

"Good." Isabelle straightened, her cue cards on her leg as she took a deep breath. "Good luck," she said in Patrick's direction as she nodded to the producer.

The cameras were now rolling.

Chapter 63

PATRICK

Patrick had only a few seconds to try to compose himself and the lights in the studio flicked on, close to blinding Patrick. However, he didn't have time to think about that. "I can't believe this; how am I supposed to do this now?"

The studio was as dark as night, the only light targeted on the stage where Isabelle and Patrick were silently waiting for the producer to yell 'action'. The heat from the giant lights beaming down left Patrick feeling roasted; his heart was pumping faster and faster in anticipation. Everything inside him told him told him to grab his walking stick and leave.

Isabelle sat, trying to compose herself. She just stared at the cue cards she had in her hands.

The hustle and bustle of the behind-camera workers stopped.

"Action!"

"Good morning and welcome. Today, we have the inspirational story of a company that has risen to the top of its field in just a few short years. A group of friends used adversity and tragedy to not only improve the lives of others but the lives of themselves and their loved ones. Today, we are going to talk to one of the founders of this company..." Isabelle's whole personality changed; she delivered her lines confidently and eloquently, smiling the entire time.

Patrick couldn't stop his jaw from dropping in awe of what he just witnessed. He didn't listen to a word she said—he just watched her; she looked like she was born for this.

Isabelle turned her chair to face Patrick, and her beaming smile almost blinded him. It was so bright and warm that he missed what she said next.

"Patrick...?"

He was frozen. She was so beautiful that he couldn't help but smile at her.

She looked at the producer and held up a finger, gesturing to wait. "Patrick?" she asked in a hushed, calm voice.

This snapped Patrick from his trance and, when he looked around, he remembered that there were people watching him and Isabelle on stage. He turned to Isabelle. "I'm so sorry. Let's continue." This wasn't the time for embarrassment.

Isabelle started again. "Patrick, the story of how you and your friends came out of seemingly nowhere and rocked the world of care with your affordable therapy and stylish yet comfortable, unique walking sticks. On top of this, you also have a new charity, is that right?"

Patrick took a second before responding. Isabelle was being professional, and he should be, too. "Thanks for having me, Isabelle; yes, our new charity is called Step by Step.

"Step by Step? Interesting, could you tell us more about that?" Isabelle genuinely wanted to know more; she'd done a lot of interviews where she'd had to feign interest, and hated doing so, but that wasn't needed here.

"In my past, I led a solitary lifestyle. I was fine with how I was and didn't see it as an issue whatsoever—but a woman entered my life a few years back and introduced me to the world…" Patrick wasn't looking at Isabelle when he said this. "After I had a terrible accident, I pushed all people out of my life and isolated myself completely; I even stopped looking after my cat. I went to a very dark place. Anyway, the idea behind the charity is—I was one of the lucky ones. I had an amazing, motherly figure who forced me to start taking care of myself and I got better. But unfortunately, not everyone is so lucky…"

The tone of Patrick's voice changed, and he became far more direct and confident. "So, I want to help people who are in similar situations to what I was for free. Not everyone is fortunate enough to have someone there or enough money to afford private care—and government funding is so backlogged that some people resort to tragic actions. I can't let this happen, so I want to help. Out n About is there for people who need that bit of help to get them back into the world." Patrick finally looked back at Isabelle, whose eyes had glassed over.

"Isabelle, the world is a beautiful, wondrous place. If I can help it, no one will miss out on finding that out for themselves—and I'm beyond grateful to the woman I met all those years ago, who changed my life forever." Patrick looked directly into Isabella's eyes.

Silence filled the studio, and a tear fell slowly down Isabelle's cheek. She didn't expect this; he had changed so much since he last saw him and she knew she was crying because of his words as much as she was the knowledge that, at last, people were seeing him as she always. Her heart filled and was ready to burst. She pulled a tissue from the side of her chair and dabbed at the tear, doing her best to hold everything together—she let out a slight cough to distract.

He was sitting less than two feet away. She wanted to lunge at him and hug him more than anything, but she knew she had to finish this interview before she could talk to him, so she went into autopilot and was her usual energetic, charming self. She tried to remember that this was like any other interview; just because it was with Patrick shouldn't mean anything should be different.

Time flew by, the two of them talking about how he, Albie, Freya and Iris—with Julia's guidance—had created their company and worked hard to get where they were. The interview finished with Isabelle explaining where to find them and encouraging those who were struggling to reach out for help.

The studio's bright lights went dim, and two people rushed over to Isabelle and took her out of Patrick's eyeline. One intern came over and took his mic off before thanking and directing him to the green room. Patrick slowly headed in the direction the intern had pointed. He was exhausted and couldn't wait to get home and chill with Doc for the rest of the day—plus, his heart was still pounding from the interview.

"I can't believe it was Isabelle," he muttered to himself. "I need to talk to Freya and Albie tomorrow."

As he was about to open the door to the green room, he heard someone call out from behind him. "Patrick! Wait up." Isabelle was jogging as quickly as she could in her heels, out of breath and trying to catch up to him. Patrick froze, gripping the door handle while the door was slightly ajar.

When she finally caught up with Patrick, she was breathing heavily and held a finger out in front of her for a second to compose herself, making him think back to how she had done the same thing after chasing him down to give him back his jeans back after their day at the beach.

Patrick stood like a deer in headlights, not moving or breathing. Isabelle seemed to notice, and it was like her nerves slipped away.

"Hey, I thought it would be nice to have a little bit of a catch-up before my meeting in twenty minutes. Would you be okay sticking around for a little while?"

Patrick didn't react at all; he was in his own little world, trapped in the past. Before Isabelle could interrupt him, Patrick was yanked back—literally—as the door was pulled open from the other side.

"'Ello, 'ello. What do we have here, then?" Albie stepped out with a smug grin on his face. He stood between them with his arms crossed and laughed aloud.

"Well, I'm gonna go wait in the car, buddy; you guys have a catch-up." He leaned in and hugged Isabelle. "Lovely to see you, darlin, don't be a stranger now." He kissed her on the cheek and started walking away. "See you in a few!" he raised his hand as he walked away.

Patrick couldn't help but grin and shake his head at Albie, which snapped him out of his trance-like state. "Well, shall we go in here, then?" he laughed to Isabelle and gestured into the green room.

Isabelle sighed. "Five years and that guy is still the same, eh?" They laughed as she walked into the room and took a seat. Patrick followed, nodding in agreement, and sat on the sofa beside her.

Chapter 64

ISABELLE

As Isabelle sat on the sofa, she watched Patrick hobble in and sit down with a big smile; the last time she'd seen Patrick, he'd looked very different from the man before her now. He looked full of life—and Isabelle couldn't take her eyes off him.

She looked him up and down and couldn't help but coyly smile. *When did he get so hot?*

Patrick sat down and looked awkward.

"Of all the people in the world, you're the last person I expected to be in my interview chair today!"

They started exchanging pleasantries, which made the situation even more awkward. The silences between grew longer and longer until Patrick asked Isabelle about her job, and she lit up and jabbered, giddy with enthusiasm.

Patrick sat, watching her, and covered his mouth as Isabelle was talking away.

"…when I first sat in that chair, it felt like home. I just wanted—Patrick? Why are you covering your mouth?" She tilted her head slightly with her eyebrows raised and Patrick pulled away his hand to reveal a big grin on his face.

His face glowed with admiration. "Isabelle, I couldn't be prouder and happier for you; you did it. Everything you've ever wanted. After everything, you've worked hard and are where you should be—you're glowing." He took her hand and looked her in the eyes. "I'm so glad I was tricked by Freya to do this today. I don't think I did as good as she does, but I'm just so happy I got to see you."

Isabelle's eyes glazed over. It didn't matter how many people were happy for her—it didn't mean anything. She didn't feel like she hadn't reached her goal yet but hearing him say that meant everything. Her face went beetroot red, and she could feel herself growing close to tears, so she turned her head away.

"Thank you, Patrick…" She felt vulnerable for the first time in a long time; why couldn't she just put up her steel walls like she had the day she'd left him behind?

Patrick dropped her hand and held his hands up. "I'm so sorry. I didn't mean to upset you. Did I say something wrong?" His voice turned high-pitched in concern, which caused Isabelle to turn around laughing. Seeing him with his hands in the air as if he was at gunpoint caused her to break into a cackling laugh. Patrick dropped his arms with a smile on his face.

"I've gotta ask, how come you aren't in a wheelchair now?" Isabelle asked, wanting to not sound rude.

"Oh, a few years ago, I had some surgery. I can now walk on it with just the aid of my walking stick. I also had a ton of therapy and physiotherapy and… I gotta say, I wish I'd done it sooner." He shrugged tone blasé.

"Well, the walking stick looks good on you," Isabelle said, not realising how much she was ogling him.

Patrick laughed, embarrassed again. "Well, at least someone else thinks so."

Isabelle realised what she had said and flushed before quickly regaining her composure. "Anyway, enough about me—what was Albie doing here earlier?"

"Oh, well Albie is a partner in the company. He shouldn't be driving me like today, but he wanted to see you." Patrick was embarrassed yet proud.

"I have to say I never expected you guys to start a company, let alone a successful one!" Isabelle was prodding for more information, and Patrick knew it.

"Is this another interview?" he laughed.

Isabelle wasn't gonna let this slide. "Yes, it is!" she said as she crossed her arms, feigning being cross.

Patrick laughed and changed his posture to look more professional. "Well, thanks for the question, Isabelle. The company came about after you left..." Isabelle's face dropped, and Patrick continued without missing a beat. "I was inspired by you chasing your goals and I didn't know what I wanted to do with my life. I thought long and hard about it before approaching Julia, Freya and Albie with the idea of creating a company to help people that had been through a traumatic experience—whether that be therapy or disability equipment. Julia jumped at the chance to help us get off the ground running and Freya and Albie loved the idea. We even have Iris with us as an office manager. We all left the office at the same time and worked hard every day until we got to where we are."

Isabelle's arms fell to her side as Patrick talked to her, her face agape, and she was in shock. "I… I didn't know any of this! Why?" Isabelle was listening carefully, and Patrick loved having all her attention again after all these years.

"Everything that had happened to me in my life and the people I held close who had to deal with me made me want to do something to help." He took a deep breath and looked down. "After you left, I started therapy—finally spoke about my parents, my anxiety and my PTSD. I'm not gonna lie, it was hard but, after some time, it really started to help. I realised how much this can help people. I was lucky—Julia paid for my therapy for me, even though I tried to tell her she didn't have to." Patrick sighed and rubbed the back of his neck "After seeing how much therapy was helping you—and how much it was helping me… I just wanted to help the people out there who don't have a Julia but need someone to guide them in the right direction and help them with the cost." He slowly raised his head and looked into Isabelle's eyes.

Isabelle sat and looked at Patrick for a moment, her eyebrows high on her forehead. "Wow, Patrick, I don't know what to say."

She leant towards Patrick and hugged him tightly. She could feel his heart beating as he put his arms around her.

Isabelle softly whispered in his ear. "I knew—I always knew you had this in you; you're just as special as I always thought." Their hug felt like time stopped; it had been five years, and it felt right.

There was a loud knock on the door, breaking their embrace and bringing them back into the room.

"Oh, God—I'm sorry but I'm late." Isabelle jumped from the sofa, looking at her watch, "I'm so sorry, Patrick, but I have to go."

The door swung open to reveal Isabelle's assistant standing in the door frame. "I'm sorry to interrupt, but we're late."

Isabelle nodded. "Yes, yes, I know… do you have one of my business cards on you?"

The assistant scrambled around and pulled out an egg-white piece of paper about the size of a credit card. "Yes, here you go; I'll explain to them that you’ll be a few moments.” The assistant handed over the card and sped from the room.

“Look, I'm really sorry I have to leave right now but please take this and get in touch?”

Patrick happily took the card from her and nodded. Isabelle headed to the door, smiled, and looked at Patrick. “Don’t be a stranger.” She grinned and winked as she left.

Chapter 65

PATRICK

Patrick was shell-shocked. He hadn't moved from the sofa the entire time and it was as though Isabelle's assistant had thrown a flash bang into the room and by the time he'd realised what had happened, Isabelle was gone.

Patrick pulled out his phone and messaged Albie to say he was heading to the car before making his way over, Isabelle's card safely in his pocket. He got to the car and Albie rolled the passenger side window open. "Ello big man, so… did she say anything about me?" He threw his head back and laughed aloud.

Patrick didn't say a thing and just got into the back of the car, lost in thought.

"Woah, sorry, bud, I need to read the room. I'll just take us to the office." Albie's attitude changed.

Patrick finally spoke. "Sorry, Albie, I'm not feeling too great. Is it okay to take me home? I'll work from home for the rest of the day."

Albie threw his arm around the passenger headrest and looked back at Patrick. "You okay big man? Did something happen?" He looked concerned.

"Yeah, I'm okay, Albie; I'm just exhausted. This isn't the norm for me." Patrick sounded and looked ragged, but Albie didn't believe a bit of it.

"Yeah, alright, if you say so bud. I'll drop you off and let Freya know." Albie's car pulled away with Patrick staring out the window, his hand still clutching Isabelle's card inside his pocket.

The drive back to Patrick's place was silent; neither he nor Albie spoke a word and when they pulled up outside his place, Patrick broke the silence.

"I'm sorry, Albie, maybe I'm more tired than I thought."

Albie looked back and threw a thumb-up. "No worries, mate. Go get yourself some rest and I'll see you tomorrow. Go on sling your hook—otherwise, I'll be late."

Patrick smiled, about to get out of the car, but paused. "Thank you for coming today, Albie. I really appreciate it." He got out of the car and closed the door behind him.

Albie rolled down the window again. "I got ya, bud." He shot him a wink and beeped his horn before pulling away, leaving Patrick on the pavement.

Patrick slowly took himself to his apartment and, when he opened the door, heard a loud meow coming from the living room. As he sat down to take his shoes off, he was met by Doc.

"Hey, Doc, sorry if I woke you. I just needed to get back today." He leaned down and stroked the top of Doc's head before heading into the living room where he flopped onto the sofa. As soon as his head hit one of the pillows he started thinking of and picturing Isabelle. He started daydreaming unable to stop thinking of her.

Doc was getting hungry, so he jumped onto the sofa, climbed onto Patrick's chest and started to stretch and paw on him.

"Doc?" Patrick groaned as. he pushed himself upright and noticed how dark it has gotten outside. "Wow, it's night-time already? I'm so sorry, Doc. I Didn't realise—it's gotta be your dinner time, right?"

Doc was sitting on his lap, looking up at him, and meowed in a way which almost seemed annoyed. Patrick leaned down, grabbed his walking stick from the floor and groaned as he slowly got rose from the sofa. Doc hopped onto the floor and headed to the kitchen.

Patrick made it to the kitchen and opened a tin which contained Doc's dinner for the evening, then leaned back on the kitchen counter as Doc jumped up, opposite him.

"You're not gonna believe this, Doc, but I saw Isabelle today; she interviewed me." Patrick couldn't help but smile as he said it. "God, Doc, you wouldn't believe how beautiful she looked. She's changed so much and seems so confident and in control of everything around her. She has this aura."

Doc looked down and started to groom his paw. Patrick pulled the card Isabelle gave him out of his pocket—it was well-made on thick card. Patrick put it on the side next to Doc, who accidentally knocked it off.

Patrick rolled his eyes at Doc and headed for his stool to pick it up off the floor. He sat on the chair and picked it up just as he got a call from Julia.

"Evening, Patrick. How did it go?" Julia seemed upbeat and Patrick could hear noise in the background.

"Where are you?" He asked wrinkling his brow at the loud music.

"I told you I was going on holiday with the wife!" she laughed down the phone. "I'm enjoying my semi-retirement just like I should."

Patrick smiled, when the business had started doing well, Julia announced that she was going to take a step back—a sort of semi, early retirement. Ever since she had, a different side had come out of her, and she was living her best life.

"What are you doing calling me all the way from Hawaii?" The music slowly got quieter and quieter.

"Freya told me what was happening today, and I had to see how it went—plus I wanted to check up on you."

"I dunno what to say Julia. She's just… wow, you know?" Patrick put his head on the island counter.

"Can we use proper sentences please? What happened?" No matter how much had changed, Julia always treated Patrick the same.

"She gave me her card… and told me to not be a stranger."

Julia immediately interrupted. "Well, did you call her?" Julia prodded.

The phone stayed silent.

"Oh, for God's sake Patrick—you still love her, don't you?" Julia raised her voice slightly.

"You know I do, Julia, but she's doing so well. I don't wanna get in her way."

Julia sighed heavily down the phone. "What did the therapist tell you Patrick? You're not a bloody mind reader. What do *you* want to do?"

There was a slight pause as Patrick lifted his head from the counter and took a deep breath in. "I wanna see her again."

"Okay, and so what are you going to do about it?" Julia prodded.

"I'll call her tomorrow." Patrick said resolutely, nodding his head.

"Good to hear," the smile in Julia's voice was evident. "I'm going to go finish off my margarita. Let me know how it goes. Chat to you later!"

She hung up before Patrick could answer. He got up from his stool and wandered to his bed, collapsing immediately.

So much has changed…

The next day, Patrick woke with a clear mind. He got out of bed, showered and got ready for the day. Because of his sleep, he hadn't gotten any work done yesterday and wanted to get to the office to catch up. After feeding Doc, he walked into the living room where the business card rested on the table. Impulsively, he put it in his pocket. "Have a good day Doc."

He grabbed his work bag and headed down to meet Albie, who was waiting outside. During the car ride, Albie told him all about the film he'd watched the night before, selling it to Patrick in graphic detail. Patrick laughed and, in turn, decided to watch that evening with Doc.

"Good luck with Freya today, mate. She's gonna chew your ear off and ask every question under the sun. I hope you're ready," Albie laughed as they started to walk in.

With this in mind, Patrick took a moment outside the office door to hype himself up before heading in.

"Good morning, Iris; nice and early as usual."

Iris was already at her desk typing away and smiled back at him. Patrick had been happy she'd came on with them. He knew that she gave everything to her job and would always keep things running. She was crucial to making things work.

"Good morning, Patrick. Your first meeting is in your office waiting for you."

Patrick frowned. "Oh, I didn't realise I had something booked so early… it wasn't on my calendar."

"Yeah, sorry about that. It came out of the blue. Best crack on."

Patrick nodded Iris' way and headed to his office. He spoke as he opened the door, "Good morning. I'm so sorry for keeping you—I've just arrived."

However, when he looked up, he found a woman sitting in the chair opposite his desk. A familiar smell flowed up his nose and he shut the door just as the woman stood up and turned.

Patrick dropped his bag.

Isabelle looked like sunshine embodied, wrapped in a striking yellow dress. Patrick was unable to speak.

Isabelle pushed her hair behind her ear, smiling.

"I've missed you."

The End

Acknowledgements

This book has been a journey of passion and self-discovery, and without the incredible people around me, I never would have dreamed of sharing this story with the world. You all gave me the confidence to step out of my comfort zone, and I will always be thankful to each of you.

Annmarie, without your challenge, I never would have thought to try writing. You helped me discover something within myself that I didn't even know existed, and I'll never be able to repay the kindness you've shown me.

Amy, you've been an incredible help behind the scenes, from crafting the questionnaire for test readers to offering me perspective when I had none. You're an amazing friend, and I'm so grateful to have you in my life.

Dad, every Wednesday, no matter how stressed or down I felt, you were there to distract me and lift my spirits over dinner. Thank you for always grounding me when I needed it most.

Chrissy, you pushed me to share my work with the world when I wasn't ready, and since then, you've been one of my biggest supporters. I'll be forever grateful for that. Without friends like you, I don't know where I'd be.

Lisa, you've been my daily support, always there when I couldn't do things on my own. You pushed me when I lacked motivation and made sure I rested when I didn't know how to stop. You've helped me not just with my book, but with my health as well, and I don't know if I would have been able to finish without you.

Gina, a random stranger emailed you asking you to test read their novel, and not only were you kind enough to read it and complete the questionnaire, but your excitement for the book gave me the confidence that my story could connect with people. Thank you for taking a chance on a stranger's work—it meant more than you know.

Connor, you were one of the few people I knew personally who read the book in its rawest form. I was anxious about sharing a story so closely tied to me with people I knew, but after you read it and challenged me on certain aspects, your feedback helped improve the book. More importantly, you helped me realize that it wasn't as scary as I thought to have people in my life read it. Thank you for that.

Simon, after the first draft, you became a mentor in so many ways. Your experience and guidance, especially when it came to taking risks, were invaluable. Thank you for your perspective and the challenges you posed—they played a crucial role in shaping the book into what it is today.

Cameron, you not only helped make my book better, but you also mentored me in improving my writing tenfold. I can't thank you enough for having such faith in my work. I couldn't have asked for a kinder, more understanding editor who constantly pushed me to become a better writer. I'll forever be grateful for your guidance throughout this journey.

And lastly but certainly not least Thank you to my test readers who didn't want to be named, you helped give me Insite and belief.

About the Author

Warne Towner's story is both inspiring and impactful. As a new author from Tonbridge, Kent, Warne's creative journey is deeply personal and filled with resilience. His first children's book, *The Hug*, reflects his efforts to help his nieces understand his medical challenges, using storytelling as a way to bridge understanding. This personal project likely paved the way for his broader storytelling aspirations.

Warne's 18-year battle with mental health issues, coupled with the physical disabilities he has faced over the past eight years, has shaped his outlook on life. The use of a wheelchair and walking aids has not deterred his creativity but has instead fuelled it. During the pandemic, he took on a challenge from a close friend to explore his buried creativity, which led him to write stories that draw from his struggles and experiences. This work is intended to support others who face similar challenges while providing a window into his world for those unfamiliar with such experiences.

By turning his personal difficulties into a source of inspiration, Warne is not only pursuing his passion for storytelling but also offering meaningful contributions to others. His writing reflects his empathy and strength, making him a voice to watch in the literary world.

Printed in Great Britain
by Amazon

9718517a-b560-42f4-9321-b8f522d12d27R01